Spinning Sideways

Claudia J. Severin

SPINNING SIDEWAYS

Copyright © February 2022

Claudia J. Severin

Published by Pella Road Publishing

Lincoln, Nebraska

ISBN: 978-1-7342-1489-5

Spinning Sideways is a work of fiction. Any references to historical events, real people, or real locales are used fictitiously. Other names, characters, places, and incidents are the product of the author's imagination, and any resemblance to actual events or locales or persons, living or dead, is entirely coincidental.

Claudia J. Severin

https://claudiaseverin.net

DEDICATION

For Lynette

CONTENTS

SPINNING SIDEWAYS

June 12, 1988
Lincoln, Nebraska

Linda Marie Bridges finished addressing the envelopes for seven of her high school girlfriends. She'd sent out scores of party invitations in her life. She'd learned to love to entertain from her parents, and they'd had a nice home where friends enjoyed gathering.

But this was not going to be the typical light-hearted party. No, she meant it to be a reunion of a more serious nature; her chance to go back and be completely honest with the friends who had once supported her unconditionally. And if she wished to clear the air, she should give all of them a chance to say their piece, and be candid about their lives and their personal struggles.

She sorted the envelopes. Four of the invitations would be strictly for an event next month on a Saturday evening. A nice meal around the pool that included two twirlers who graduated two years ahead of her, and two twirlers who graduated a year after her. She would invite her core group, Yvonne Adams, Debbie Washington, and Nancy Thompson to spend Friday evening with her as well. In those three invitations, she'd tucked an additional typewritten piece of paper explaining the agenda and details of the Friday night event.

I typed out letters to these three friends almost a year ago. Those messages read much differently. I was going to say goodbye and explain why I'd meticulously collected a variety of barbiturates to swallow in rapid succession, chasing them down with my favorite rosé wine. Thank goodness the past twelve months of therapy have taken me to a different place. A better place. I hope.

1

But would they understand what Linda hoped to share with them now? She read a copy of the note she'd sent them one more time to judge its clarity.

My dear Nancy, Debbie, and Yvonne,

I hope you can come to the twirler reunion party on Saturday night, but I also wanted the four of us to have a special gathering the night before. Although we have kept up with the basic family stuff pretty well over the past twenty years, there has never been a time when we have gotten together to share our deepest fears and hardships. If you are like me, life has taught you many lessons you weren't prepared for. For my part, there are things about me that I have learned that are hard to talk about. When I wondered who could understand my struggles the best, I thought about the three of you.

I am asking something unusual of each of you. I'd like you to share some stories about your lives over the past decades that will surprise us, secrets or insecurities that you have never even told your husbands. Maybe something you have done that you regret or something you wish you had done. I hope we can refrain from judgments and embrace the women we have become today. I can't express how much your support will mean to me, and I promise to do my best to reciprocate.

Only the four of us will be included in the Friday evening event, but the time and

2

place are identical to the Saturday details.
Please say you'll come.

Linda sealed and stamped the envelopes and tucked them into her purse. She'd swing by the post office before work the next day.

CHAPTER ONE

June 12, 1962

"You can't be best friends with a boy, Linda. It just isn't right." Thirteen-year-old Sarah Bridges sat at her dressing table, brushing out her long golden hair. Her ten-year-old sister sat on the edge of her twin bed watching her. Elvis Presley crooned from Sarah's clock radio as local station KLMS unfurled the weekly Top 40 hits.

"But Brian is my best friend. He likes to do the same things that I do and he always makes me laugh. Isn't that what a best friend does?" Linda smiled thinking of Brian Walker, the boy in her grade who lived across Lyncrest Drive. They'd been best pals since first grade when they had both come down with chickenpox at the same time, and Brian's mother let him stay at her house to try to prevent his three siblings from catching it. Naturally, they had all gotten chickenpox the next year when his little brother picked it up in kindergarten.

"Pretty soon, when you are my age, you will start to like boys and maybe he can be your boyfriend then. But for now, you should find other girls to play with," Sarah insisted.

"But Brian and his brother Cody play fun games. Sometimes we kick the football around. They have a pool table. Brian even said that he'd go hunting with us whenever Daddy thinks I am old enough to shoot."

"You can't be serious. You are not talking Daddy into taking you hunting. That is strictly a boy's activity." Sarah opened her drawer and took out a mother-of-pearl barrette. "Do you think you're the son he wanted? Here's a news flash. You're a girl. You could even be a pretty girl if you'd start combing that rat's nest of a hairdo. And one of these days, your buddy Brian will prefer a cute little girl to a tomboy. Then you can spend as much time with

4

him as you like." She pulled up a section of her hair on the side of her head and snapped the barrette into place.

Linda scowled. "Maybe I am not like you. You are trying to be like Mom. I mean I love how Mom takes care of us and makes us nice meals, but I don't know why she wants things to be so fancy. I am never going to grow up, get married, and have to take care of babies. Instead, I am going to find a job that makes me rich and famous, and I can hire someone to cook and clean for me."

Sarah laughed and stood. "Good luck with that, Babydoll. I'm going to take a walk with my best friend, Trudy. We are going to walk by that new boy's house and see if he is sitting outside tonight."

Linda thought about what her sister had said the next evening when she was sitting on a blanket with Brian's younger sister, Mary, and his brother Chris. Brian's mother was standing up watching the Little League game. Mr. Walker had taken the oldest boy, Cody, to his own baseball game that evening.

Brian isn't that good of a baseball player. He looks bored out in left field most of the time, but he seems to enjoy being on the team. I could play baseball. I have a good arm, even Cody lets me pitch to him, and I can catch a fly ball on the run. Why don't they let girls play in Little League? If I weren't friends with Cody and Brian, I would have never even learned to play baseball.

When the game was over, Mrs. Walker took them all to A & W for root beer floats. The carhops brought the junior-size mugs for kids. Linda and Brian sat in the rear-facing back seat of his family's station wagon.

"I'm sorry you lost the game, Brian." Linda stirred her vanilla ice cream in her mug. She liked how the flavors melded together.

5

"There's always next week." Brian shrugged. "Cody is the baseball star in our family."

Linda studied him. "How old is Cody?"

Brian licked ice cream off his upper lip. "He's almost fourteen. Why?"

"I'm wondering about something my sister said. Does Cody have a girlfriend?"

Brian chuckled. "A girlfriend? Yuck. Why would Cody want a girlfriend?" Then he glared at her. "Wait, you don't mean you want to be Cody's girlfriend, do ya?"

Linda nearly choked on her sip of root beer. "Oh no! Not at all. I don't ever want to have a boyfriend. But Sarah acted like it was inevitable. You get older, you want to have a girlfriend or boyfriend."

"Not me. Promise me you won't start getting all gushy on me. I need someone to help me practice catching fly balls."

"Don't worry. I don't ever plan on getting gushy with anyone."

CHAPTER TWO

July 1, 1963

"Girls, we have something important to discuss with you after dinner," Linda's mother, Mary Jo, announced as she was bringing out the baked Alaska dessert.

"What about, Mom? Are we getting a dog?" Sarah asked.

Mary Jo smiled. "No, at least not yet. Eat your dessert and then we'll adjourn to the living room."

Linda looked at her father. This did not sound good at all to her. You couldn't judge such things from her mother's demeanor; she would put a positive spin on a murder scene. But Michael, her father, had a pleasant expression on his face too. He raised his brows playfully when he caught Linda watching him.

What could it be? She remembered last week when Brian's cousin, Bart, stayed at Brian's house for a week. He'd confessed to Brian and her that his parents had called the children into their living room and told them they were getting a divorce. Bart's father was moving into an apartment and the rest of the family would stay at their house. They were only going to see his father once a week.

She hoped that wasn't what her parents wanted to tell them. Her father had been gone more than usual these past few months, and when he was home, he was often working late in his study. She hated to think what their household would become without him there. Sometimes, when he was working at his desk, he'd let her come into the study and sit on the floor reading a book or doing something quietly. She felt happier knowing he was nearby.

Linda sat fidgeting on the couch next to Sarah, watching her parents' faces as they stood before them. Sarah didn't seem very concerned. *Maybe she knows something I don't. It wouldn't be the first time Mom had confided in Sarah.*

7

"I'm sure you've noticed how busy your father has been lately. He's had to bring work home and has been on the telephone more," Mary Jo began. Her smile seemed genuine enough. "That is because he got a big promotion at work. He is now the president of the company, and he got a sizable salary increase."

"Golly Gee, Daddy! Congratulations," Sarah exclaimed, getting up to throw her arms around her father's neck. "Does this mean we're rich?"

Linda furrowed her brows. She had a feeling there was more to this story.

Michael laughed. "I wouldn't say we are rich yet, but we are moving in that direction at least." He cleared his throat. "But here's the part that affects you girls. We are moving to a bigger house in Piedmont. Your mother found a lovely home, and we put an offer in on it. It has been recently remodeled and even has a swimming pool in the backyard."

"A swimming pool? Oh, my goodness!" Sarah grabbed Linda's hands, pulling her to her feet and started bouncing in place, shrieking. "Lindy, a swimming pool! Of our very own!"

Linda's mind was racing. She bounced with her sister but wasn't sure what it all meant. The pool sounded fantastic. But she didn't want to leave this house. She liked Eastridge and she knew everyone on Lyncrest Drive. She could walk the few blocks to school and the community pool. She liked her friends in the neighborhood, especially Brian. She couldn't leave Brian behind.

"What's wrong Lindy, aren't you excited?" her father asked when he saw her biting her lip.

"I dunno. Do we have to move away from here? What about school and our friends in the neighborhood?"

"That is why this is perfect timing," Mary Jo beamed. "Sarah will be starting high school at Southeast and you will be starting junior high at Millard Lefler. You'll only be a few blocks from school again. And this will be the perfect place to entertain all of your friends."

"But my friends all live here. How far is the new house from here?"

"Hmmm. It's about a mile, I guess. An easy bicycle ride," Michael said.

"Oh, I don't think anyone Linda's age should be riding a bike on those busy streets. But don't worry. It isn't that far away," her mother assured her.

"I can't wait to see the new place! Will our bedrooms be bigger?" Sarah asked.

"Oh, yes. They are much nicer. And we'll have such fun decorating them too. We should be able to finish that before school starts. Won't you enjoy that, Linda?" Mary Jo said.

Linda rolled her eyes. "I guess you're not getting a divorce then?"

Michael shot a look at his wife before answering. "What gave you that idea?"

"Oh, it's just ... when you said you had something important to tell us, I thought... Never mind. I guess this is better." Linda smiled ruefully.

"Well, I'll say. This is what your mother and I have worked for since we were married. It's going to be much easier for all of us to have this kind of money. You'll see."

"Of course, Daddy. I'm sure it will be swell."

CHAPTER THREE

October 4, 1966

"Linda, hold still. I about have your hair the way I want it." Mary Jo put the final hairpin in Linda's bouffant updo and let loose with a cloud of hairspray.

Linda choked. "Mom, my God. Are you trying to suffocate me?" She hid her face beneath her hands. "Why do I have to get all gussied up anyway? I'm not the one who is making her debut."

"It's important to your sister that we all look our best even though this isn't a real debutante ball like I had back in Atlanta. In my day, it was much more formal. We're having a fancy party for Sarah because she is turning eighteen. You'll have your turn when you are her age."

"I will not be doing anything resembling this for any of my birthday parties. Maybe I'll have a costume party and ask people to dress like hobos."

Mary Jo shook her head. "Well, no need to think about that now. We just have to make it through tonight. Look at me, Lindy."

Linda sighed and pressed her mouth in a line, allowing her mother to study her appearance.

"Okay, help yourself to a bit of Sarah's lipstick, and maybe a little blush. You look a tad pale, Dear. I will see you downstairs." Mary Jo smiled at her daughter in the dressing table mirror and left to tend to party details.

Linda stuck her tongue out at herself in the reflection. She was only fourteen years old, but this atrocious hair made her look like she was thirty. She dutifully went into Sarah's bedroom to find the lipstick her mother mentioned. Sarah had already departed for the main floor to greet early arrivals. Linda plopped down at Sarah's dressing table. If the hair wasn't enough sophistication, she had on a full-skirted sundress in pale orchid. Orchid, really? In October?

She rummaged through Sarah's drawer looking for her makeup. She found several tubes of the brand Sarah favored. She put a little pale pink on her lips. Then she spotted a bright coral and put that on top. She kept searching and put a fire-engine red shade on top of the other two. She hadn't worn lipstick, but now that she tried it, she realized she had pretty full lips. That ought to attract some attention. This is kinda fun. What else? She spotted some lavender eyeshadow. That would match her dress, sort of. She caked that on and then found Sarah's favorite mascara. Sarah said a girl was positively naked without mascara. She'd watched how her sister applied it and imitated her. She blotted her mouth and under her lower lashes with a tissue to try to minimize the rub-off.

She laughed at herself in the mirror. She certainly didn't look like Sarah's little sister now. Maybe tonight she would have fun pretending to be someone else. Someone older and more worldly.

She tried to sneak downstairs without attracting attention. The first people she recognized were Cody and Brian Walker. They were the only ones Linda wanted to see tonight anyway.

"Linda?" Brian squeaked out when she approached them. "What happened to you? You look like you were caught between a propeller and a crayon box."

For a moment, she thought she should flee back upstairs.

"Brian, be nice," Cody said. "Linda's dolled up for her sister's party. You look pretty, Lindy. Ignore my idiot brother."

Linda suddenly locked eyes with Sarah across the room. Sarah squinted and then made a beeline for her little sister. She grabbed Linda's hand and ushered her into the first-floor powder room, decorated in whimsical florals.

"You have to clean off some of that before any more guests see you. Did you think you were finger painting? Sit down here

11

and close your eyes." Sarah pushed Linda down on the closed toilet seat cover and took a tissue to her eyelids. "Fourteen-year-olds don't need to be wearing so much makeup. You look like you are auditioning for a streetwalker."

"Mom told me to put a little of your makeup on," Linda complained.

"A little would be okay. You want it to look natural, so your beauty shines through. This makes you look like a freak." Sarah eliminated most of the eyeshadow and some of the mascara. Then she began rubbing the lipstick off with a wet tissue. Sarah opened the medicine cabinet and pulled out a jar of Vaseline. "Here, put a little of this on your lips. A smidge of color and lots of shine, that's all it takes." She cleaned up the mascara that had smudged on Linda's cheeks with the petroleum jelly.

"How did you learn to do this so quickly?" Linda asked.

"Mom taught me some of it. But I have to read *Glamour, Mademoiselle,* and *Seventeen* to know what is really in style for young ladies. You look much better now. Sorry about the hair. You may be stuck with that tonight." Sarah discarded the dirty tissues and marched out of the bathroom as though it was perfectly normal to be sharing a bathroom with her sister.

Linda studied herself in the mirror. Sarah was right; this looks much more wholesome. She emerged from the powder room and went in search of someone she knew. Most of these kids were in Sarah's grade, and there were about twenty-five of them milling around now. Cody and Brian were near the door chatting with Sarah. She didn't want to interrupt, so she slipped out of the big patio door and descended the stairs to the pool deck area. It seemed quiet out there, and she admired the twinkling lights festooned around the perimeter of the pool.

"Are you having fun?" a deep voice called out to her.

Linda whirled around to find a young man with coal-black

hair, wearing a suit and smoking a cigarette. He sat at one of the tables they had placed on the patio for overflow seating. She didn't recognize him.

"I'm not sure about the fun. It's too early to tell. Are you a friend of Sarah's?"

"I'm Billy. Billy Kidrow, but most of my friends call me Billy the Kid. You know, like the outlaw. I was Sarah's tennis instructor at the country club last summer."

"Tennis, huh?" Linda asked. She vaguely remembered Sarah going on about her dreamy tennis coach. But then Sarah was enamored with a lot of different boys. "Are you any good? At tennis, I mean."

Billy smiled mischievously. "I was a state champion in high school in Kansas. I don't know that I have what it takes to go pro, though. Not exactly ready for Wimbledon. You like tennis?"

Linda sat down at the table with him, propping her chin in her hands. "Eeeh. It's okay. Not my sport, I don't think. I'd rather play baseball or do gymnastics. My dad promised to teach me to play golf last summer, but then he got too busy."

"I'll bet you could find a nice boy willing to teach you golf if you want to learn."

Linda shrugged. "I suppose I'd better get back inside. Who knows what activities Sarah has planned for tonight?"

"Well, aren't you the thoughtful friend? Let's go." Billy extinguished his cigarette in a glass ashtray and followed Linda back inside. They followed the noise into the walkout basement level where the party had moved. The guests were now gathered near the snack tables.

When they went into the crowded family room, Sarah came up and gave Billy a quick kiss.

"There you are, Bill. I wondered where you'd run off to. You

13

met my sister, Linda?"

"Your ... sister? Oh, I didn't know she was—"

Linda didn't stay close long enough to hear his explanation. She found Brian and Cody and started doing the twist with them as the music of Chubby Checker filled the room.

Billy the Kid became a frequent visitor to the Bridges' home. He was two years older than Sarah and attended Nebraska Wesleyan University in Lincoln. His father, Royce Kidrow, was a prominent businessman in Omaha, and Royce played golf with Michael Bridges at the country club sometimes.

One night at dinner the following spring, Mary Jo asked Sarah about applying for admission to colleges. "I know you have been accepted by the university here, and also Wesleyan, but is there anywhere else you might want to attend college? It might be a chance for you to see another part of the country. You know, more of an adventure."

Sarah got a dreamy look on her face. "I don't know why I'd want to go away to school. Everything I want is right here. I mean, Bill is here. I don't know how long I will attend college before we get married. He has two more years as an undergrad. After that, I suppose he'll go to law school, but I can't imagine we'd wait that long to get married."

"I don't think you want to rush into marriage so young," Michael said.

"Your father's right," her mother said. "Now is your time to see the world, meet a lot of different people. You'll have the rest of your life to settle down. I think some colleges even let you study abroad. Can you imagine spending a semester in Paris?"

"That sounds cool. I'd jump on a chance to travel for school." Linda finished eating and set her silverware across her plate. "You should do that, Sarah. Why would you want to marry ol' Billy the Kid anyway?"

"I'm sure you're too young to appreciate true love," Sarah said.

The following Saturday, Linda came home from her gymnastics club practice to an empty house. Her parents had gone to a bridge party. She checked Sarah's room and was surprised that it was empty. It was a pleasant evening, so Linda decided to do some of her homework on the back deck.

She'd gotten herself settled on a redwood chaise with a soft drink and books when she thought she heard noises coming from the pool house. They had fixed up the pool house the previous summer, and it was equipped with a bedroom and full bathroom, so guests could change clothes before or after swimming. They also stored pool equipment and patio furniture in there during the off-season.

After a few minutes, the noise turned into an argument, and Sarah came rushing out the door heading toward the main house. She didn't seem to notice Linda sitting near the far corner of the pool deck. A minute later, Billy came out, buttoning his cuffs. He looked around for Sarah and spied Linda.

"Hey there, Kiddo. Did you see Sarah go somewhere?" he asked. He walked over to her, and she noticed he'd left his shoes next to one of the chairs. Sarah's Keds were nearby, and one of her cardigan sweaters was draped on the chair.

"She went inside the house. You two fight?"

Instead of putting on his shoes, Billy pulled out a cigarette and lit it. "Yeah, we are not seeing eye-to-eye today. She acts like she wants me to kiss her, but then when we have the whole place to ourselves, she doesn't want to take advantage of it."

15

"And you want to take advantage of it? Sounds like you are trying to take advantage of her." Linda lifted her nose in the air over her book.

"Nah, it's not like that. You seem like an open-minded chick for your age. I mean, I've seen some of the kooky clothes you wear and heard some of the music you like. Hey, you wanna cigarette?"

Linda hesitated, then nodded. He lit a cigarette for her and handed it to her. She closed her book and moved to the end of the lounge chair, close to where he sat.

Billy went on, "I dunno how to get Sarah to loosen up a little. She drank a little beer. I thought that would help. How about you? You ever take a boy to the pool house?"

Linda snickered. "No, what for?"

"What the world needs now."

Linda's brows furrowed.

"Love, sweet love. You know, like the song."

She scoffed. "No, I don't take my boyfriends into the pool house."

Billy scooted his chair closer to hers. "So, you have had boyfriends. I guess I'm not surprised. You're more of a wild thing than your sister, right?" He nearly growled when he said "wild thing."

"Have you been drinking Billy? Cuz you are not making much—"

Linda was flabbergasted when he grabbed her head in his hands and pulled her in for a kiss. Not a little peck but a forceful wet kiss meant to shock her. She got her bearings and backed away on the chair, knocking her book to the cement deck.

"What are you doing? Gross, Billy." She picked up her book and stomped into the house. Her heart was racing as she climbed the stairs and knocked on Sarah's door.

"Come in," Sarah's tear-stained voice requested. She was sprawled on her bed, a tissue box nearby, apparently engaging in a pity party.

Linda plopped next to her. "What is wrong with that boy?"

"He expects too much of me. Maybe I am being stubborn. After all, if we are getting married eventually, it won't matter. Did you hear us fighting?"

"He kissed me. For no reason whatsoever."

Sarah bolted upright. "What do you mean, he kissed you?"

"Billy. We were talking, and then he grabbed my face and kissed me."

"Billy kissed you? No. That can't be true. Why would you say something like that? Can't you see I'm already upset?"

"You're upset? How do you think I feel? I never wanted to kiss him! You should break it off with him. He's weird."

Sarah scowled at her sister. "That makes no sense at all. Why would he kiss you just because I ran out on him? Did you flirt with him?"

"No. We were talking about you. He was complaining that you were too uptight. But you think whatever you like. I never want to see that creep again. He's not a nice guy."

Linda got up to leave.

"You're the one who's not being nice. Don't be telling that lie to anyone else. Bill would never try to kiss my little sister. That's absurd. Keep your mouth shut."

Linda shook her head and went back to her room. When she looked out her window at the pool, she didn't see Billy. Good riddance. Maybe her sister would come to her senses.

"He kissed you? Your sister's boyfriend kissed you?" Brian asked. "Isn't he like twenty or something? Why would he kiss a fifteen-year-old?" It was a warm May afternoon and they were sitting on the side of her swimming pool with their legs in the water. It was still too cool to swim.

"I don't know. I was hoping you could shed some light on the subject. You're a boy, after all. Do you go around kissing girls on a whim?" Linda asked. She wanted to see what his reaction was, but she doubted Brian had kissed anyone.

"No, that would be rude. You shouldn't make any moves on a girl if you're not sure she is interested. That's what Cody told me."

"Hmmm. How do you know if she's interested?"

"Well, let's see," Brian mused. "If you were sitting by her and you moved closer, that might tell you." He slid over so that their bare knees were touching.

"Then what would you do? Let's see if you have any moves."

"Well, maybe you would take her hand like this and see if she objects." Brian picked up Linda's hand that was resting on her leg and wrapped his fingers around hers. "If she doesn't pull away, that might mean she's interested."

Linda didn't move, but she was a little surprised he was playing along. She looked at their hands, then looked into his eyes.

"If that works out, you might move in even closer." Brian moved his head right in front of Linda so that their faces nearly touched. She didn't flinch.

He chuckled and sat back. "See, you're acting like a girl who might be interested. Did you do that with what's-his-name, your sister's fella?"

Linda frowned. "No way, I am certainly not interested in Billy. Yuck."

18

"Oh, but you are interested in me?" He moved back to where he had been nearly touching her face. When she started to laugh, he kissed her quickly.

"You can't kiss me. You're my best friend!"

"Consider it a friendly kiss. Who else should you practice with?"

"I suppose we could give each other pointers. So that we are ready for that first real kiss with someone we are mad about."

"Linda, there is something I have to tell you. The reason I wanted to see you today."

"Is something wrong, Brian?"

"It's my father. He got a better job, like your dad."

"Great, maybe you can move into a house around here then."

"We are moving. To Chicago."

"Chicago? No! That's like three states away. You can't go to Chicago! We're about to start high school."

"We're moving as soon as school is out. I'll go to high school in Illinois."

"Then that was a kiss goodbye? That's not fair. We didn't even get to practice."

"I know. It's a bummer. But at least it isn't in the middle of a school year. And Cody is graduating and going to college in Illinois anyway." Brian pursed his lips. "Maybe you could visit me sometime."

"It won't be the same. We won't even have the summer to horse around. Who am I going to play ball with? Or go pheasant hunting with? I think I am going to go inside now and be depressed."

When Linda got up, Brian followed her. He took her arm.

"Don't get all mad. We can write letters. It doesn't have to be the end of our friendship."

She sighed. "And just when I was beginning to like you, Brian Walker."

CHAPTER FOUR

Linda tried to forget about that kiss that Billy planted on her. She wanted to forget about him altogether. But that summer, he was at their house almost every evening. Often Sarah and Billy went out somewhere, but he was always there chatting up her parents before their date. And it was clear Sarah was becoming more enraptured by his charm.

Most of the time when he came by, Linda excused herself and went into another room. But there were times that she couldn't, without being obvious. His favorite trick was to make a little joke at her expense or to wink at her when no one else was looking.

"What happened to your little friend, Brian?" Billy asked one evening as Linda cleared the dishes from the table. Sarah had gone upstairs to change clothes. Her parents were in the kitchen.

"Brian moved. He left in June." Linda said, stacking the plates to carry.

Billy glanced around, then moved in right behind her. Too close behind her for comfort. "You must be lonely without your boyfriend."

Linda whirled on him. "He's not … I miss my friend, sure. But I have other friends."

Billy stroked one hand down her arm which was laden with dishes. "Funny, I haven't seen any of your friends keeping you company."

She bristled. "If you want to help, grab those glasses. You may as well make yourself useful."

"Nah," Billy said. "I like watching you work; watching how you move and how cute you are when you are annoyed."

She bustled into the kitchen and put the plates in the sink. Why wouldn't he leave her alone? Why didn't Sarah see what a

21

jackass he was? She was going to have to do something to stop him or he might end up becoming a permanent part of their family.

After she finished loading the dishwasher and Billy left with Sarah, Linda went to her room. She liked to draw and paint there. But tonight, she started making some notes, drawing some diagrams. How could she expose Billy in a way that Sarah could not dismiss? She'd thought about talking to her parents, but she wasn't sure they'd believe her either. He made her uncomfortable. He was doing it intentionally, but it was hard to explain to anyone else.

Finally, a plan began to form. It was potentially risky, but she thought she could keep things under her control.

The next time he tried to flirt with her or touch her, she smiled and acted friendlier. When he put his hand on her bottom as she passed in front of him, she whispered, "Careful, you don't want Sarah to see that." He seemed to think she'd changed her mind and might be more receptive to his advances.

After a few weeks, a situation developed that fit into her scheme.

"Your father and I are going to dinner at the Parsons' down the street," Mary Jo told Linda as she was getting dressed for the evening. Linda liked watching her mother put her outfits together. She had to admit Mary Jo had style and knew how to flatter her figure. "They are having a cocktail party at 6:30 p.m. and then dinner, so we probably won't be home too late. I imagine it will be around nine. You and Sarah can order a pizza or whip something up."

"That sounds fine, Mom. Have fun." She was leaving her parents' bedroom when her father came up the stairs to change for the evening. The phone rang in the hall and Linda answered it.

"Sarah Baby, that you? What are we doing tonight?" Billy asked.

"This is Linda, Billy. But Sarah asked me to give you a message. I don't know exactly what she meant, but she said the coast is clear tonight. She asked you to meet her in the pool house at seven o'clock."

"She said that?"

"Yeah. I don't know why she didn't want you to ring the doorbell, but I know my folks are going out. You can come around the side of the house. The gate will be unlocked."

"Interesting. This sounds very mysterious. Tell Sarah I'll be there."

Linda hung up and went back to her room. She had a couple of handwriting samples of Billy's from when he'd sent Sarah greeting cards. Sarah didn't even know she'd taken them from her drawer. She wrote a note to Sarah, trying to replicate his handwriting, and sealed it in an envelope with Sarah's name on the outside.

Sarah arrived home a few minutes after her parents left. Linda went to her room at once.

"Billy stopped by earlier. I mentioned that you and I would be home alone tonight. He wrote you this note and asked me to give it to you."

Sarah opened the note. It read, "Tonight will be very special. Meet me at the pool house at 7:05 p.m." Sarah squinted. "What do you suppose this means? Did Mom and Dad go out?"

"Mom said they were going to dinner down at the Parsons' house. I'm waiting for a phone call from Brian tonight."

Linda went back to her room and took a deep breath. The stage was set. She just hoped this would work. She put on her blue bikini and a white swimsuit coverup. She wasn't sure everything would go as planned, and she may have to appear that she intended to take a late evening dip in the pool.

She was in the pool house before Billy arrived at seven. She'd brought several candles and lit them. There was a main room in the pool house, which contained a bed and a kitchenette. The rest was the bathroom and storage area.

Billy came in promptly at seven. He squinted, adjusting his eyes to the candlelit room. "Sarah, are you here?"

"No, it's me, Billy. Sarah's not home. I thought this would give us a chance to talk," Linda said. She knew he wasn't there to talk. That was the point. She needed to get him to kiss her again and have Sarah walk in and catch them. But she had to time it perfectly.

"Well, Lindy. Aren't you the sneaky one? And all this time you've been pretending to ignore me. But you've been hankering for a little piece of Billy the Kid too." He walked up to Linda and slid his arms around her waist. She took a step back bracing her hand on his chest, trying to fight her nausea.

"Well, I think we should have a little chat first. Are you really in love with my sister? Cuz she seems to have this silly idea you want to marry her." Linda tried to sound flirtatious.

"Marry her?" Billy laughed. "I'm certainly not thinking about marrying anyone. I'll be in school for years yet. Marriage can wait. I do like Sarah. She's just a little too prim. But I had a feeling about you. I could really go for you." He kissed her neck, pulling at the neckline of her coverup.

Hurry up, Sarah! I'm not going to be able to stall him all night.

"You didn't answer my question, Billy. Are you in love with Sarah?" *You need to hear his answer, Sarah. Come in now!*

"I don't want to talk about Sarah. I want to think about me and you, Sweetie Pie. There's no point in wasting time. We know why we're here." He wrapped his arms around her again and kissed her, lifting her off the floor. Once her feet left the floor, it was difficult to push away and move back. He stumbled onto the bed a few feet away and laid on top of her.

"No, no, Billy! You're going too fast. We need to talk. Let me go." She struggled to free her mouth but he was stronger than she'd expected. When he started pulling at her clothing, she panicked. "Stop, Billy. You can't—" Shock made her pulse skyrocket and stole the words from her mouth.

"Don't fight it, Linda. You know you want it. You asked for it. Just relax."

He started pulling his pants down and she couldn't get away from him. This was not part of the plan. Linda started screaming.

The door to the pool house burst open.

Thank God, Sarah! Help me!

But the next sound she heard wasn't Sarah's voice. It was the slide racking on her father's Remington shotgun.

"Freeze!"

Billy froze. Linda couldn't breathe.

"I'm going to give you three seconds to get off that bed before you're picking buckshot out of your ass." Michael's voice was steely.

Billy rose slowly, hiking up his pants as he did. Linda rolled off the bed, gathering her coverup tightly around her. She burst past her father without looking him in the eye. She dashed out of the pool house, nearly upending Sarah. Linda didn't stop until she was in the upstairs bathroom she shared with her sister, where she flung herself into the shower.

Mary Jo came into the bathroom when she heard Linda crying hysterically.

"Linda, what's going on? Are you okay?"

Linda sank to her knees, still wearing her coverup and bikini top. It was going to be a long night.

"Linda, I need to know if I should call the police." Michael sat on a footstool facing his younger daughter.

Linda was wrapped in a chenille bathrobe, her long blonde hair twisted into a towel. She hugged a throw pillow to her chest on the sofa and couldn't stop trembling. She hadn't uttered more than a few syllables since she was attacked.

"We're lucky we came home when we did," Mary Jo said. "I started getting queasy after drinking a cocktail at the party and didn't want to expose anyone else if I was getting the stomach flu, so we left." She searched Linda's face for answers.

"Sarah, what can you tell us about tonight?" Michael shifted his questioning to her.

Sarah was wearing a long robe too and hugging her legs to her body on the opposite corner of the sofa. Her expression was pinched. "I got a note," she said softly. "Billy sent me a note asking me to meet him at 7:05. That seemed kinda odd."

"Meet you where?" Mary Jo asked. Linda ducked her face into the pillow.

"He said to meet him at the pool house. I don't know what Linda was doing there."

All eyes fell on Linda again. *I shouldn't say anything. That will only make this worse. At least Sarah saw what kind of creep she was dating. I oughta let him get arrested. But that will drag this out and no one needs that.* She merely shook her head.

"You don't want me to call the police?" Michael persisted.

Linda shook her head again.

Michael sighed. "All right then. We'll leave it for now. I already told Billy he is never to come within 100 feet of either one of you. He will never be welcome here again and shouldn't call

26

here. If he doesn't quit his job at the country club, I will go to the manager and tell him what happened and he'll be fired. I have a good mind to call his father, but I hate to drag Royce through this. He's a good man."

"That may be a reason to tell him, Dear," Mary Jo said. "If Billy does this to some other poor girl, Royce may be shelling out a lot of money for a lawyer."

"Let's think about that some more. You may be right." Michael stood up. "You girls think you can sleep tonight?"

Linda got up and trudged up the stairs. She left the lamp on when she went to bed. Her mother came in and rubbed her arm just as she had done when Linda and Sarah were children. Mary Jo stayed until Linda fell asleep.

I'm not crying anymore over that creep. I have to put him out of my mind. I hope Sarah would have done the same thing for me.

CHAPTER FIVE

"I can't believe my mother made me sign up for this charm school class," Linda said, sinking onto a folding chair in the shopping center auditorium. She looked at the girl sitting next to her, who was tall with dark blonde hair nearly to her waist. When she smiled, her braces gleamed in the overhead fluorescent lights. "I'm Linda Bridges, by the way. I suppose you're excited to be here."

"Janet Sparks," the girl said patting her chest. "I am pleased to meet you, Linda, although that may not be the correct thing to say upon meeting someone. I think we will go over how to do introductions in this class. Did you pick up a handbook?"

Linda saw the red and blue booklet in Janet's hand and went to the front of the room to fetch herself a copy. She opened it and began to read about what the course would cover over six hour-long sessions.

"How to walk and move like a model, how to sit, how to exit a car gracefully, writing thank-you notes, setting a table …I think my mother could teach this stuff," Linda said as she returned to her seat.

"Wait until you get to the part about boys in the last section. It talks about how to speak sweetly and let him show you how masculine he can be," Janet chuckled.

Linda was glad she'd found someone who wasn't going to take this too seriously. "I've had it up to here with boys trying to assert their masculinity. I hope it teaches us how to get a boy to chill out," Linda said. "I'm going to be a sophomore at Capital High. How about you?"

"Same here. We probably should have taken this last year. Most of these girls look younger."

"My mom wanted me to go last year but I managed to put her

off until now. I had too many swimming and gymnastics meets last summer. Of course, my older sister took this course and loved it."

Linda and Janet had some fun in charm school even if they were older than the rest of the class. Janet was particularly good at walking down the makeshift runway with a book balanced on her head. She'd pulled her hair back into a ponytail which helped support the book.

Linda had a turn to shine when they covered how to be a proper hostess. She already knew how to set a table for a seven-course dinner; and which fork to use for any course. Mary Jo had drafted her daughters to help her prepare for elaborate dinners once a year when she invited Michael's executive committee and their wives to dine.

By the last class in August, they had gotten to the chapter on how to interact with boys. The instructors, who were middle-aged matrons, had drafted a couple of college girls and their boyfriends to lead a discussion about what boys wanted from teenage girls.

"If you all would turn to Chapter Twelve in your handbook, we're going to talk about ways to talk to a boy, especially a boy you like," a peppy little brunette named Gretta explained. "First of all, don't necessarily pick out the boy you think is the most handsome or charming in a group. You need someone to practice on, so pick out a boy who looks like he is a little nervous, just like you are. Be sure your voice is soft and sweet." Gretta walked over to Rick, one of the college boys they'd brought to help demonstrate.

"Hello there. What brings you here today?" she cooed to Rick.

Rick played his part well. "Oh, I thought I'd come to the mall today. I was bored at home. My name is Rick. What's your name?"

"My name is Gretta Malone. I came to the mall with my family. We saw that movie about the Martians. Have you seen that?"

"Yes, I saw it last week with my brother."

"How nice. I wasn't quite sure I understood the ending. Can you explain it to me?" Gretta said this to Rick in a sweet voice, moving in closer and studying his face. Then she turned to her audience. "Now, of course, I understood the ending of this movie. But it is a good way to get a boy to talk to you for a few minutes, and it might make him feel like he is a little smarter. He'll find out soon enough that you're not really dumb."

Linda's hand shot up, and Gretta nodded to her.

"Why would you ever want a boy to think you are dumber than he is?"

Gretta smiled. "It's a ploy to get him talking. No harm in it. Go ahead, Rick."

"Well, the ending of the movie was all about what might happen to the earth if we don't take care of it. If we continue to dump garbage into our oceans, life might not survive. If we continue to waste water, we might run out. It is really a warning to be more careful."

"Really?" Gretta said, leaning closer to Rick. "Tell me more about how we can save our planet." She looked back at the girls. "The idea is to keep him talking. Even if he changes the subject, he'll feel good telling you his opinions and he will think you are a great conversationalist."

Linda snorted loudly. The other girls turned to look at her. She shrugged.

Another young girl raised her hand. "What if you want him to kiss you?"

Gretta turned back to Rick. "What should a girl do to indicate she'd be interested in kissing you?"

Rick blushed. Before he could answer, one of the instructors, Mrs. Mattingly, spoke up. "I don't think that is a subject for our curriculum. These girls are too young to be kissing boys."

"Not all of us," Linda piped up.

Mrs. Mattingly glared at her. "Gretta, why don't you move on?"

Gretta called on the other college coed, Sharon, who joined her. Then she motioned to a few of the girls sitting in the front row to come up and stand with them.

"Okay, ladies, now let's say you are at the mall or even in the school hallway, and you are forever surrounded by your friends. They are always chatting, and you are paying attention to what they are saying." She turned to the girls standing there, "Pretend you are all talking together about something or someone." The girls giggled and acted as though they were gossiping. "So, then a boy you like comes along." Gretta beckoned for Rick to approach. "How does it make a boy feel when he sees a girl surrounded by all of her friends?"

Rick stuck his hands in his jeans' pockets. "I wouldn't want to interrupt. I'd probably wait to talk to her another time."

"What if you never find her without friends around?" Gretta cocked her head.

"I'd probably find some other girl to talk to."

"Exactly. See, that's what you want to avoid. Make sure you aren't always with a crowd." Gretta smiled and motioned for the front-row girls to sit back down.

Sharon took the floor then and signaled to her boyfriend, Hal. "Okay, now let's talk about things you might do that would drive a boy away. No one likes someone who is sarcastic, a smarty pants, or crude. That is not very attractive on a girl. What else do girls do that turns you off, Hal?"

Hal appeared to be on the intellectual side. He was thin and wore glasses and long hair. "You want a girl to look like she takes pride in her appearance. She doesn't have to be a raving beauty; not everyone can achieve that. But anyone can be neat and clean. Somebody who has wild hair or kooky clothes is not attracting the right kind of attention. No one wants to be seen with a girl like that."

Linda stood up. "What are you saying? You wouldn't date a girl unless she looked like every other girl in school? What if she wants to show her individuality? I'm not sure I'd want to date a boy who looked so boring."

Gretta jumped into the fray. "I think you can tone it down while you are looking for a boyfriend. Once you are dating, that might be the time to experiment with unusual styles."

"It sounds wrong to think a girl should change who she is just to attract a boy who might not be her type. Maybe he should change to catch her attention. Girls aren't so desperate." Linda was enjoying taking a stand.

"The point is that it is up to the young lady to show that she has been raised with good manners and has class," Mrs. Mattingly said. "Those are qualities any young man would appreciate."

Linda smirked and sat back down. *These ladies have escaped from the 1950s, disciples of Emily Post. Catch up to the real world where women are claiming their rights.*

Janet and Linda walked out of the auditorium together. All they had left was the final tea, where the girls could demonstrate some of their new knowledge.

"Do you buy that, what they were saying in there? Do you think boys want a girl who has manners and class?" Janet scrutinized Linda who had a distant look on her face.

"I don't think boys give a damn about manners or class." Linda sighed and looked at her new friend seriously. "I think they just want to get laid."

Janet's brows shot up and her cheeks colored, but before she could say anything else, her mother drove up to the curb to pick her up. Mary Jo pulled up a few minutes later and Linda got into her sedan.

"Mom, do you remember when you suggested I might want to talk to a therapist?"

"Of course, Dear. I find talking to my therapist always makes me see things more clearly."

"Go ahead and make the appointment. I feel like I am on a different planet than other girls sometimes. I don't like feeling this way." Linda ran her hand through her hair and breathed heavily.

"Oh, Sweetheart. I'll call tomorrow. Don't worry. Everyone feels like that sometimes."

CHAPTER SIX

June 16, 1988

Yvonne fingered the invitation from Linda, frowning at the words she used. "I'd like you to share some stories about your lives over the past decades that will surprise us, secrets or insecurities...maybe something you have done that you regret or something you wish you had done."

Didn't they all know what Yvonne's biggest regret was? Debbie certainly knew, although, Yvonne had avoided talking about it after things had gotten so intense. So, what could she tell them now? Maybe it would stop them from making the same mistake she had.

The babies were so little back then. She'd just given birth to Gigi and Jesse when Michael Conyers showed up in her hospital room. She remembered she'd been a mess, as they hadn't even let her shower or put on her own clothes. And there he was, looking like a million bucks in his expensive suit. She'd no idea Daniel had hired him at his law firm. And Daniel had no clue that Michael had been her first lover.

And Yvonne hadn't told him. That was Michael's request. He didn't want things to get awkward between him and Daniel. Later, she questioned Michael's real motives. And she knew it had been a mistake not to tell Daniel right away.

Things came to a head the same day that Daniel won a big case. Well, technically the case was dismissed. Daniel was defending Debbie's brother-in-law, Donald Washington. From what Yvonne gathered, many factors led to the case being dismissed, but certainly part of the credit belonged to Daniel and his team of investigators. Michael had been on Daniel's team and had provided some key information.

34

Yvonne remembered that night like it was yesterday. She'd tucked the twins in bed and waited for her husband to come home. He finally came through the door about midnight. She'd found him in the kitchen with his palms planted on the counter. He seemed unsteady on his feet.

"Daniel, it's late. Where have you been?" she said, walking up to him. He'd set two cans of beer left in a six-pack on the counter. She put them into the refrigerator.

The look he gave her could have frozen her heart. For a moment, he merely stared. "I went over to Donald's place. They were still having a party. Debbie and Robert were there."

She reached out to touch his arm and he flinched.

"We need to talk. Daniel, you have to listen to me." She put a hand on his cheek and he turned his face away from her.

"It's been a long day. I'm tired. Kids in bed?"

"Naturally. It's after midnight. Let's go into the living room."

"I'm taking a hot shower and going to bed. We can talk tomorrow." He brushed past her and went into the main bathroom.

She went back to bed and listened to the shower running. Tears spilled down her cheeks. She'd better get the crying out of her system before he came to bed. He'd accused her of using tears to try to manipulate him before, and she didn't want to be guilty of that. She had enough to be guilty about.

He got into bed and laid on his back after fumbling with a pair of pajama pants. He usually didn't wear pajamas to bed. She pretended to be sleeping, but sleep had alluded her so far that night.

After fifteen minutes, Daniel spoke. "Yvonne, how could you do that?"

She was thankful he'd broken the silence. "Do what?"

"You've been lying to me for what…six or seven months? You had a previous relationship with Michael Conyers."

"Yes. He asked me not to mention it. At the time, it seemed unimportant because it was ancient history."

"Today wasn't ancient history. He was here with you. He was supposed to be at work, in court with me. You said you were going to work. But you were both here together. So, what exactly has been going on behind my back?"

Yvonne swallowed hard. She was thankful that the darkness hid her trembling chin. "I am not having an affair with Michael."

Daniel exhaled slowly. "What were you doing here today?"

"He called and asked me to meet him here. I had already dropped the babies off at daycare and was about to leave for work. It sounded important, so I waited for him."

"Why did he need to see you?"

"He asked me if I wanted to—um—well, I guess he wanted to know if I still had feelings for him, if I wanted to get involved romantically again."

"So, he wanted to have an affair."

"Well, I'm not sure. I think he intended to get it all out in the open if I'd said yes. But I said I wouldn't do that. He asked me to choose and I did. I chose you."

"Pardon me if I don't sound appreciative. You made that choice years ago when you said wedding vows." Daniel sat up in bed. "He came here to ask you to leave me and what, move in with him?"

"No, he didn't say that. He said if I wanted to be with him, we needed to tell you. If I didn't want to be with him, he said he'd try to forget about me."

"How damn noble of him." She could see his eyes flashing

36

even in the semi-darkness. "What has been going on between you two that you didn't tell me about? What happened in the courthouse? Apparently, you were the subject of a lot of gossip."

"The courthouse? What do you mean?"

"No, don't play dumb. You were seen going into a meeting room on the third floor."

"Oh, um, that was silly. I don't know what he had in mind. He kissed me, then I left."

"You don't know what he had in mind? You're not that naive. You knew exactly what he had in mind from the moment he told you not to tell me you knew him. I don't take a lot of comfort in knowing you chickened out when he started pressuring you."

She got out of the bed and paced the room. "What do you want me to say? I handled this badly. I'm sorry. I thought it was harmless. We were just teasing each other. Then suddenly it started getting complicated. I never meant to hurt you."

"Well, you did. Make no mistake about that." Daniel got up, grabbed his pillow, and left the bedroom.

Even after all these years, thinking back to that night tore her heart out. Did she really want to tell her friends about it, especially Debbie?

She'd had the next day off, but she took the children to daycare in the morning. Daniel was still in bed when she left, but she hoped they could talk when she returned. But when she got back, he was packing a suitcase.

"You're taking a trip?" She asked when she found him zipping his bag in the bedroom.

"No, I'm staying at a hotel downtown for a few nights. I'd

stay with my folks but I don't want to drag them into this, and I have a lot of extra work I need to concentrate on. I neglected my other cases during Donald's trial. And I have to decide what to do about Michael." He hauled his suitcase into the living room.

"What do you mean?"

"I hired the guy with a civil servant's salary and gave him a nice career shot in a major law firm. He charmed everyone in the office but meanwhile, he went after my wife. I don't think I will ever be able to trust him. I have to get him off my team, maybe out of the firm. But to do that, I will have to explain this to at least one of the managing partners. That's going to be embarrassing. I vetted the guy pretty thoroughly, but it never occurred to me to ask my wife about him."

"You're going to fire Michael? But I told you, nothing happened."

Daniel's eyes narrowed. "Just because you didn't sleep with him, you think nothing happened? He's been courting you for months. I found phone calls from his extension to our number at times when I would have been working down the hall. There was a receipt for flowers sent to your office that he expensed. Once I started looking, the signs were there. Secretaries at our office knew something was going on; they just didn't know who his lady friend was. Once Donald's trial was over, he probably figured I'd be home more, and he'd better take his shot before that happened."

"You make this sound so calculating. It wasn't like that; it was an occasional flirtation."

"It may have been that way for you." Daniel shook his head. "But attorneys have to be calculating; their success depends on it. He was setting you up to see if you'd take the bait. I see you find that hard to believe, but if it is not true, if he was acting on some romantic impulse with his boss's wife, then he's just plain stupid. I have no use for stupid." He fixed her with a tense glare. "Do not try to warn him."

Yvonne gasped. There were times that Daniel seemed so driven, it scared her a little. But it also turned her on to think he had the power to alter Michael's career. "I won't talk to him again. He wasn't very happy with me when he left yesterday."

Daniel didn't return home until the weekend, and then their time was filled with the children and her parents coming over for dinner. It was Sunday evening before she had a chance to talk to him privately.

"You didn't tell me what happened with Michael," Yvonne said as they sipped wine on the patio.

"I don't think I can go into it. He'll likely be leaving the firm though. Things are in flux."

"Did you have to tell one of the partners what happened?"

Daniel sighed. "They all know about it now. Not the best thing for my reputation, let alone his. But there is something I need to tell you. I spoke to Tony Williams, one of the divorce attorneys in the firm. He's an expert, been there about thirty years."

Yvonne's heart leaped to her throat. "A divorce attorney? You can't mean that."

Daniel studied her. "You sound surprised." Then he smirked. "I wanted to ask Tony about marriage counseling, whom they usually recommend. He said when they have a client who asks them to file a divorce petition, the judge wants to see that they have participated in marriage counseling. Tony said most of the time, by the time one party files, they have already decided they want to move on, and the counseling is too late. I thought it made more sense to do counseling when you're trying to work on the relationship."

Yvonne frowned. "You want to go to marriage counseling?"

"Seems like it might be smart. Maybe I'll find out who this

mysterious woman is who married me. The one I thought I knew."

"Daniel! You know me. You know me better than anyone."

"Will you make an appointment for us?" He fished a business card out of his wallet and handed it to her.

She stood in front of his chair to take the card from him, then wrapped her arms around his neck and pulled him to her. He got to his feet, sliding her back so that he could embrace her.

"Is it time to make up?" Daniel started kissing her cheek working his way toward her lips.

She nodded and let a faint smile escape. The burden of the past week lifted at least a little.

They'd gone to six weeks of marriage counseling. On the final night, they surprised the therapist by revealing that their third child was coming. Yvonne remembered how amazed they had been considering her history of endometriosis. But it ushered in the next phase of their lives.

CHAPTER SEVEN

June 14, 1968

Brian was back! Linda couldn't believe it. She opened the front door one day in June, and there he was. She was so happy she threw her arms around his neck.

"Whoa there, Sailor. Give me a little breathing room. Let me look at you." The blonde tomboy he'd grown up with now had a pixie haircut, a girlish figure, and long tanned legs emerging from skimpy shorts.

Linda pulled him by the hand into the kitchen. "What can I feed you? You always used to be hungry. Do you want a milkshake?"

"It's not even noon, Linda. A soda or glass of juice is fine. Let's go outside and catch up."

She took him downstairs and out to the pool deck. Sarah was already lounging in a chair working on her suntan. They went to the opposite end of the patio and sat on a metal glider under a tree.

"What are you doing here? Why didn't you call me?" Linda asked.

"It was sudden. My dad drove us here yesterday. Mary, Chris, and I are staying at my grandparents' house for most of the summer. My dad already started driving back to Chicago this morning. My mom, she's uh not doing so well. She's going to be gone too, at some sort of rehab place."

"Rehab? What happened to her?"

Brian dropped his voice. "She's an alcoholic. My parents have been fighting. My dad convinced her to go to this spa place or something for treatment. He didn't want me to have to take care of Mary and Chris all summer, so we came back here."

"Well, I just got a job. I kinda shocked my parents because I didn't tell them about it beforehand. But I am going to be a carhop at this German drive-in called Runza. They gave me a pair of lederhosen to wear. I have to buy some yellow knee socks and a yellow T-shirt to wear with it. At least I'll have money to put gas in my car."

"You got your own car, that's right. I'm driving my grandma's Ford Galaxie. But it will probably be roomy when we go to the drive-in movies."

"Are we going to the drive-in movies?" Linda laughed.

Across the pool, Sarah lowered her shades and stared at Brian.

"You said you got a job. You can take me. I'll probably try to get some work mowing lawns around my grandparents' neighborhood."

A couple of weeks later, Brian came over to swim, and no one else was home besides Linda. After about an hour of horsing around in the pool, he asked, "Nobody else is here, huh? Maybe we should go someplace more private."

"What do you mean? This is private."

Brian hoisted himself onto the edge of the swimming pool. His dark curly hair was plastered to his forehead. He was growing rapidly, like most sixteen-year-old boys, and was already three inches taller than Linda. "It wouldn't be very private if someone came home and walked in on us."

Linda pulled herself out using the ladder and grabbed a beach towel to rub against her wet skin. "What do you mean? We're not doing anything embarrassing."

He wiggled his brows. "We could be. You have a bedroom, don't you?"

"Brian!" Linda covered her mouth in mock surprise. "You want to see my room? It is pretty cool. I can show you my art."

Brian grabbed his street clothes off the lawn chair and followed her upstairs. She handed him a towel and told him to get dressed in her bathroom. She put her shorts and T-shirt on too.

Linda wrapped her wet suit in the beach towel and left it on the bathroom floor when Brian came out. "Okay, this is my room. My mother hired a decorator for the whole house, and she was the one who thought these cabbage roses were so great." The wallpaper, bedding, and draperies were variations of the same red and coral roses pattern. "I can't say I cared, but these batiks I made myself, and of course I have my rock and roll posters." She pointed to one wall where she had covered most of the wallpaper with her own choices.

"Cool. I guess," Brian said. "I don't know anything about decorating. My room is painted white."

"So why did you want to see my room?"

He closed the door and locked it. "I thought we might do a little experimenting." He pulled her into his arms and slowly moved in for a kiss.

Linda laughed. "I don't know if you should kiss me. We're friends."

"We're friends. But that doesn't mean I don't want to kiss you. Then you can tell me if I do it right."

"Oh, I think you're doing fine—"

He backed her against the bed and they tumbled down onto it. He hadn't toweled off his hair and she felt the cool wetness hit her forehead when he ran his lips across her face. She supposed Brian was a good kisser but it seemed wrong somehow, like kissing a brother.

When he slipped one hand onto her bare back, she pushed him

43

off. "What do you think you're doing, Brian?"

"Experimenting. Like I said. Has anyone kissed you before?"

"Yes. You've even kissed me before, did you forget?" Linda squirmed away until she could sit up on the bed.

"I remember. But there's kissing and then there's serious kissing. I want to know how people get to that point where it drives them crazy."

"Oh no. I don't think so. Why would you want to lose control like that?"

Brian sat up and raked a hand over his face. "Okay, well, I have to tell you something that happened to me. But it's kind of embarrassing. Whatever you do, you cannot tell my brother."

Linda moved around so she could face him on the bed. "You can tell me anything, Brian."

"About a month ago, I went downstairs to my favorite little reading spot. I think I might have told you before. We have a guest room in the basement, and I put a bunch of pillows on the floor in the closet and put a little reading lamp in there. It's a cozy quiet little spot. Anyway, I was reading a mystery I got at the library."

"That's embarrassing?"

He held up his hand to signal there was more. "I heard voices outside the bedroom door, so I turned off the light and mostly closed the closet door. Then Cody comes barging in there with his girlfriend. They jumped on the bed and started going at each other like animals."

Linda started laughing. "And you were stuck—"

"Yes, I didn't dare breathe. But God, he was kissing her like he was trying to swallow her whole. I stopped looking but then the sound effects were worse! He'd say things like, 'I can't keep my hands off you. Your skin is so soft.' I kinda wanted to puke. Then she'd sorta squeal and he'd moan and it was awful."

"They had sex right in front of you?"

"I dunno exactly, but man, they were carrying on. Then I heard a door bang from upstairs and Cody scrambled up and the two of them left the room as quickly as they'd come in. When I turned the lamp on again, the bedspread was all rumpled up and a pillow was on the floor. But I don't think they figured out I was there. I didn't go upstairs for a while, and I didn't tell Cody. But later, I started wondering what made them get so crazy. So, I thought maybe if I tried kissing you, I'd find out."

"Did I miss the part where you went crazy?"

"No. I mean, you have nice soft lips and you do smell good, mostly like chlorine. But kissing you didn't make me act as Cody did. I am really confused now."

"Brian, Cody is three years older. Maybe we're too young to feel that way."

"Maybe," Brian said. "But what if there is something wrong with me?"

"I think you should just relax. Be glad you aren't a crazy fool like some boys. Find a real girlfriend whom you haven't known your whole life."

"Yeah?" Brian said, taking Linda's hand. "I guess we'd better get off your bed before someone comes home."

CHAPTER EIGHT

Linda was thrilled when she and Nancy Evans were selected as the newest baton twirlers for the upcoming marching band season. She imagined creating fun dances and routines that were more original than the ones she'd witnessed so far in school. And it was nice of the senior twirlers, Yvonne Edison and Debbie Adams, to invite them over to Yvonne's for a pizza party. The main event, however, was going to an all-city Keentime dance that evening.

Linda was a little nervous about that. She knew Brian wouldn't be there as his father was coming back for a visit that night. She tried to put on an air of confidence, but she dreaded meeting new boys. And Yvonne had put a lot of mascara on her lashes, making her feel like she was at a costume party imitating Twiggy. Twiggy may have been the hottest fashion model on the planet, but she was pretty sure the boys were plastering pin-ups of Jane Fonda as Barbarella on their walls, not Twiggy.

As soon as she tried to talk to a boy she thought might be attractive, she knew something wrong would leap out of her mouth. She tried to recall the lessons she learned in charm school, but all of that seemed so artificial. What was worse, being fake or being crude? The next thing she knew, her new twirler pals were running around the dance pavilion and she was adrift in a sea of strange teenagers.

She floated around the perimeter of the crowd. It was hot and loud inside. Most of the kids seemed to be talking to other friends. She would probably find the twirlers again if she kept moving. She looked up and saw a familiar face, a girl with big hazel eyes and long dark hair. *Where have I seen her before? Charm school? Gymnastics?*

"Linda, is that you?" the girl said. "Madeline Ambrose. Remember from fifth grade? God, it's been forever, but you look great!"

"Oh sure, Madeline! How are you?" Linda was so glad to see someone she recognized that she hugged Madeline. *Geez, why did I do that? I never hug people. Now she'll think I'm weird.*

But Madeline was apparently a toucher. She embraced Linda with gusto, ushered her over to a side bench and introduced her to two other friends. "Maisy, Phoebe, you must meet Linda. We had the most fun in fifth grade trying to survive that awful Mrs. Potter. You remember how we drew little cartoons of her with her screwed-up face?" Madeline laughed and wrinkled up her nose, imitating their fifth-grade teacher, "You children must show respect for your surroundings. A clean classroom is essential for healthy learning!"

Linda cackled. She'd never done that before. How had she let Madeline out of her life? She was a breath of fresh air. "And remember, we thought Mrs. Potter had the hots for the principal, Mr. Bates. He was bald and overweight and seemed like her type. I might even still have that picture I drew of the two of them."

Linda and Madeline crowded onto the bench with Maisy and Phoebe. Her new companions all attended Lincoln Southeast and were soon pointing out various boys in the crowd and sharing choice tidbits about them.

"That hunky guy over there is Jeremy, a big football hero. He's a senior next year and thinks he's pretty hot stuff. But my friend Patty went on a date with him and he talked about himself all night. Boring," Maisy said.

"Oh, and your ex is here, Maddy," Phoebe said. "That's him over by the far wall with the blonde hair. You see who I mean, Linda? Maddy went with him for two months, and then he just stopped calling."

Linda looked at Madeline for confirmation.

Madeline shrugged, "It was not a big loss. Plenty of fish in the sea."

Linda nodded. "I like your attitude."

"Besides, it is much more fun to hang out with my buddies." Madeline wrapped her arms around Linda and Phoebe's shoulders and pulled them toward her, nearly spilling everyone off the bench. They all started laughing.

"So, you gotta boyfriend, Linda?" Maisy asked.

"I dunno. Sort of. There's a boy who has been my friend forever. He moved to Chicago, but he's back for the summer. We hang out, but it's not romantic."

"But he's cute, right?" Madeline asked.

"Sure, he's cute enough."

"He didn't come with you?" Phoebe asked.

"No, he was busy. I came with my new twirler friends. See, there's one of them now." She pointed to Nancy, who was dancing with John Anthony Turner, a senior at Capital High.

"Wow. Who is that guy she's dancing with? He's a dreamboat!" Madeline asked.

"John Anthony. He's got quite the reputation. Most of the girls go a little ga-ga for him. But the story I heard was that his last girlfriend left town because she was preggers. I don't know him very well." Linda sighed, wondering if she'd said more than she should have.

Phoebe made some remark Linda couldn't hear and then Phoebe and Maisy started laughing again. Soon, the girls exchanged phone numbers and all agreed to come swim at Linda's house soon.

The next time she looked at the dance floor, Nancy and John Anthony had disappeared.

"I should probably go see what happened to the friends I came with. I enjoyed talking with you girls. I'll call you, Madeline, and

48

we'll set something up." Linda took her leave and went to search for Nancy, Yvonne, or Debbie. She spotted Yvonne on the dance floor with a tall red-haired boy. Before she found Nancy or Debbie, she nearly ran into John Anthony.

"Ah! There you are, Linda. I've danced with Yvonne and Nancy, so I think it is your turn," he said.

"What does that mean? You specialize in twirlers? I'm not so sure how that worked out for Barbra."

"Oh God, not you too!" He swiped his open palms apart in a gesture of denial. "Not my baby, all right? Turns out I must be the biggest chump in town because I didn't know Barbra was seeing anyone else. Now I have to prove to all the girls at school that I can be trusted. So please dance with me."

He looked so forlorn; she had to be sympathetic. "Why not?" Linda said and let him lead her to the dance floor. She caught a quick glimpse of Madeline watching them, and she stuck her tongue out, panting. Linda laughed. She'd never noticed how handsome John Anthony was with his athletic build and blonde hair that fell in layers framing his large brown eyes. Now that his eyes were taking her in, it was hard not to be mesmerized.

After dancing for about twenty minutes, they went outside. Many of the kids had left and the Keentime dance was winding down.

"So, what's your story?" he asked her. "Is it exciting to be one of the new twirlers?"

Linda smirked. "I think it will be fun, sure. I like to try new things. I'm hoping to add a few gymnastics moves into some of the routines, spice things up a little."

"You like to spice things up? Are you adventurous?"

"Hmmm. Not sure I know what you mean. I like to go pheasant hunting. I like target shooting."

"Oh, that's not what most girls like. Have you ever been water skiing?"

"Once, about three years ago. We went to a friend's house on a lake."

"Would you like to go water skiing with my family at Capital Beach? I can show you how to do it if you forgot."

Linda's brows shot up. *Is he asking me on a date? At least water skiing sounded fun.* "I might like that," she said.

"Okay, give me your number, we'll set something up."

And just like that, she was dating John Anthony Turner. Who would have thought it?

CHAPTER NINE

The summer was coming to a close. School would start right after Labor Day, but Linda had band camp the week before that. She was enjoying one of the last days of leisure, lounging around her family's swimming pool, drinking soda, and watching John Anthony try to do a flip off their low diving board. He bounced so high on the board, she was afraid it would snap in two, but he almost got his feet in first when he hit the water.

She'd enjoyed getting to know him. His family had a nice home facing Capital Beach Lake, and she'd been water skiing and boating with him several times. He seemed to appreciate that she was a quick study, and Linda's family liked having John Anthony around. He had good manners, and even Sarah said she liked him.

"Maybe you should try doing a handstand on the board first," Linda suggested, as J.A., as she had started calling him, emerged from the water.

"Can you do that?" he asked.

Linda sighed and put down her magazine and sunglasses. She ambled over to the diving board and stepped upon it. Then she began concentrating, hands at her side, and took a deep steadying breath. When she was sure he was watching, she leaped forward, did a handspring on the end of the diving board, and flipped over into the pool. She didn't rotate quite far enough and caught some of her backside as she went in.

"You didn't have enough height," J.A. told her when she surfaced. "Did that hurt?"

Before she could answer, she saw Brian coming out of the lower-level entrance to the house. He was dressed in his swimming trunks and had a towel and a bag with him.

Linda squinted in the bright sun reflecting off the water. "Brian? What are you doing here?"

Brian's gaze roamed from Linda to John Anthony. "You invited me to come over on Saturday. It was last week. Did you forget?"

"Oh," Linda was able to hide her reddening cheeks by ducking her head back underwater. "I guess I forgot that was today. But it's fine. Come and meet John Anthony."

Well, this is a little awkward. But Brian is still my friend, not my boyfriend. And J.A. is what? I dunno what J.A. is, but there's no reason for anyone to be jealous.

Brian and John Anthony seemed to be getting along well enough. Brian pulled the floating basketball hoop out of the pool house and they shot some baskets.

"Is that your Mercury Cougar convertible parked in the driveway?" Brian asked.

"Yeah, it's mine," J.A. said.

"Can I drive it?" Brian asked.

"Brian! He just got that car a few months ago. I haven't even driven it," Linda said.

"No, it's okay. You have a license, right? You're sixteen?" John Anthony pushed back up out of the pool. "We'd have to get dressed; I don't want it all wet."

"Yeah. Let's get dressed then go bomb Southeast King's," Brian said.

Linda laughed. "I can't believe you've heard that expression. You're not even living here."

"Cody used to talk about bombing King's; driving through to check out who's at the drive-in. But I've never gotten to do that."

They all changed into T-shirts and shorts and piled into John Anthony's Cougar. J.A. insisted on sitting shotgun in case Brian had any trouble with the car's operation.

52

They made a pass through the drive-in parking area at the King's Restaurant on South Fortieth Street and hollered at some of the teenagers there, just to be rowdy.

"Wait, go through again. I think I saw Madeline!" Linda cried.

Brian circled back to drive through the cars again.

"Madeline! Are you here?" Linda said loudly, and Madeline opened the passenger door of a Volkswagen Bug and jumped out. She ran out to see Linda, and Brian stopped the car, effectively blocking traffic. Horns blared behind them.

"Look, there's a spot next to us. Park right there," Madeline said.

Brian pulled in next to the VW. Madeline's companion, a tall, dark-haired boy named Gus got out. He climbed onto the backseat of the convertible and helped Madeline in. They joined Linda on the back end of the convertible with their feet on the seat.

Linda spoke up, "Madeline Ambrose, these are my friends, Brian Walker and John Anthony Turner. It's John Anthony's car but he let Brian drive. What are you doing today?"

"Nice to meet you boys. This is Gus. His real name is Wally Gustafson, but everyone calls him Gus. I'm so glad we ran into you, Linda. You have to come with us tonight." Madeline linked her arm through Gus's.

"Where?" Linda asked.

"We're going to check out Hobbitsville. Have you ever been there?" Gus grinned.

"What's Hobbitsville?" J.A. asked.

Gus's eyes widened. "It's this big ol' house, like an estate. It takes up a whole city block on Sheridan Boulevard. Supposedly some kids died there in one of the reflecting pools or they fell into a well. Now it's supposed to be haunted. But you have to watch out for the old lady who lives there. She has a gun."

"I've never heard of this," John Anthony said.

"Me neither," Brian said. "But it sounds like fun. What are you going to do?"

"We're going to walk around the outside of the fence to see what we can. Then, if we get inside, I'm going to take a picture," Madeline said.

They made plans to meet Madeline and Gus at nine thirty that night. They parked about two blocks away from their destination. Linda brought a flashlight and Madeline had her camera.

"If we go into their yard, we're trespassing, you know," John Anthony whispered when they approached the gate. "I don't want to scare a little ol' lady."

"It's an adventure. I thought you liked adventure, J.A." Linda flashed him a smile.

They stopped talking when they reached the designated location. There was a decorative wrought iron fence surrounding the property and they followed the fence around the block.

"Look there," Madeline said. "I think it's a pool." She grabbed Linda's flashlight and shone it through the fence. They could make out what appeared to be a section of a cement structure that might have been a shallow pool. "This is where they said the ghosts are. Let's go."

There was a brick section of the fence nearby, and Gus boosted Madeline up so that she could see over the wall. She swung her leg over and sat on the wall. Gus jumped and pulled himself up to join her. Then they both dropped to the ground on the far side.

"Now or never," Linda whispered.

Brian and John Anthony exchanged glances, then boosted

Linda to the top of the wall. They scrambled up the same way Gus had. Within minutes, they were all standing a few feet from the long cement pool. Linda shone her flashlight on something in the center of the pool. The fountain was dormant, but calcium pocked pipes seemed to vibrate in the dancing light. She jerked when the beam illuminated slimy algae floating ominously in the dark water.

For a moment, no one moved.

"You hear something?" Madeline whispered. The branches were thick overhead and rustled in the breeze. A nearly full moon slithered through the canopy, shifting shadows on the brick path at their feet.

"It sounds like someone is crying," Brian offered. He motioned with his hand to follow him down a path. They came to a limestone grotto which was rough and slippery. The flashlight beamed across the water's surface. It appeared that someone may have splashed water on the rocks.

"Do you think someone was swimming in here?" Gus asked.

"It's not deep, maybe three feet," Linda said.

Madeline climbed onto a spot on the grotto where there was an opening in the rock. She slipped off her thongs and scooted to the edge to dip her feet in the water. "The water is warm!" she said.

"There's something in there!" John Anthony said. "Like a snake."

Madeline jerked her feet back and tried to scoot off the rocks the way she came, but her cotton shorts snagged on a sharp part of the rocks.

"I'm stuck! Help me!" she cried out.

Brian was closest, so he reached out to tear the fabric away from the rock, making a hole in her shorts. Just then, a light turned on outside the back door of the house, and dogs began barking.

"Run for it!" Gus yelped. He grabbed Madeline's hand and her shoes and they sprinted for the fence where they'd entered. Brian, John Anthony, and Linda were on their heels, but Brian stumbled when they hit four steps that descended to the pool area.

When they made it to the wall, Madeline and Linda were boosted over first, then John Anthony and Gus scrambled over. Brian was struggling to get a foothold to help him over the wall. John Anthony boosted himself back up so that his chest was atop the wall and extended a hand back to Brian. Once he crested the wall, they all collapsed at the base, panting. They heard the dogs snarling on the other side. In a few minutes, a flashlight beam shone above them. Apparently, the person on the other side was too short to look over the six-foot-high wall and see them.

Linda covered her mouth with her hand to stifle her laughter. Madeline looked at her and also started to giggle. She buried her face in Gus's shoulder.

"I still hear it," Brian said. "The crying."

"It's the dogs. They're whining. They didn't get a bite out of us," John Anthony said.

"Did you take a picture?" Linda asked.

"Oh, I forgot!" Madeline said. She fished her Instamatic out of her jacket pocket and took a photo of Brian, John Anthony, Linda, and Gus all leaning together against the brick wall. When the flash went off, they all gasped a little. Madeline dropped back to the ground, hugging the wall.

When the light went back off near the backdoor, they rose and took a different route back to the car, so no one could see them through the open fence.

When they returned to Linda's house, Brian jumped out of John Anthony's car, into his grandmother's car, and headed down the street.

John Anthony and Linda lingered reflecting on the evening's activities.

"Is that the kind of thing you do for fun, Linda? Breaking the law?" he asked, leaning his head against the back of the seat gazing at the moon and stars.

She smiled coyly. "I can't say I've ever broken the law before. I may have driven my Camaro over the speed limit on the straightaway if you count that."

"You do drag races on O Street?" he clicked his tongue in mock dismay.

She shrugged, "Only when I'm challenged."

"You're kind of reckless, aren't you?" he said, leaning over the console toward her.

"Is that a problem?" she asked as his mouth got closer to hers.

He kissed her then, without even reaching out to touch her head or her back. Not easy with bucket seats. But it was sweet the way he snuck up on her mouth.

"You're not used to reckless, is that it?" she laughed when he pulled back a little.

John Anthony didn't answer, but this time when he kissed her, his hand wrapped around the back of her head, pulling her partway over the gearshift divider. It wasn't timid; it was a kiss designed to shake her down to her knees.

"I can get used to it. Goodnight, Linda."

CHAPTER TEN

Sarah had picked Linda up in her Pontiac Firebird, and they were speeding up Interstate 80 towards Omaha. "I can't believe Mom is letting us shop by ourselves," Sarah said. "My sorority sister, Janice, told me all the best dress shops to try in Omaha, so you will probably find something for homecoming that you wouldn't see on any other girl in Lincoln. I'm looking for something to wear to the Aksarben coronation. This is the first year I get to watch. Daddy thinks I have a good shot to be a princess the year I am twenty-one."

"I don't understand that Aksarben king and princess thing. Isn't the man they select for the king an old guy, like Daddy's age? So why wouldn't they select an older lady to reign with him, or better yet, have a young man and woman?" Linda asked.

"I'll probably learn more about it once I attend the coronation. But from what Mom said, it's all based on the civic contributions of your father. That applies to the king and the princesses. I guess they think it's more fun to have a young princess. I have read the resumes of the princesses too, and they are all very involved in charitable organizations. I may have to add a few activities this year. Of course, if I hope to be tapped for Mortar Board, that will help."

"Good luck with that. I certainly won't be anybody's princess," Linda said.

"Ha! You've always been Daddy's little princess. You know that," Sarah said. "But don't sell yourself short. Maybe Aksarben isn't your cup of tea, but you are certainly turning into a pretty girl. I mean, look at that hunky boyfriend you picked up this summer! He must think you're groovy."

"J.A.'s nice, and he's handsome, I guess. But we have more fun when we're doing something exciting, like racing around in his boat. I can't say I'm madly in love with him. Although he did offer to take me to Paris."

"Paris? Paris, France?"

"Oh, his father owns a travel agency. John Anthony's been to Europe about five times already. So, Paris might not be that extravagant for his family."

The first store they entered was in an upscale shopping center right off the interstate. Sarah went right to work, pulling dresses to try on. Luckily for Linda, they usually wore the same size. Sarah's choices were feminine and sophisticated, whereas Linda was drawn to styles that felt more avant-garde. They claimed adjacent dressing rooms and modeled each dress for the other.

Linda studied Sarah's reflection as she pivoted in the three-way mirror. This dress didn't do her justice. She'd always admired Sarah's confidence. Her bounteous blonde hair was always carefully coiffed. Her skin had a healthy radiance rarely seen, and her figure looked like she only ate the healthiest food. It didn't seem fair that Sarah rarely committed to any exercise regimen, but she still looked fit. She was nearly as tall as Linda's five-foot-six, but Sarah was more curvaceous like their mother. They shared the same blue eyes inherited from Nordic ancestors, but Sarah's always seemed to draw attention. Linda supposed the eye makeup she was never without might have made the difference.

"You know what we should do," Linda said. "You should let me pick your dress, and I'll let you pick mine."

"Really?" Sarah broke into a grin. "You'd wear one of the classic styles I picked out?"

"If that means I can dress you in something funky."

"It can't be too funky. This is for Aksarben. But as long as I get the final say, let's try it."

They switched dressing rooms, and Linda tried on Sarah's picks and vice versa. They did the same thing in the subsequent stores, but at least then they knew whom they were styling, which is how Linda ended up standing in front of the mirror in a dress that was much too pink for her taste.

"I dunno," Linda mused. "I guess this dress fits me nicely, but it is so girly. So Sarah." The pink wool sleeveless dress stopped three inches above her knees and had a hidden zipper down the front. The girlishness was accented with baby blue nylon ruffles framing the neckline. "Do you think it makes sense to have a wool dress without sleeves? I thought sleeveless was for summer wear."

"You haven't thought this through. You'd be dancing close with a boy and your shoulders and arms would be bare. Boys like bare shoulders, they are sexier than you think and unexpected in cold weather. I guarantee any boy would find a way to put his hands on your shoulders at a dance, especially if you mention that you are a little cold."

"Hmmm." Linda tried to imagine J.A. putting his hands on her shoulders. She didn't think he'd done that so far. "It might be too long."

"It fits divinely. And I'll bet this is a dress you could wear for years, at least in college. If you don't buy it, I may have to. But if you buy it, I can borrow it." Sarah folded her arms and circled Linda appraisingly.

"I'll get it if you choose the green one," Linda said. "Any guy who sees you in that will flip out."

Sarah had tried on a fitted emerald green dress with a V-neckline and a slit up the back. The silk fabric made you think of a tropical rainforest, but the style had an Asian influence. As soon as Sarah had zipped it up, they both had spoken just one word: sexy.

"All right, but I am not sure I can wear it to the coronation. It might attract the wrong kind of attention."

"Aren't you the one who told me that attracting attention was the point of wearing pretty clothes?" Linda grinned. "Whip out

Daddy's charge card and let's get on the road, Sister."

They made one more stop at the shoe department to find matching pumps before their shopping trip was complete.

"Who is taking you to this coronation thing anyway, Brad?" Linda asked, watching her sister parade around in shiny black patent leather heels.

"No, not Brad. James is taking me. He knows a lot about Aksarben. His family is involved."

Linda had lost track of her sister's suitors. At least they all seemed to be a cut above old Billy the Kid. Sarah would find the perfect mate. It was good that she was shopping around.

CHAPTER ELEVEN

When Debbie got Linda's letter, it was easy for her to pick a problem to share with her friends. She knew neither Yvonne, Nancy, nor Linda would have dealt with this issue. But maybe they'd give her new insight.

November 2, 1980

Debbie went into her eight-year-old son's bedroom and found him playing with the dog on the floor. "Jamal, have you been finishing your homework?" Debbie tried to make sense of his teacher's note.

"Yes, Momma. I do it every day." Jamal gave her the big puppy dog eyes that always melted her heart.

"This note from Mrs. Wiggins says you are daydreaming in class and have trouble with the reading. You don't seem to have trouble when we read at home."

"Mrs. Wiggins is mean to me."

"Jamal, that can't be true. She's trying to help you develop good habits at school. Did you bring home any assignments today?"

He shook his head. "I got my work done in class."

"This note says that you sassed her back. What did you say?"

"No, Momma. I didn't say anything. She aksed me a question and I didn't answer. Some other kid called out something snotty but it wasn't me."

Debbie was puzzled. Jamal was a bright and eager student, at least he had been until third grade. What had gone wrong? Robert had left town for a work assignment that morning, so she figured it was up to her to sort this out. André hadn't had a problem in third grade, but he'd had a different teacher.

She had the next day off work, so she decided to visit Jamal's classroom. She didn't even warn Jamal she was coming. She knew very little about Mrs. Wiggins, except that she was new to Jamal's school this year.

Class had already begun when she walked into the room and took a chair in the back. There was another mother already visiting. Jamal didn't even notice her. *That's good. Maybe I can get a better picture this way.*

They were talking about arithmetic. Mrs. Wiggins seemed to be pleasant enough and asked several questions of the class. Jamal always raised his hand, but she called on other students. When she asked a more difficult question, no one raised their hand except for Jamal. Mrs. Wiggins didn't call on him. She told the class the answer.

Why did she do that? Didn't she see his hand? Or did she figure if only one kid knew, she should just tell them the correct answer?

Debbie glanced at the other mother. "Which child is yours?" she whispered.

"Mary Alice. She's in the blue sweater about in the middle," the lady replied.

Debbie nodded. Little Mary Alice had brown hair and freckles like her mother. Cute girl.

Mrs. Wiggins gave the class some work to do, then walked around the room and looked over the children's shoulders. She'd nod or stop to point something out when speaking to some of the kids. But, when she passed Jamal, she didn't even glance at him; she kept moving. Debbie frowned. *What is going on here?*

Then they started doing their reading groups. The class was divided into two sections. Mrs. Wiggins had one group and a teacher's aide had the other group. Two other Black boys were in the same group as Jamal. All of the other children in his class appeared to be White. Debbie moved closer to Jamal's group, and then he noticed her and looked surprised, but kept his seat. She could tell from overhearing the other group that it had the more advanced books.

When it was Jamal's turn to read aloud, he read every word correctly. He even added a little emphasis on certain words, making it more dramatic.

"Just read the words, Jamal. This isn't supposed to be funny," the aide warned him.

But can't it be fun?

After reading class, the children went out for recess. Debbie decided it was time to investigate. She waited her turn to speak to Mrs. Wiggins.

"Hello. It was nice of you to visit. What's your name?" the teacher asked.

"I'm Debbie Washington, Jamal's mother."

"Oh, Jamal. I heard about his family. Are you his foster mother, or is he being adopted? It must be so challenging raising a crack baby!"

Debbie's jaw dropped. For a moment, she couldn't respond. Then, finally, she drew in her breath and spoke softly. "I don't know what you're talking about. He's my son, not a crack baby."

"I was talking about his birth mother, of course. I've seen this quite a bit when I taught in the inner-city schools. It's the poor little kids that suffer, and sometimes the schools don't know what to do with them."

Debbie shook her head. "I gave birth to Jamal. There was no crack or any other kind of drugs involved. Where did you get such an idea?"

"But you are so light. You can't be his momma."

"He's the spitting image of his father if you must know. But why did you think there was something wrong with him?"

"I heard stories. Like I told you, I've seen this before. And when I ask him questions, he gives me strange answers sometimes. Like when I showed a picture of a dog and asked what it was, the other kids said 'dog.' Jamal said it looked like a mix between a cocker spaniel and a poodle. He never gives a straight answer, so sometimes, I don't give him a chance to derail the class. I have to ignore him."

Debbie's eyes widened. "Maybe he is more creative or informed. We have had dogs that are mixed breeds. Why is he in the lower reading group?"

"That's another thing. When he reads aloud, he changes his voice like he's acting out a play. It makes the other children laugh and we need the time to get everyone learning the words."

"He is being funny when you need the class to be serious? We can work on that."

"I figured his behavior was unavoidable due to his mental defects. I mean, those other two dark boys in the class are behind too."

Debbie was having trouble containing her temper. She wished her husband was home to give this woman a piece of his mind. But she couldn't wait for his return, She had to take matters into her own hands.

"Mrs. Wiggins, I am not at all sure you are the right person to be teaching Jamal. He will be leaving with me today." The class came running back into the classroom from the playground. Debbie marched over to Jamal and took his hand.

"We have to leave today, Sweetie. Grab your bookbag."

"But Momma ..." he started to say. "Hot dogs for lunch."

65

Debbie hadn't thought about what it would be like to raise biracial children. When she fell in love with Robert, she couldn't deny that part of the attraction was that he was Black. At first, she convinced herself that she had paid no attention to that. But as time went on and their relationship became more intimate, she appreciated all the ways he was different than any other boy she'd known. And she'd learned over time, watching him interact with his family members, that his heritage shaped not only his appearance but his mindset, his personality, his ambition.

But they'd jumped into parenthood without much time to consider what effect their races might have on children. Debbie had been surprised to learn that her offspring were all considered Black. She'd never heard of the one-drop rule: that anyone with any Black ancestor within four generations was automatically classified as Black. She didn't understand how her own White DNA had been obliterated.

Like most offspring, her sons and daughter had inherited various physical traits from both of their parents. André and Chantelle were both light-skinned enough that strangers rarely questioned her role as their biological mother. One of her church friends had approached her once, telling her that she had used a chemical straightener on her hair, and when Chantelle was older, she might consider that. If her hair was smoother, she could pass for a White girl. Debbie had been a bit horrified. Why should Chantelle pretend to be someone other than herself? But then she decided she'd leave it up to Chantelle once she was a teenager and dying to fit in.

Then there was Jamal. He resembled his father so closely that it was hard to tell the difference between a photo of Jamal at age two and a similar one of Robert at that age. As he grew older, she occasionally would see traits in him she recognized in herself, or she would catch herself thinking Jamal reminded her of her twin brother, Daniel. But how did Jamal see himself? Did he set himself apart from his two siblings? Did he see himself like the dog in the teacher's picture, a mixed breed?

Debbie gasped. She'd never considered that. Was that why he'd answered the question the way he had? Did he want to be seen as two separate entities? She had been angry at the teacher, but now she was worried about Jamal. She needed to talk to her husband.

The children were in bed by the time Robert called her. He was in Florida working on a project with some NASA engineers. "Sorry to call so late. These guys know how to turn dinner into a three-hour event," he said.

She relayed the events of her morning. "I really wish you were here to confront that Mrs. Wiggins. Maybe she'd get the message if you got in her face."

"You want me to go all angry Black man on her ass?" he asked.

"Yes. At least it would be fun to watch."

"Hold on there, Momma Bear. You sure you didn't overreact a bit?"

"No, I didn't. You would have been just as mad. She not only ignored what Jamal needed, she assumed those other two boys were stupid or crack babies or something, just because they were Black."

"Do you know if those two other boys are having trouble in school? Do you know who they are?"

"Well, no. I didn't get their names. Jamal probably knows them."

"Okay, let's take this one step at a time. You could complain to the principal, maybe get Jamal moved to the other third-grade classroom. That might be a good solution for him, but in the short term, he'd have to adjust a whole new class and teacher."

"But isn't that better than some racist—"

Her husband continued, "Or maybe you could engage the principal and the teacher together and try to have a meaningful dialogue. Maybe they would allow the parents of the other two Black boys in his class to participate. That would take longer, but you might be doing all of the kids in Mrs. Wiggins' class a favor for years to come. Once she sees you're trying to help, Mrs. Wiggins might be more receptive."

"You want me to be more diplomatic."

"It's a good place to start. If it doesn't work, you can always try something more drastic."

She'd taken his suggestion. The principal was receptive to inviting the parents of the other two boys she'd identified for a meeting. It turned out one of the two had a learning disability, and the other was somewhat shy. They had both expressed to their mothers how much they admired Jamal. That nearly brought her to tears to think of her eight-year-old setting an example.

After a while, Debbie found the meetings were worth the effort. Jamal was moved to the higher reading group, and he began to talk excitedly about school again. He even made friends with several classmates, including the other two boys the teacher had singled out. She found that Mrs. Wiggins mellowed a little bit. In a couple of years, she transferred to a different school again, before Chantelle started third grade.

Debbie thought about how to explain this episode that had happened eight years earlier to her twirler friends.

I always knew I'd be a mother; I took it for granted growing up. Of course, I didn't expect to start at age eighteen. But had I doomed my future children to extra hardships by marrying someone of a different race?

No, that was stupid. She could search the world and not find a better father for them than Robert Washington. He was intelligent, hard-working, successful, and gave back to his community. But no matter what else was on his plate, he always had time for her or the children, to talk with them, to listen, to offer ideas.

No, she may not have taken the easiest path, but it was the one she believed in. If other people in society didn't like it, that was their problem.

CHAPTER TWELVE

Linda walked into the homecoming dance holding John Anthony's hand. She was wearing the pink wool dress her sister had picked out. She felt the other girls' eyes on her. After all, her date was a candidate for Homecoming King. It should have been perfect, a sixteen-year-old girl's dream come true. He certainly looked the part of a Prince Charming. His blondish hair was slicked back to show off more of his beautiful face.

Most boys she knew were still a little round-faced like the children they'd been, or they were battling acne or scattered whiskers coming in. But John Anthony's face looked like it had been chiseled to perfection, and no amount of dirt, sweat, or bruising from the football game could mar his countenance. He had the face of an air-brushed fashion model. Not necessarily a male model.

But she couldn't help but think something was missing. It had been nagging at her since they left her house. They'd had to wait for Peter to come to meet Nancy, who had gotten dressed for homecoming at Linda's house. Peter was late because he'd been in some sort of fight with his brother.

But when he came into the living room, he'd kissed Nancy. No, that wasn't right. She'd kissed him first, very gently. Then he'd practically exploded and grabbed Nancy and laid such a passionate kiss on her that they both came up panting. Linda had found her breath taken away just witnessing that kiss.

That's what kept haunting her tonight. She remembered something that Brian Walker had told her about his brother kissing his girlfriend with such enthusiasm. She'd never been kissed like that, never even expected it. But now she wondered why. What had Nancy done to make Peter kiss her like that?

Partway through the evening, she and John Anthony went outside to the courtyard. When they returned to the dance floor,

Nancy and Peter were gone. It made her wonder if they had wanted to spend more time alone. But John Anthony seemed perfectly content to keep dancing.

After the dance ended, he took her home. There was a driveway at Linda's house that circled to the back of the garage, where a second garage door allowed entry to park two cars nose to nose or, in this case, a big riding lawnmower parked in the rear. John Anthony pulled around the driveway circling the garage which hid them from the street view.

"Did you have fun tonight?" J.A. asked, pushing a lock of hair back from her forehead.

"Yes, it was nice. Last night was nerve-racking doing all those twirling routines, but tonight was relaxing." The previous evening at the football game, Yvonne, Debbie, and Nancy had joined her in twirling fire batons, flags, and hoops. It had been a lot to learn, but it had been a fun challenge. Of course, he was a halfback on the football team, so he'd had his hands full too.

He leaned across the console and kissed her gently.

"John Anthony?"

"Hmmm?" He'd moved his mouth around to kiss the side of her jaw.

"Do you still think about Barbra?"

He leaned back in his seat. "Sure. I've tried to picture what she must look like now. She must be seven or eight months pregnant. I haven't heard from her though."

"Did you love her?"

John Anthony looked away through the windshield and huffed out air. "I suppose I did. I guess I didn't even realize it until the whole mess blew up. Her father came storming over to my house. That's how I learned she was pregnant. I guess I told you that."

"I don't think I heard that story."

"Oh. Well, her father assumed I was responsible since Barbra and I had been dating for about three months. But we didn't ... that is, I haven't had sex with her or anyone else. I think you should wait for something like that. If not for marriage, then at least when you are ready to get married. I guess that makes me pretty square."

"No, I think you should follow your conscience."

"I'm done talking about my messed-up love life. Tell me about yours."

Linda sighed. "Not much to tell. You met Brian. He and I have been pals forever. He did try kissing me once. I don't think it felt right for either of us. I guess the friend thing got in our way." There was no reason to tell John Anthony about her more sordid history.

He moved in closer to her and pulled her raincoat off her shoulder so he could plant a kiss on her skin. *I guess Sarah called that one. Boys do like bare shoulders.*

"Just so you know, I don't want to be friends with you." He kissed her shoulder again and then her cheek and then her mouth.

Linda tried to relax and enjoy it. He smelled like English Leather, and his caresses were warm and gentle. Of course, with the console between them, it was a little uncomfortable.

Maybe he'd read her mind because he said, "Do you want to get into the back seat?"

Linda glanced behind them and yawned. Immediately she slapped her hand over her mouth. She hadn't meant to do that.

John Anthony chuckled. "Or maybe you're tired and need to get some sleep."

I know I am blowing this big time. The best-looking boy in the senior class is trying to make out with me, and he thinks I'm bored.

72

"I'm so sorry! I guess I am kinda sleepy. Maybe I could get a rain check on the backseat thing." Linda figured she was probably the first girl ever to turn John Anthony down, and maybe it would signal the end of their relationship.

CHAPTER THIRTEEN

Linda didn't need an excuse the plan a party. She'd thrown some epic ones already. Every year, her mother let her have her school friends come over for her birthday in February. Once she got to second grade, Linda had begun planning her party with a theme, or something unusual that would make everyone talk about it for weeks. One year, it was a Miss America contest, where the guests had to have a talent display. One year it was a "Bring Your Pet" party. That had ended badly with a literal cat and dog fight.

But Linda loved hosting, especially once they moved to the large house that was designed for entertaining. She was now focusing on throwing a holiday party in December.

This party wasn't going to have a theme, but of course, there would be Christmas decorations. Mainly she wanted to have fun entertainment for her friends. She'd gotten an idea from Madeline to play "Spin the Bottle." Madeline said she'd played it with her group, and she was surprised when boys and girls kissed someone other than whom they'd been dating. Linda thought that might be fun to orchestrate.

She jotted down a few rules for the game. She supposed if they spun a bottle sitting in a circle, it would point to someone of the same sex about half the time. They'd have to be able to spin again when that happened. Oh, but what if they didn't want to?

I don't know if I would want to kiss all of the boys I'm inviting. But maybe it would be fun to kiss some of the girls. That would shock everyone for sure. And let's face it, girls smell sweet and have soft lips. From a practical standpoint, they were more appealing.

So, she'd give the spinner the option. And with the right girl, Linda might try something new. She reviewed the list of girls she'd invited. They were juniors and seniors who knew each other from band class. There were only two girls she thought she could get away with kissing. Yvonne Edison and Nancy Evans. The other twirler, Debbie Adams, was nice enough but perhaps too naïve. Linda couldn't be sure how she'd react, and it could blow up in Linda's face, especially since Debbie's twin brother, Daniel, would be there.

But Yvonne and Nancy would probably be comically outraged, and Linda could handle that. And she had to admit, she thought both of them were beautiful. Yvonne was tall and graceful with wavy mahogany hair. She had the kind of classic beauty that boys couldn't help but notice as though she'd stepped out of a magazine. Nancy was cute, but her striking long red hair and emerald eyes were captivating.

After the party was in full swing, Linda brought out the empty wine bottle and had the fourteen guests sit in a circle, alternating boys and girls.

"If you spin the bottle and it points to someone who is the same sex as you are, you have an option to keep spinning until you get someone of the opposite sex. Or you can kiss the person it points to. Up to the spinner," Linda explained.

John Anthony started the game, and the bottle landed on Nancy. It didn't take too long before it was Randy Sparks' turn and the bottle pointed to Linda. Randy was sitting right next to her but moved very slowly toward Linda, trying to be funny. Finally, Linda gave him a quick peck on the lips.

She took a deep breath and spun the bottle. It pointed to Yvonne, who was sitting on the other side of Randy. This was the opportunity she'd wanted. She put her hand on the bottle as though she was going to spin again. Then she quickly pounced past Randy and landed on Yvonne. When Yvonne fell back from the impact, Linda climbed on top of her and kissed her before Yvonne could stop her. Randy, who was dating Yvonne, started laughing. When Linda pushed herself back to her knees, he helped her get back to her place in the circle.

75

"Linda! What the—? What'd you do that for?" Yvonne rubbed her mouth.

Linda laughed, wondering if she'd have another chance to do that or if anyone else would dare try something similar. But the next thing she knew, Yvonne was in the center of the ring kissing Daniel. It was such a prolonged kiss that everyone pretty much forgot about Linda's antics. So, there was something still going on between Yvonne and Daniel. They hadn't been dating for at least six months.

But Randy, who was dating Yvonne, and Andrea, who was dating Daniel, were not happy after this show of affection. The whole party wound up soon after the "Spin the Bottle" game ended.

Linda had almost forgotten about the game by Monday when Yvonne cornered her after school in the hallway.

"Linda, why did you kiss me Saturday night?" Yvonne folded her arms and grimaced.

Linda grinned. "It was supposed to be funny. Randy got it, he laughed."

"I didn't find it funny."

"Oh, lighten up, Yvonne. My therapist told me I should be more open to exploring my inner child. That's all I was doing, trying not to be bound by society's constraints."

"Well, there are some constraints that are there for your own good. Girls simply don't kiss other girls like that."

Linda shrugged. "I didn't mean to offend you. I was just playing. Besides, you're the one who got the room buzzing after you laid that big one on Daniel. And here I thought the two of you were over." Yvonne's cheeks colored, and Linda felt like she'd shifted the focus.

"Daniel and I are over. Otherwise, he would have called me, right? And apparently, Randy and I are over too, or at least he's mad at me. So, I guess I shouldn't have been so bold either. That is a dangerous game."

"Daniel's the one you really like, isn't he?" Linda asked.

Yvonne glanced down the hall to see if anyone was within earshot. "I suppose I do. But I'm not sure he feels the same way."

"Maybe you should tell him. Don't wait for him to make a move. Boys can be so dense."

"No, I—" Yvonne dropped her eyes. "I think that might be worse."

"Suit yourself. But you could get tired of waiting." Linda raised her brows and sauntered down the hall toward the outside doors.

CHAPTER FOURTEEN

January 1969

Linda was proud of herself for getting her job back as a carhop a few days into the holiday break. Of course, she hadn't asked her parents' permission to start working again. But Mary Jo and Michael were too busy sniping at each other to spend time with her anyway.

She tucked her long-sleeved yellow T-shirt into the forest-green lederhosen. With her matching yellow knee-high stockings and black loafers, she looked like a German boy. She'd added a green knit cap to match the lederhosen and keep her ears warm. She wore a ski jacket over her top half most of the time, but she kept it open to show off her uniform. Running back and forth between the Runza drive-in and the patrons in their cars didn't keep her warm.

Still, she was having fun. The tips weren't great, but most of the customers were friendly, and she liked the staff at the restaurant. For her first job, she felt lucky.

There were occasionally abusive customers, especially toward closing time, when they might have been drinking or smoking pot. But even if they made a snide remark, she could retreat pretty easily when they were in their cars and she was on her feet.

Tom Case became a regular customer. If the other girls saw his green 1966 Jeep with the zippered windows, they immediately maneuvered Linda into taking his order. At first, she didn't even think she liked him.

"Good afternoon, Farmer Boy. What's it going to be today?" Linda narrowed her eyes at his smiling face peeking under a black Stetson.

"That's Rancher Boy if you please." He leaned out the window to give her the once-over. "And I don't know that you are in any position to criticize someone's wardrobe choices. Who are you supposed to be, Pinocchio?" His blue-grey eyes squinted behind black frames.

Linda rolled her eyes. "Pinocchio is Italian. Everyone knows that. Lederhosen are Bavarian." She parted her blue ski jacket and gestured to her short suede pants with the leather braces joined by a panel featuring an Edelweiss.

Tom's brows shot up. "Nice. You give everyone that show?"

She frowned. "Do you have a food order to place?"

"Hey, don't be mad. I apologize. Your legs are much better than Pinocchio's. Give me one of those Runza sandwich things and some French fries. Are the fries really French, or are they German too?"

She stomped back to the restaurant without asking what size fries he wanted. When his order was ready, she suggested another girl deliver it, but no one would get her off the hook.

"One Runza sandwich and one medium fry." She held out a small brown tray with the food to Tom. He unzipped the Jeep's window.

"Oh, I guess I forgot to order coffee," Tom said pursing his lips. She scowled and turned on her heel. "Black please!" he called after her.

He's going to stiff me now. He'll drive off with his food without paying.

But he was eating his ground beef and cabbage bread pocket when she returned with a large coffee. He smiled at her and handed her a folded five-dollar bill, which was much more than his order cost. When she fished her fingers into her change apron, he held up his hand.

"Keep the rest. I can see you work hard. And this job gives you goosebumps."

79

She narrowed her eyes at him again. The only place she had goosebumps was on her thighs. Why was he looking at her thighs? He must be a creep. She'd already met enough creeps on the job.

"What's your name?" he asked when she didn't retreat.

She sighed. *He is not going to intimidate me.*

"My name is Linda. Who's asking?"

"Tom. Tom Case. When do you work again?"

She squinted. He was pushing it now. "I work again on Friday, eleven to four."

"Good. I'll be hungry for another one of these by then. See you Friday, Linda."

This became a pattern for a few weeks. He'd show up almost always during her shift and ask about the next time she worked. And even though it appeared he might be a college student; he always gave her a decent tip.

After a few weeks, she began to trust him more. "What are you having today, Mr. Tom Case Rancher Boy?" Her pencil was ready on her order pad.

"Man, that is a long name. How about just Tom? I'd like to have your phone number, Linda."

Her gaze darted to his eyes. He looked like he was serious. Was it against the restaurant rules to go out with a customer? She had no idea. "I don't know if um ..."

"Look, it's nothing major. You give me your number. I call you. We find out more about each other and take it from there. I can't monopolize your time while you're at work. I don't want you to get in trouble."

She studied him. She'd never seen anything suspicious in his car. He hadn't given her any reason not to believe him. Sometimes you had to take a chance. She gave him her teen line number and took his order.

Tom called her the next day. "Are you still wearing lederhosen, or do you sometimes impersonate American girls?"

"I'm not telling you what I'm wearing." She had learned how to tease him and he seemed to like it.

"Oooh. Now my imagination is going a little crazy," he laughed. "How about you tell me all about Linda the carhop. Do you have a last name?"

"I do. It's Bridges. Linda Bridges. I'm a junior at Capital High School. I'll be seventeen next month. Wait. How old are you?"

"God, are you worried that I'm thirty or something? I'm eighteen, will be nineteen in July. I'm a freshman at the university. I live with my cousin in an apartment on K Street, about a mile from campus."

"You called yourself a rancher."

"My family lives on a ranch in the Sandhills near Gordon. There are more cattle than people there, so coming to the university was a bit of a shock. Right now, I'm studying botany, but I am thinking of switching to landscape design."

Linda chuckled. "You really are a rancher boy."

"You betcha. Have you thought about going to college after high school?"

"I'm sure I'll get to college one of these days. I would kind of like to travel a little after high school though. Maybe backpack through Europe."

"Gee, you'd better save your tip money if you want to fly to Europe. Staying in hostels might be cheap, but getting there won't be."

Linda smiled. How long could she make him think she was struggling to hang on to her meager wages from her part-time job?

81

"How about you? How do you pay your rent and tuition?"

He groaned. "Oh, Daddy had to sell his prize steer for my first-semester tuition. Good thing he's got a couple of hundred head of cattle. I wish I could do a student work-study, but my family income is over the limit to qualify."

"You mean you can make money raising cattle?" Linda realized she knew very little about agriculture, despite the fact it was a major industry in her state.

"You can make a shitload of money in the cattle business. But after spending my formative years shoveling shit, I decided I'd rather work with plants."

On Saturday evening, she invited him over to her house to watch television. Her father was going out and her mother retired to her room early, so she didn't even have to introduce Tom.

By the time she'd led him to the family room in the basement, Tom was laughing.

"What's so funny?" she asked.

"This was not what I pictured. I thought you were a poor high school girl trying to help your family make ends meet. This place is a palace."

She smiled. "My father runs an insurance company. The biggest insurance company in town. We're doing okay." She plopped on the leather couch in front of the television. "I thought it would be smart to earn a little money on my own."

He shook his head and sank next to her. She had a better look at him then, without the cowboy hat or suede jacket. He was taller than she'd realized, at least six feet. Now that he was not pinned behind the steering wheel, she thought he moved with a certain confidence, not only in the way he walked, but his stance, and even the way he moved his arms down to his fingertips. As if his reflexes were always on high alert. At close range, his grey-eyed gaze was more intense, putting her slightly off-balance. He exuded a very male aura.

His well-cut brown hair fell over his ears and kissed the top of his collar. His light blue sweater covered a plaid shirt and rust-colored corduroy jeans. When he sat back, cowboy boots sprang under his boot-cut pants. Someone had purchased his clothes with care. Most likely, it was his mother.

Linda went up to the television and tuned it to the Saturday night movie. "Oh good, *How the West Was Won* is on. They probably filmed this in your backyard, didn't they?" She smirked and sat back down on the couch, tucking one foot under her. Linda was wearing new jeans and a snug black poor-boy sweater, basically a thick T-shirt with a cable pattern.

"What exactly are you implying, Pinocchio? Do you think western Nebraska still looks like it did in the last century? We have TV out in the sticks, you know."

"How many channels?"

"Um, one. Well, sometimes we get a Rapid City station on a clear day, but you can't hear it. We sit around and pretend we know what the people on the screen are saying. It's quite the game in my family. Or we play board games." Tom reached out and ran the back of his fingers down her lower arm.

"How many are in your family?"

"Well, it depends who you count. I have a brother who is four years older than I am. Then a sister one year younger'n me and another four years younger. Then the last brother is seven years younger than I am. My big brother, Jerry, went to Chadron State for a couple of years, but now he's back trying to take over the ranch. Trouble is, my father and his father are still running things. It's kind of a multiple-generation thing. My great-grandparents settled there first. In addition to my parents and five kids, we've got my grandpa, who everyone calls Chief, living there in one of the other houses on the ranch. We bring in extra help, during the busy season, which might mean five or six more people staying in the bunkhouse. Been like that all of my life."

"And you're not planning to be a rancher?"

"I don't think so. I like the outdoors. Can't see myself working at a desk for a living, but I could get a job helping farmers plant the best seeds or planting ornamentals around fancy places like this one. My mom let me design the landscape around her house, and she gets a lot of compliments. Next summer, I'm going to install a fountain."

"I think I am going to try dental school myself."

"You want to be a dentist?" he asked.

"Well, I am not sure about that part. I know I need a job that pays me well enough to hire someone else to cook and clean for me, so I don't have to do that. Several dentists who live around here seem to do well financially. I don't want a job like my dad has. He is always going to meetings at night or working in his study after hours. That's too much stress. My goal is to make the most amount of money, wasting the least amount of time doing it. Dentists seem to have limited office hours."

"I guess you could marry some man who makes a lot of money. Then you could stay home and still hire someone to do housework."

Linda scoffed. "Then I might get stuck taking care of kids. That might be worse than housework." She grimaced. "I think I'll stick with the dentist idea until I come up with something better."

"You're pretty funny. But I guess you have plenty of time to reconsider what you want to do," Tom said.

They watched the movie in silence for a few minutes. They'd taken off their shoes to put their feet side by side on a large hassock in front of the sofa.

"Are you cold?" Linda asked, getting up to pull a quilt out of a chest near the outer wall. She spread it over his legs and then snuggled back up next to him, a little closer than they'd been before. She could feel his eyes on her as she moved around.

"January," Tom said, "is snuggling weather. You get a big fire going out there in a log cabin in the Sandhills, snow three feet deep all around you, and you just want to eat hot soup and snuggle close with someone. Preferably a warm girl like you."

Linda felt her cheeks coloring. "You live in a log cabin? Like in the movie?"

He laughed. "No. But my grand-pappy did back when. We do have a log cabin we use as an outbuilding, and some knotty paneling in our house, but it's pretty modern. Even indoor toilets." He slipped an arm around her waist. "I was talking about snuggling. It's an excellent way to conserve heat." Tom nuzzled her ear and kissed the back of her neck, making her shiver.

She leaned her head back on the sofa, sure he was about to kiss her when they heard a ruckus on the stairs.

"Oh! Linda! I didn't know anyone was down here. My goodness, it is cold out there!" Sarah exclaimed. A blonde broad-shouldered young man was on her heels, wearing a ski coat and knit cap. They walked up to the couch where Tom and Linda sat up a little straighter. "Thad, this is my little sister, Linda. She's a junior in high school. Linda, meet Thad Benson. He plays football at the university, and he was in my economics class."

Linda studied Sarah's latest beau. Good-looking and well built. Her taste had improved.

"Nice to meet you, Thad," Linda said. "But what are you two doing here? Don't you usually spend Saturday night at the sorority house?"

"Yes, but Thad and I wanted some time alone. I didn't know you'd be here watching TV with …?"

Tom stood up and reached out to shake hands with Sarah and Thad. "Tom Case. I'm a freshman at NU. Is that where you go to school?"

"A college boy? Lindy, how did that happen?" Sarah winged her brows.

Linda prickled at her sister's tone, as though she wasn't allowed to meet anyone outside of school. "I met him at work," Linda narrowed her eyes. "We're trying to watch a movie here."

"Oh yeah? Who's in it?" Sarah glanced at the console television.

Linda looked at Tom for help. "Um, what's-his-name. The guy from that Christmas show, *It's a Wonderful Life*."

"Jimmy Stewart?" Sarah asked.

"And Debbie Reynolds," Tom added.

"Yeah, her." Linda nodded.

Sarah scoffed. It was pretty clear they'd taken over the spot she'd wanted on the basement sofa. She led Thad over to the bar on the far side of the room. She took two cans of beer out of the refrigerator under the counter and settled on a barstool next to Thad. "Do you wanna beer, Tom?"

Tom looked at Linda who shook her head.

"No, thank you. I'm good." Tom leaned back onto the couch.

Linda put on a pretense of watching the movie then, but Sarah and Thad's hushed voices and laughter distracted them. She crossed her arms over her chest tightly and set her jaw. Tom pulled the quilt up around their shoulders and scooted his hips right next to hers. His arm was back around her with his hand resting on her thigh. The romantic mood, however, was ruined.

"Maybe I should go," he said softly in her ear.

"I'm sorry," Linda said.

"You could come to my apartment sometime," he suggested. "Not this nice, but no sisters."

Linda shot a glare toward Sarah who had her hand on Thad's shoulder and was leaning close to his face. Her gaze returned to meet Tom's. She planted a soft kiss on his lips. He took the hint and wrapped his hands around her head and took her mouth. Linda heard Sarah gasp.

I couldn't have planned that better if I'd tried.

When they broke apart, Linda was chuckling and Tom was smiling. He stood and grabbed his cowboy boots and headed for the stairs under Sarah's disapproving glower. Linda followed him to the door to say goodnight.

CHAPTER FIFTEEN

Tom woke to loud voices and the front door banging in his first-floor apartment. The old house he lived in with his cousin, Warren, had been divided into this ground floor apartment, where he was, and two smaller ones on the second and third floors.

Who the hell was that? Warren had gone home two days ago. Warren had returned to Valentine quite a few times since they moved in last September. How did he expect to fit in if he wasn't here to meet new people on the weekends?

Tom's feet hit the floor, and he pulled on his blue jeans. Was someone breaking in? They had nothing worth stealing. Maybe someone was whacked out on drugs or something. He picked up his trusty baseball bat he'd tucked inside the closet and carefully opened the bedroom door. His cousin, Warren, and Warren's mother, Donella, stood in the hall. Tom let out his breath.

"Put a shirt on, Tommy. It's January, for Christ's sake," Donella said.

"I thought you were burglars. What's going on?"

"I'm moving out, Tommy. Sorry. Quitting school," Warren said, studying his shoes, which were muddy and untied. Warren was related to Tom through Donella, Tom's mother's older sister. When Tom looked at old photographs of Donella and his mother, Denise, as children, he could see the resemblance. Their coloring, their eyes, their noses were taken from the same mold. But time had separated the two sisters along with their offspring. Like everyone in Tom's immediate family, his mother was lean and kept fit working on the ranch.

Donella, Warren, and his father, Butch, carried excess weight. Warren, in particular, was overweight by ninety pounds, and Tom knew he was sensitive about his appearance. Tom couldn't help but wonder why his aunt had not helped her son before it had gotten so extreme. Warren was also not very tall. When Tom and Warren were both in the ninth grade, they were about the same size. Then Tom had shot up six inches, eventually topping six feet and Warren had just gotten heavier.

"Wait a minute. You're dropping out of school? I thought you liked it here." Tom pulled on a sweatshirt he'd dropped on a chair the night before.

"My grades weren't great. I didn't always understand the teachers," Warren said. "It's better that I try something else. I'm sorry to leave you with twice the rent. Maybe you can find another roommate."

"C'mon, Warren," his mother snapped. "Get the lead out. Pack up the rest of your clothes. Strip the bed so we can carry the mattress." Donella turned back to Tom. "Did Denise get over the hissy fit she had on New Year's Eve?"

"I don't know what you're talking about," Tom said, brows furrowing. His mother spent too much time complaining about Donella, and he assumed the reverse was true.

"Oh, she wanted us to book a cabin with your family in Estes Park this summer. I told her that no one in my family wanted to go mountain hiking or fishing or any of the things she had in mind. She acted like we were crazy. She gets on her high horse. She forgets I know what she was like when she was younger."

Tom dropped onto his bed and pulled on socks and sneakers. "What was Mom like when she was younger?"

Donella stood in his bedroom doorway. "Oh, I'm sure you've heard the rumors. When your daddy was up in Canada those five years working on the pipeline, I don't think she even set eyes on Jake for two years before you were born."

Tom laughed, "Well, Aunt Donella, she must have seen him at least once about nine months before I was born."

"I don't think so. I think they were what you call separated back then. Then Jake comes crawling back, gives up the oil gig, and reunites your family pretty as you please. You were born a few months later." Donella turned and walked back to the door of the house and hollered to her husband, "Butch, get on in here. We've got to get that furniture loaded."

Tom went out to the main living area where his aunt stood. "What exactly are you implying about my mother?"

"C'mon, child. You ain't that dumb. I know you won several scholarships; your mother told me more than once. Didn't you ever wonder why you're the only one of your brothers and sisters with light eyes? Why both of your brothers have Jake's cleft chin, but you don't?"

"That's ridiculous. I can't believe you would accuse your own sister of …"

"Don't take my word for it, Sweetie. Ask Chief. He knows who was helping out at the farm when Jake was working up north. Denise was living there with baby Jerry, and helping with the house chores, cooking for the hired men."

Mom must have really pissed Donella off this time. She's never tried to spread vicious lies around me before. If she doesn't stop it, I may have to shut her up myself.

Tom flexed his fingers and tightened them into fists. He grabbed his coat and car keys. Then he made a beeline for the door. He didn't even speak to Butch, who was ambling up the driveway. He headed toward the street and his Jeep.

He pulled into his usual parking spot at Runza. He wanted coffee, but he'd come twenty minutes before they opened.

Why had Donella said those things? Was she mad at Warren and decided to take it out on me? Donella had always been jealous of us. Mom had hinted at that many times. But I can't believe she'd go so far as to tell me... what? That I was illegitimate? That Jacob Case isn't my father? That made no sense. Jake would've known if he hadn't been with Denise before she'd gotten pregnant. He would have never put up with that kind of farce. Would he?

It was true about the blue-grey eyes and cleft chin. But hello? Recessive genes.

Tom was so tangled in his thoughts he was surprised to see Linda's smiling face at his window.

"Do you have an order, Rancher Boy?"

Was he even a rancher by blood? Was that sprawling cattle ranch even his birthright? Or was he an imposter? Holy shit. He unzipped the window.

"Coffee. Large. Black."

"Nothing to eat?" Linda studied his face.

"Uh...I don't know."

"Tom, what's wrong?"

It was those cheerful bluish-green eyes staring back at him. He couldn't take it. He couldn't fake it. How could she help him or understand?

"You know what? Forget I came by here. I gotta go."

He put the Jeep in reverse, and Linda backed up quickly, squinting at him. He drove around until he found a diner, then sat and nursed his coffee for an hour.

When he got back to the apartment, the first thing he noticed was that the door was left open. The storm door was closed, but the inside door was wide open, letting the cold air in. He slammed the door. Guess who was paying the gas bill now? Then he surveyed the room. Not that it was a large room. It had been just big enough

91

for a three-cushion sofa and a chest that held a black and white television. All of which were now missing.

Damn.

Okay, the TV and chest were Warren's, but I'd found that couch in the newspaper ads. I found the friend of a friend with a pickup truck who hauled it over here and who helped me haul it to this very spot where it happily resided for the last four months. Warren didn't even pay for his half of the twenty bucks I spent.

The only evidence that the couch had been there was the dirty bowl and spoon left on the floor. It looked like it had contained ice cream or cereal—something that left a coat of soured milk stuck to the bowl. And the remains of a few candy bars and potato chip bags, all of which Warren had hidden under the sofa instead of putting them in the trash or the sink.

Tom picked up the trash and the bowl and took them into the kitchen. Warren had not been the neatest roommate. Tom had been taught to clean up after himself at home. When he got to the kitchen, he rinsed the bowl and washed his hands. But the towel that usually hung by the sink was missing. He opened the nearby drawer where the towels were. All gone. *Shit.* He pulled open the refrigerator, which had come with the apartment. He might be having a beer today after this. As if. The beer and most of the food in the refrigerator were gone. A few ketchup packets and a stick of butter remained.

God, this was like a bad divorce. Was Warren pissed at me for some reason? Or was this his psycho bitch mother's doing?

He walked into Warren's room. It was empty, but that was expected. At least he could clean it. He went to the utility closet for a broom. All of the cleaning supplies, including the broom, his mother's old vacuum cleaner, and spray bottles of cleaner were gone. Even the supply of toilet paper had been taken.

That prompted him to check the bathroom.

You've gotta be kidding me. Now I know what happened to the toilet paper. It looks like two rolls of paper are jammed into the toilet. Then someone used the toilet. Of course, the plunger is gone too. They're trying to mess with me now. Was this supposed to be funny? Your loser son flunks out of college after three months and you take it out on his cousin?

After that, he was afraid to open his bedroom door. His furniture was still there, thank goodness. But all of his clothes were pulled out of the closet or chest of drawers and now littered the floor. What was that smell? Oh, of course. His aftershave, which he'd saved for special occasions had been poured on his sheets, and his stick deodorant had been smeared on the mirror that was attached to the closet door. Toothpaste was decorating his prized black Stetson hat.

Warren must have a death wish. I'd like to pound that worthless slob into the ground. Or was it his mother? Maybe even big ol' Butch. How do I know?

One thing was certain: he should never have agreed to live with his cousin.

He wanted to scream or cry. But he did neither. He looked for a pen and paper to make a list of things he had to replace. When he couldn't find either, he started cursing. Then he discovered his bookbag had been left untouched and found paper and pen inside.

The phone rang. Warren left the phone, at least. It was on the floor in the living room.

"What?" he barked when he picked up the receiver.

"Tom, is that you? Are you okay?" Linda sounded concerned, almost timid.

"No, I'm not!" Tom took a deep breath. "Warren just…um, Warren moved out, and he left me with a big mess. Are you still at work?"

"Yeah, I get off in thirty minutes. Do you some help?"

He thought about it. He could use the moral support. But he didn't want her to see this place in its current condition. "I tell you what. I need to go to the store and pick up some things. I'll call you later, and maybe you can come over."

By that evening, he had cleaned the apartment thoroughly and restored order. Most of the damage was superficial. He'd run his sheets and some clothes through the washer in the basement. Once he'd cleaned out the mess in the toilet, it still worked fine. He wasn't sure what to do about his felt cowboy hat, which appeared to be stained, even after he washed the toothpaste off. He called Linda and gave her his address.

The only thing good about his day so far is that the shopping and cleaning had kept him from thinking about the first thing that had upset him. Linda could keep his mind busy the rest of the evening.

When she walked in an hour later carrying a hot pizza, he wanted to kiss her. So, he did.

"What's that for?" she laughed.

"I didn't know how hungry I was until I smelled pizza. All I've had to eat today is a burger from McDonald's."

"Uh, Tom. You don't have any furniture in here. Is there a table in the kitchen?" Linda walked around the front room as though the furniture was hiding somewhere.

"No. We had furniture in here, but Warren took it all. No table, I'm afraid. I have a bed. That's about it."

He led her to his bedroom and they sat on the bed. Everything in his room had been washed and put away by then. Linda pulled off her boots and sat cross-legged. They tore open the paper-wrapped pizza and dug in.

"You are a sight for sore eyes," Tom said. "It's been a helluva day."

Linda dipped her chin, smiling at him through her lashes. "He left a mess?"

"Well, yeah. He made a mess before he left. I mean, who does that? I got it taken care of. But that wasn't all."

"What else?"

He looked at the ceiling. "I don't know if we know each other well enough yet. Maybe I shouldn't get into the rest of my family drama."

"I can keep a secret. How do you think people get to know each other?" A long string of mozzarella cheese trailed off her piece of pizza. Linda arched her tongue around it and reeled it into her mouth. She closed her eyes, savoring the hot cheese.

Tom could only fixate on her tongue. "What? Oh. Right. My aunt. This morning, she went off on some rant about my mother, her sister. She was pissed at my mom, for God knows what. They're always bickering. But then she accused my mom of …well, she told me that um…she claimed that my father isn't really my father."

"Huh? If that's true, then who is your father?"

"I have no freaking idea." Tom picked up another piece of pizza. "But that can't be true. I mean, my parents would have told me something like that, right?"

"I guess so. But you're not sure, are you?" Linda was studying him.

"I don't know what to think. I mean, I know before I was born, my dad, that is, Jacob Case, was working in Canada on a pipeline. Then after I was born, he came back to help run the ranch. My older brother was born in Canada, but my mom said that since my dad was gone so much, she decided to move back to Gordon, Nebraska, which is where I was born. I suppose the thing to do is ask my mother, but I don't want to do that over the phone. If I drive home on the weekend, I'll spend most of the time on the road, so I usually wait until I have at least a few days off."

"What would you do if you found out it was true?"

"I can't wrap my head around it. Maybe I shouldn't even ask."

95

"You have to ask. You need to know."

He sighed. "I guess I'll have to think about it. My Aunt Donella said to ask my grandpa. She said he'd know. That might be easier."

"I'm sorry you had to deal with this today," Linda said.

"Well, there is one good thing that came out of it. You can come over here and we will have privacy. Maybe I won't even try to get another roommate."

"Why do you think we need privacy, Rancher Boy?" Linda cocked her head.

Tom stood up and put the rest of the pizza on the dresser. Then he sat down hard on the bed, bouncing Linda up and he pushed her down on the mattress, wrapping her in his arms. "In case we want to do this." He pushed her hair back from her face and looked at her at close range.

"You are very pretty, you know that?"

"No," she blushed. "My sister is the pretty one. I'm just—"

"You're wrong," Tom leaned over her and pulled her into a kiss. "But I know you're only sixteen. I don't want you to do anything you're not ready for."

"I'm not sure I was ready for you. But it feels right." She wrapped her arms around his neck and held him close. She let him hold her for a long time.

Just what he needed.

CHAPTER SIXTEEN

What is wrong with me? I'm falling for Tom.

She hadn't planned for that to happen. Up to that point, she'd felt like she'd had her love life under control. She'd been friends with Brian, and neither of them had wanted a romance. She'd been mostly friends with John Anthony, although they'd made out a few times. Still, she appreciated the discipline he'd shown, and things hadn't gotten out of hand. But shortly before Christmas, he'd stopped calling or showing up at her locker, and she assumed he was moving on.

I'd done that too. Let's be honest.

Tom hadn't pressured her. At first, he seemed happy to kiss or cuddle with her on his bed. A double bed was much more comfortable than a cold car in the wintertime. But slowly, things had progressed.

On the weekends, they usually went out for dinner or a movie, then ended the date at his apartment. During the week, she only spoke to him on the phone or when he showed up while she was working. She found Tom very easy to talk to, sometimes easier than her girlfriends. He called her nearly every night.

"Tom, you seem to have this boyfriend thing down. You must have had a girlfriend in high school," she told him one evening on the phone.

"Well, yeah. I had a girlfriend last year. But I knew it wasn't going anywhere. She was determined to go to college in Colorado."

"Did you have sex with her?" Linda knew this was a loaded question, but she hoped Tom trusted her enough to be candid.

There was a moment of silence. Linda wished she could take that back.

"That's pretty blunt, even for you," he said slowly. "I think that's for me to know and you to wonder."

"You don't want to ask me the same question?"

"No, I don't. I suppose I might figure it out. But there's a stupid double standard surrounding whether someone is a virgin. Like boys are supposed to have sexual experience and girls aren't. That makes no sense. A guy who has had sex in high school is a stud, but a girl who has had sex is a slut. Ridiculous. I think you should do what you want and not make it public knowledge."

"I suppose no one talked about this in your high school."

Tom laughed, "That's all they talked about. That's why it bugged me."

Linda felt a certain detachment from her friends dating an older guy. Was she missing out on events you could only do in high school? She didn't think he'd want to go to her high school's Sweetheart Dance held on Valentine's Day. She didn't even tell Tom about it. Sometimes she envied her girlfriends who were dating boys in their grade.

I wonder what it would be like to date Randy Sparks, Yvonne's boyfriend. Randy was the star of the basketball team and he seemed very focused on that. Linda knew Yvonne was frustrated that he wasn't giving her more time. She also knew Yvonne secretly cared for Daniel, Debbie's brother. But Daniel also seemed distracted between his school activities and his on-again-off-again girlfriend, Andrea. Neither of those numbskulls appreciated how special Yvonne was.

Then there was Debbie. She and Robert seemed to be gaga for each other. Linda didn't know Robert well, but she'd seen how well he danced. By Debbie's account, he was devoted to her. But they had been sneaking around to date, as both sets of parents were against their relationship. That would be a problem. Linda was dating Tom openly; he'd been to her parents' house for dinner. She just kept the fact that she'd spent time in his apartment a secret.

Nancy has the sexiest boyfriend. It's exciting watching how Peter gets possessive and physical in trying to keep other boys away from her. But what would it take before he crossed the line and scared Nancy?

There had been an incident where he'd made Linda nervous. The band went to Kearney to play at a basketball game. Peter should have gone, but he'd been suspended from school for fighting. On the way home, Nancy had been kissing another boy, Chad Duncan, in the back of the bus. Linda was sitting in the last row and couldn't miss it. They weren't the only kids necking that night.

But when they arrived back at the school parking lot, Pete had been there to meet Nancy, who was still standing with Chad.

Linda saw the look on Pete's face, even if Nancy chose to ignore it. He was ready to hit someone, and he wasn't going to be particular about who it was.

"You should ride home with me, Nancy." Linda had made her way to stand between Peter and Chad. She should get her best friend out of there before she got hurt. She tugged on the corner of the blanket Nancy had wrapped around herself.

Peter put his forearm up to block her path. "Back off, Linda. This is none of your business."

But Nancy was her business as much as she was Pete's or Chad's. She may not have been dating Nancy, but they'd become close and she was not going to stand there and watch if things got violent.

Instead of wasting time at charm school, I really should have taken some lessons in self-defense or karate like Pete had. I can't even defend my girlfriends.

What happened next was even more humiliating. Chad, who was about Linda's height, came up next to her and put his hand on her as though protecting her from Pete. Linda scowled and shook his hand off.

If I'd only brought a gun. Imagine blowing both of those posturing boys away.

Okay, that was stupid. They'd never let her on the bus with a gun. She didn't want to injure anyone. She just wanted to be treated with respect.

So why would she want to date a high school boy? Tom was looking better all the time.

Linda heard about Randy dumping Yvonne right after the Sweetheart dance. The idiot. She heard about Debbie and Robert sneaking into a vacant house. Pretty risky. And Nancy had told her she'd sworn off parking with Pete because she had no self-control.

Somehow Linda had avoided these problems. Her boyfriend was patient and considerate. He had his own place, so they didn't need to lie to anyone. He had even offered to take care of birth control.

Yep, that threw me for a loop.

CHAPTER SEVENTEEN

Children learn how to do almost everything from watching their parents. Parents are usually eager teachers. Here's how you talk, how you walk, how you hold a pencil. Here's what you should eat and not eat. Linda's father had even taught her to drive, which was beyond some parents' patience.

But who is there to teach you how to act when you want to make love? Or even how to know when the time is right?

Oh sure, she'd heard lots of jokes about it. So many television shows alluded to sex, but she needed some clear guidance. She couldn't even ask Sarah, because she thought Sarah was clueless too.

That only left Tom. While she was wondering whether she wanted to partake in this particular activity, it became more apparent that he was onboard. Of course, he was nearly two years older, and according to the article she'd read in *Cosmopolitan*, boys his age were much more likely to be sexually active. *That was a dumb thing to call it. It sounded like they trained for it. Do you have an active lifestyle? Yes, I am sexually active. Yikes.*

It was Valentine's Day when he first brought it up. Her seventeenth birthday was a few days earlier. They had gone out to a restaurant, and he had brought her a red rose. Like most evenings, they went to his apartment afterward. He still hadn't gotten another couch or a television, so they always ended up lying on his bed.

"You know we've been dating for five weeks. Sometimes it seems like I've known you forever," Tom said, running his fingers down the side of her head. They were lying on their sides facing each other, wearing the fancy clothes they'd worn to dinner.

"Uh-huh. I never expected to date someone older than me. Does that seem funny to you?" Linda took his necktie in one hand

and slid her hand down the length of it.

Tom's eyes flicked to the tie and then back to her face. He cleared his throat. "Uh, what did you say? Oh, dating someone younger. You don't always seem like you're in high school. Like right now, when you're wearing a pretty dress and makeup. You look like you could be in college."

"You look older in a sports coat too. You probably wore this to your high school graduation. Maybe even for your senior pictures."

Tom rolled over on his back. "Busted." Then he gave her a sidelong look. "You look so beautiful tonight; I might forget you're young and innocent." He picked up the rose laying between them and ran the bud gently down her nose.

Linda sat up, leaning on one arm. "I'm seventeen. Shouldn't I look more mature? Only one year younger than you now."

He took a deep breath. "Okay, I'm going to say what I'm thinking about. At some point, I'm going to want to take advantage of having you on my bed."

Her brows rose slowly. "You mean...?" She cast her eyes down at the bed as though she'd forgotten it was there. Then she stole a glance back at him.

"What do you think about that? Does it scare you?"

She swallowed. "Maybe. Isn't that a little dangerous?"

"I have condoms if that's what you're worried about."

She scooted toward the end of the bed.

"Where are you going?" He put a hand on her arm to stop her. "Darn it. I spooked you, didn't I?"

"I don't know. This seems so fast."

"Hey, don't freak out on me. I don't mean tonight. Not soon. I wondered if that is something you'd want to think about." He slid down to the bottom of the bed and they both sat on the edge with their feet on the floor. "You know I find you irresistible." He put his arms around her, and she let him pull her close.

"Tom, a year or so ago, a friend of my sister's kissed me when I didn't want him to."

He pulled back frowning and took her head in his hands. He watched her eyes fill with tears.

"And then a few weeks after that, he tried to rape me."

His mouth flew open on a gasp. "Oh my God."

She looked down and stammered, "He did sort of rape me; he was pushing inside. My therapist said there is no such thing as half-raped, but that's what it seemed like. I couldn't push him off, but we were interrupted and I escaped." She swiped at her eyes. "But I suppose that's still messing with my head. You know I like you, but I have to go slowly."

He pulled her back into a tight embrace. "Jesus, Baby. I had no idea. Now I feel like a monster."

She shook her head, but stayed nestled on his shoulder. That should slow him down until she figured out what she needed.

CHAPTER EIGHTEEN

It was a month later, and Tom brought Linda back to his place after a movie. It had been sprinkling earlier, but when they got out of his car in the driveway, a cloudburst drenched them both. By the time they got to the porch, they were laughing.

Linda shook her arms. "I am soaked to the bone. My raincoat didn't even help. I feel like I went swimming in my clothes and shoes."

"I've got clean towels at least. I washed a load this morning," Tom said. They stood on a small rug right inside the door, dripping onto the floor. Tom tore off his boots and socks and put his boots over a heat register. Then he removed his jacket and put it on the coat tree. The bottom half of his boot-cut jeans were soaked and dragged across the floor when he made his way to the bathroom.

He returned with several bath towels and handed one to Linda. He took a towel himself and rubbed it over his hair. "Can't even see outta my glasses." After wiping off his glasses, he propped them on one of his boots. "Here, let me help you."

She let him run the towel through her hair, which had gotten a little longer, the back nearly shoulder-length now. She hung her coat up with his, and her knit blue dress was soaked from the hips down, and her white tights were sodden.

"My shoes might be destroyed," she said, pouring water out of her Old Main Trotters. "These were my favorite loafers."

"Sorry. Maybe they'll be okay once they're dry." He pulled on the bottom of her dress that was clinging to her thighs. "I think maybe you should take off the dress and tights. I can throw them in the dryer with my jeans."

She studied him for a moment before pulling down the back zipper on her dress. "You should turn around."

"What fun would that be?"

104

Linda rolled her eyes but slid her arms out of the long sleeves of the dress, holding the bodice up to her chest. Then she picked up one of the towels he'd brought in and held it in front of her as she pushed the dress off her hips. She wrapped the towel more tightly around her and pulled down her tights.

Tom dropped to his knees and helped her by pulling the wet tights from her feet. Then he stood up. "Anything else wet?" She surprised him by sliding one hand beneath the towel in the back and then sliding black panties down her legs. She stepped out of them before he could snatch them off the floor. He could see black lace bra straps above the green towel she was wrapped in, so she must have had a matched set.

He swallowed hard and picked up her wet clothes.

"I'm going down to the basement to put these in the clothes dryer. Why don't you go get under the covers to get warm?" He remembered to grab another towel before going to the basement to put their clothes in the dryer. He hoped none of the other tenants would wander down there while he stripped off his jeans and shorts, adding them to her clothes and turning on the dryer. He squinted at the controls, realizing he'd left his glasses upstairs, and hoped he'd set the timer correctly. He wrapped the towel around him and headed back to his apartment.

He couldn't put aside that Linda was already in his bedroom without most of her clothing. *Thank you, Mother Nature.*

Gotta play this cool. She's already been emotionally scarred once. Take my time; she may not be ready. Where did I put those condoms anyway?

He found Linda was snug in his bed, covered to the neck with the blanket and quilt his grandmother had made. Thunder rattled the old windows. He pulled open the top drawer of his chest and found the green and purple sock where he'd stashed a supply of condoms. He put the sock on the wooden crate next to his bed and

105

climbed in next to her. He slid the towel off as he got in, and pulled his shirt over his head.

When he laid his hand on Linda's shoulder and realized the bra strap was missing, his eyes widened. He pushed the covers down enough to see that she'd shed her towel as well. He was getting overheated rapidly just by the prospect.

He sank into the pillow facing her, kissed her gently, and ran a hand down her back. "How are you feeling?" he asked when he pulled away.

"I don't know," she said licking her lower lip. "How do I feel?"

Jesus. Does she have any idea what she's doing to me? Going slowly? That notion crashed into a million pieces on the floor.

He hardly considered himself an old hand at this. His only previous partner, Jillian, had never even taken off all of her clothes. Of course, being parked in a pasture in a pickup truck hadn't guaranteed them privacy.

But Linda—sweet little innocent barely seventeen-year-old Linda—was buck naked in his bed. And he was too. He rolled on top of her trying to get as much skin contact as possible and started kissing her mouth, her neck, her shoulders, anywhere and everywhere he could reach. His hands were in her damp hair, then on her shoulders, her back, her bottom. It all became frenetic and heated.

Linda laughed and seemed to embrace the spirit. She wrapped her arms around him and kissed him back, parting her lips when his tongue asked for more. She stroked fingers through his hair and ran her mouth along his jaw.

How much of what they were doing was new to her? Aside from the attack she had mentioned, he had no idea.

They were both breathing harder by the time he pulled the

covers away from her to get a better look at her lean athletic body. Her protruding ribs and hip bones were a lovely contrast to rounded breasts and thighs.

"You know, it's a crime for you to wear clothes at all. Your body is amazing."

She ran her fingers down the middle of his chest. "Yours isn't too bad either." Tom scowled, and she laughed.

"Not too bad? I'll show you 'not too bad,'" He pulled her on top of him and began smothering her mouth with kisses.

She moaned when he parted her legs with his hand and began grinding against him.

She certainly acts like she knows what she's doing. Maybe I'm worrying for nothing.

She pushed herself up, and he ran his fingertips over her breasts. She murmured but didn't move away. Her eyelids fluttered half-closed. His stroking continued until she started making high-pitched gasps. He realized he'd better get the condom on quickly. He nudged her back next to him on the bed and reached for the sock with the condoms.

There were packages of two different colors. He couldn't recall which kind he used before. He hadn't bought any himself. One of his father's friends gave him some for high school graduation. He assumed it was a joke when he opened the card.

The others he'd found in the bunkhouse when he was a senior in high school. His mother had asked him to strip the beds when the summer ranch hands left. In a rickety chest of drawers, he'd discovered a paperback, *The Last Call for a Gunfighter* by Bliss Lomax. The middle of the book had been carved out as a hidey-hole. Six condoms quickly made their way to his pocket.

He didn't remember which ones were which, and without his glasses, he couldn't read the print on the package. They were all for the same purpose. He randomly opened one and put it on. Linda's eyes were wide open now, watching this maneuver. "Shit, did I scare you again?"

"I never realized how..."

"Do you want to stop?"

"No! I don't want to lose my nerve." She pulled him toward her again and brushed against his chest. "Come and get it, Rancher Boy."

She always made him laugh. He moved in slowly, gently running his hands across her baby soft skin on her hips and thighs. Random thoughts kept popping into his head. Song lyrics about love and passion. Movie scenes that only showed lovers in the shadows or tight closeups. How thankful he was that Warren wasn't sitting in the living room eating onion dip and making crude noises, listening to them making love. When he couldn't wait any longer, he slid home with less resistance than he expected. His thoughts were obliterated, pounding down in rhythm with the driving rain on the window. It might not have been as dramatic as the movies, but it was certainly worth an encore. How soon could he get an encore?

Linda was wrapped around him as he pulled the covers back up to warm them. Once his pulse stopped thundering, he rolled off the bed and went to the bathroom to dispose of the condom. That's when his heart nearly stopped. The jolt of adrenaline made him focus.

The condom had split. Not a tiny little hole; a great big messy gash.

Holy shit! Aren't these things guaranteed to at least hold together? This is not good, not good at all. It probably leaked on the clean sheets, on Linda. All inside...oh no. No, no, no.

He washed himself off and grabbed the pajama pants he'd hung on a hook on the bathroom door. What was he going to tell her? Did he have to tell her?

He made a detour to the front room and snatched his glasses up where he'd parked them on his boots. He returned to the bedroom and picked up the condom packaging he'd dropped on the floor. The wrapper was brown. He vaguely remembered these were the ones from the bunkhouse. The printing was faded, but he saw what might have been an expiration date. That couldn't be right. The date was four years ago. No wonder someone abandoned them.

Tom felt a knot forming in his gut. "Uh, Linda?"

Her eyes were closed, and she reached out a hand for him to come back to the bed.

"How long has it been since you had a period?"

She opened her eyes and frowned at him. "Why do you care? I don't always pay attention. I usually feel a little bloaty a few days before, so I know it's coming. I suppose a week ago."

A week ago. That's probably safe. He knew more than most city boys about reproduction from watching their animals mate and give birth. It would be fine. But he decided to throw away all the condoms with the brown packaging.

He took a deep breath. *Stop panicking.* "Are you okay, Linda?"

"I'm fine, Baby. But it's getting late. Are my clothes dry yet?"

Over the next month, Tom used up the supply of condoms in the blue packaging. The material in those seemed a little more flexible.

One day when Tom was sweeping the floor, he found part of one of the blue packages under the bed. He hadn't thought he needed to read that one but stopped to do so. It looked like this one was also past its expiration date, but only nine months past. So, they had been expired when he'd gotten them! *Damn.* He jerked open the drawer where he'd put the new ones he'd just bought. They were good for nearly four years. Looked like he could relax a little.

He pulled out a Marlboro from the package next to the condoms and a disposable lighter. He didn't smoke often, only when he was tense.

What about Jillian? Which condoms had he used with Jillian? It had to have been the ones from the bunkhouse; he hadn't graduated from high school the first time, so he didn't have the others. He hadn't seen or talked to Jillian since August. Surely, she would have contacted him if she'd gotten pregnant. Maybe she'd been on the pill. He had to stop leaving these things to chance.

CHAPTER NINETEEN

In early April, Tom had spring break. It was his first chance to go home for more than twenty-four hours. He knew he'd have to confront his mother, and he was dreading it.

He'd spent time with Linda every weekend, and he wasn't looking forward to missing time with her either. She also had two days without classes.

"I'm going home next weekend, you know," he told her. "I don't know what's going to happen when I ask my mom about what Donella told me."

He'd finally sprung for another second-hand couch and a small television, and they were moving the furniture around in his front room, trying to decide the best angle.

"When are you leaving?" Linda asked.

"Leaving Friday morning, coming back Sunday afternoon after Easter dinner."

"Can I go with you?" Linda gave him a soulful look.

"You want to meet my family? Don't you have to be home for Easter yourself?"

She shrugged. "My parents aren't speaking to each other at the moment. So not much fun at casa de Bridges."

"Oh. Well, in that case, I guess you could come. There are plenty of bedrooms. I can always bunk with Chief in his cottage, if necessary."

It was a long drive to Gordon from Lincoln. They'd already had one major skirmish over which radio station to listen to. His choices were strictly country-western and she kept tuning it to rock and roll as soon as they lost the signal from his station.

About an hour from their destination, Linda appeared to be asleep.

Tom was a little apprehensive about the weekend. How would his parents react to Linda? She could be a little outlandish at times. Mostly he was worried that they would think he should be dating a college girl. When he said he was bringing a guest, he hadn't mentioned that she was a junior in high school.

"What are you going to say to your mom?" Linda asked, opening her eyes enough to give him a sidelong look.

He sighed. "I think I'd better wait until we are ready to leave Sunday before saying anything. If it gets awkward, we can bolt for the door." He hit the brake because he was approaching a large grain truck going ten miles under the speed limit.

"What are you expecting her to tell you?"

"The truth, I hope. Whatever that is." He drummed his fingers on the steering wheel. "Now that I have had time to process it, I believe it is most likely one of Donella's fantasies. A way for her to hurt my mom. But that's why I decided I have to mention it. My parents deserve to know what Donella has been up to."

Linda nodded. "Are Donella and Warren going to be at your house for Easter?"

Tom turned to glance at her. "Jeez, I hope not. They don't usually come. But it's not impossible. You may get a ringside seat to some family arguments."

It was nearly six o'clock when Tom's Jeep wound up the long driveway to the Case Ranch. Three barking dogs ran up to greet him, which brought his youngest brother and sister to the porch.

Linda watched through the car window as the coonhound and Doberman jumped up on Tom to lick their greetings. He reached down and snatched the cocker spaniel up and let her lick his nose.

112

Tom laughed and opened the passenger door. "Ya comin'?"

Linda pressed her lips into a line and glanced at the dogs eagerly awaiting her descent from the car. "Do they bite?"

"Nah, they're affectionate." He held out a hand to her, then turned to the dogs. "Down mongrels, no jumping." When the coonhound approached Linda, Tom repeated, "Tootsie, stay back." The dogs sat patiently by the Jeep until Tom and Linda reached the porch.

"Are you afraid of dogs?" twelve-year-old Brent asked.

Linda looked surprised and glanced back at the dogs who were now running in the yard.

"Linda, this is my kid brother, Brent. We're still trying to teach him to be shy. And Susan is over here giving you the once over."

Linda broke out her killer smile for the youngest siblings. "Hi, kids. What are you up to?"

"Mom says you're late. Dinner is almost ready." With that, Brent turned and marched back into the house.

"Sorry. None of the Case men like to have their meals delayed," Tom smirked. He ushered her into the house with Susan following them.

His mother, Denise, was directing where the food was set on the large dining table. Tom's father and grandfather were choosing chairs to sit on, while his older brother Jerry, and Jerry's fiancé Molly, were bringing bowls in from the kitchen. Brent had disappeared. His sister, Theresa, stopped short carrying in a plate of ribs when she saw Tom and Linda.

"Tom! There you are. We were about to give up on you making it for supper." She planted a kiss on his cheek. "And you said you wanted to bring a friend. You didn't say it was a girlfriend."

113

Tom felt his cheeks redden, but this was expected. He wanted to see the looks on their faces. "I know. This is Linda Bridges." He paused, glancing back at his mother. "My girlfriend."

"Well, Honey, I'm sure she wants to freshen up before we eat," Denise said. She turned to Linda. "The powder room is right down that hall if you want to wash your hands. Although who knows what kind of mess these men have left it in. There are clean towels under the sink."

Linda looked like she was happy to escape for a second and headed to the bathroom.

Tom sat down with the rest of the boisterous family. When Linda returned, he pulled out a chair for her next to his younger brother, and there were a few whoops and jeers from the men.

"You've been learning manners up there at the university, huh, Thomas?" his brother Jerry teased.

Tom had learned to ignore most of the jabs from his family. "Okay, Linda. Remember, this was your idea." He gestured to his brother Brent sitting next to her. "Starting with Brent, you met him outside. Then there is Molly. She's engaged to Jerry, the oldest, who is next to her. My mother, Denise, then Susan, she's fifteen. Then over here is my grandpa Chief, and my dad, Jake, and finally, my sister Theresa, who is graduating from high school in about six weeks."

"It's nice to meet you all," Linda smiled demurely and put her napkin in her lap.

The cocker spaniel that she'd seen outside made his way between Linda's chair and Brent's. Linda was wearing a sweater and mini-skirt and jumped a little when the dog put his wet nose on her bare knee.

"How come you don't like dogs?" Brent asked her, feeding the cocker spaniel half a dinner roll.

Tom scowled at his brother, but Linda smiled sweetly. "It's not that I don't like them. I'm not used to them. I don't have a dog."

"Your mom probably wouldn't want a dog to mess up that fancy house of yours. You should see her parents' place." After putting two ribs on his plate, Tom tucked his cloth napkin into the top of his sweater. "It's like a mansion with columns, a balcony, and a swimming pool out back."

"What does your father do, Linda?" Denise asked.

"He's the president of an insurance company in Lincoln."

"Oh, so did you and Tom have a class together at NU?" Jake asked.

"No," Tom said. He didn't want her to correct the assumption that she attended college. "I met Linda where she works. She's a carhop."

"What's a carhop?" Susan asked.

"It's like a waitress, but you have to take the orders and deliver the food to the customer's car. I have to wear little suede shorts called lederhosen. It's kind of a German restaurant."

"Except she looks like Pinocchio in her little costume." Tom grinned.

Linda raised her brows. "And apparently you have a thing for Pinocchio."

That elicited groans from Jerry, Jake, and Chief. Tom's eyes went wild.

"You gotta watch this one, Tommy. She's a live wire." Jake leaned back in his chair chuckling.

"Believe me, I found that out." Tom shook his head grinning.

The plate of ribs had made its way around to Linda and she took one but seemed unsure how to eat it. She tried cutting it with

115

her knife and fork but saw the others picking up the bones and getting barbeque sauce on their fingers.

"Don't you pick up your ribs to eat them, Linda?" Molly asked.

"I guess I've never eaten ribs before. They're kinda messy, huh?" Linda laughed as sauce ran down her chin.

"City gal," Jerry scoffed.

"Don't worry. I'll have her roping calves by tomorrow afternoon," Tom said.

"Not sure I brought my calf-roping outfit," Linda said.

"Not a problem. Two sisters, we'll find you some sturdy jeans and boots."

They made it through dinner without anyone questioning Linda's age or where she attended school. Tom thought that discussion could wait for a later time if they continued dating. He'd avoided telling his family he was taking her to her high school prom.

The next morning when Linda came downstairs in Levi's and an oversized pullover sweatshirt, Tom studied her. "I thought you didn't bring anything like that," he said.

"I didn't. I brought nice clothes. Your mother found these for me. She said you outgrew them a couple of years ago, and she was saving them for Brent."

He walked up to her and circled her, trailing a hand on her hip. "You're wearing my clothes. That's a little strange, don't you think?" He kept his voice low enough that the rest of the family didn't hear. She filled those jeans out differently than he had. They were loose at the waist and tighter on the hips and thighs. She even made that sweatshirt look sexy.

Linda brushed his hand off her. "Be nice."

"I am being nice. I thought it would have been nice if you'd snuck into my room last night."

"Tom! Hush!"

He laughed and wrapped his arms around her. "What do you want to do first? Feed the horses or the calves?"

Her eyes grew wide. "You have horses?"

"Of course. You herd the cattle on horseback."

"Can we ride horses? I used to have a horse when I was eight or nine. Sarah had one too. We had to board them on the edge of town, but I haven't gotten to ride in years."

They went out to one of the barns, where they fed both the calves and horses. Tom saddled up his horse, Cheyenne. He intended to let Linda ride one of the older mares. But she mounted Cheyenne before he could stop her.

"That one is mine. I'll find you an older horse since you haven't ridden for a while." Tom put his hand around her leg. He'd help her down if she wanted him to.

"I'll take this one. Can you shorten the stirrups a little?" Linda stretched her legs, but they didn't quite reach.

Tom frowned but fixed the stirrups as she requested. He supposed this was part of being a gracious host. "All right, but keep him reigned in. I'll get on my dad's horse, Brazen. Wait here."

Tom went to fetch the other horse, which was saddled at least. When he brought Brazen out to where he'd left Linda, he saw Cheyenne trotting along the path to the pasture.

"Hey! Wait up. You don't know where that leads!"

It was too late. Without even a backward glance, Linda was galloping on Cheyenne with her blonde hair trailing behind. She didn't look like she was in trouble. She looked like she was urging

117

the horse on.

Tom pushed Brazen in pursuit, but he wasn't used to this horse, and the horse wasn't used to him. Brazen was a workhorse, not a racer. He finally caught up to Linda about two miles away when Cheyenne had to stop for a fence that marked the end of their land. Linda had the horse walking in a circle.

Tom dismounted and ran to her. "What the hell was that? You can't just take off. You didn't even know where you were going!"

Linda swung off the horse. "I often don't know where I'm going. The horse did though. I was along for the ride."

Tom took the reins of both horses and walked them around to cool down. "That was irresponsible. You had no idea whether this horse could run like that or whether he'd try to throw you."

"The horse was great. I like to ride like that, don't you?"

Tom glared at her. Then he tied the horses' reins to the fence and walked back to Linda.

"I changed my mind. I don't want you to wear my old clothes. Take them off." He started pulling at the hem of the sweatshirt she wore.

She laughed, but his expression remained steely. "You want me to strip out here in the middle of a field?"

"It's a pasture, but yes. I want my clothes back. Right now." He started unbuckling the belt she wore, and she tried to push his hands away. In the struggle, she lost her balance, and they both tumbled to the grass. Linda fell onto her back. He managed to pull the sweatshirt over her head and pin her arms in it above her on the ground. Her breasts heaved threatening to escape her low-cut lacy pink bra. He pinned her arms with one hand and unbuckled the belt with the other, shoving the jeans down to her hips.

Then he rolled on top of her, kissing her forcefully and letting his hand slide down into her matching pink panties.

Maybe I went a little too far.

Tom pulled back to search her face. She made no move to escape his grasp and lifted her head to kiss him back. His response was to jerk the sweatshirt off of her arms and slide his mouth down her neck to her cleavage. He rolled over, pulling her on top of him, and slid the jeans off her bottom.

She pushed on his chest so that she was half-sitting. "Is this safe out here?" She looked around to see if anyone was watching.

"Safe? A minute ago, you didn't care about safe! You were running my horse into the ground for no reason at all. Well, this is me being impulsive. So don't talk to me about safe."

She rolled off and hiked her jeans back up. "It's not warm enough to get naked."

"Oh, I'm burning up. I'll keep you warm," Tom smirked. He pulled her back into a kiss. He thought she'd be more indignant after his reckless advances.

"I'll bet you don't even have a condom."

He sighed. She was right. He hadn't thought that far ahead. "That's true. Take off my old jeans, and you can ride back in your underwear."

She jumped up and buckled the jeans. "I can't do that. You want your family to see me in my—" She reached for the sweatshirt, but he folded it up as though he was going to put it in a knapsack. "You're just pissed about the horse."

"I'm pissed because you didn't wait when I asked you to. I know this land. You don't. I know these horses, you don't. You can't always have things your way."

Linda turned and walked back to the horses. She stroked Cheyenne's head and talked softly to him. Then she untied his reigns and got back into the saddle.

Damn. She's playing with me now. She knows I won't let her go back without a shirt. And I can't keep my eyes off that pink bra. It's not like she's got huge tatas, although they're generous enough for her thin frame. But she knows how to dress them up for maximum appeal. And she doesn't try to hide them like my last girlfriend.

"Do not leave without me. I'm serious." Tom narrowed his eyes.

Linda smiled and slowly walked Cheyenne in a circle.

"You forgot this," Tom grumbled and tossed the sweatshirt back to her.

She smiled. "You're sure you want me to wear it?"

Tom growled and slapped Cheyenne on the flank, causing the horse to take off. She nearly dropped the sweatshirt, and he laughed as he mounted Brazen and followed her back.

The family was cleaning up after Easter dinner when Tom approached his mother.

"Mom, we have to leave soon, but there is something I need to ask you about." He motioned for his mother to go into the laundry room off the kitchen.

"What is it, Dear?" She threw the tablecloth they had used for dinner into the washing machine.

"Um, it's…my hat. My Stetson got toothpaste on it, and after I wiped it off, it left a stain. Do you have something to clean suede with?"

"Yeah, I think there is some suede and leather cleaner in that cupboard behind you."

Tom opened the door to the kitchen. "Linda, would you bring me my black cowboy hat? I think it is in the front room."

Linda appeared with the hat, and he motioned for her to come into the laundry room. He grabbed the cleaner and a rag and started working on the stain. Linda squinted at him.

"Actually, Mom, there is something else I need to ask you." He glanced at Linda before locking eyes with his mom. Tom took a breath. "Donella told me something pretty strange. Something about you and Dad being separated before I was born. She implied Jake wasn't my biological father."

Tom had set down the hat, so Linda picked up the cloth and started working on it.

Denise dropped her gaze back to the washing machine lid and stood very still. Then, after a moment she spoke. "She threatened to say something like that. She thinks she knows everything that happened, but she doesn't. Jake and I did see each other more than she knew. We saw each other and I got pregnant. Donella didn't know. But she shouldn't have said anything to you. That was spiteful." Denise rubbed her hand over her cheek and covered her mouth with her fingers.

"So, Dad came home from Canada about nine months before I was born?"

"I kind of forget. I think I went up there to see him." She looked up at the ceiling. "We'd been back and forth over the four years he worked up there." Denise put her hands on Tom's shoulders and took him in. "You remind me so much of your father; I can't believe you'd buy her bullshit. She's always been so jealous of our family." Then Denise's gaze moved to Linda, who was putting the lid back on the cleaner.

"Linda knows about this," Tom said. He turned to her and picked up his hat. "That looks better. Thanks for finishing it. I guess we'd better head out."

Denise put her arms around her son. "I'm sorry you had to hear that, Baby."

"It's okay. Thanks for letting me bring Linda for the weekend."

After saying goodbye to the rest of the family, they got underway in the Jeep.

After a few miles, Tom said. "I guess I was worried about that for no reason."

"Tom, I don't want to burst your bubble. But you know I have been going to a therapist for years. One time she told me how she can tell when her patients are lying to her. Of course, I had lied to her myself, so it was kind of embarrassing. I was watching your mother, saw her body language. I noticed how she phrased her answer."

"You think she was lying?"

Linda sighed.

Tom tossed his Stetson into the back seat. "Damn."

CHAPTER TWENTY

"You are so lucky, Lindy," Sarah gushed over the phone. "I talked to the most qualified candidate for twirler at your school. And she's even a sophomore, so it's perfect. Do you know her? Her name is Dawn Gray."

It was April, and practices for twirler auditions would start soon. Linda heaved an exaggerated sigh. Her sister liked to think she knew a lot about every activity at Capital High School. Sarah had been in as many activities as possible when she was the head cheerleader, homecoming queen, and student council president. But she'd never been a twirler. The very idea that Sarah was impressed by this girl made it almost impossible for Linda to like her. Linda's taste was often diametrically opposed to Sarah's.

"How did you meet her?" Linda asked.

"She moved into a house across the street from my friend, Bambi. You remember Bambi? She was on the cheer squad with me, and we have an English Lit class together now. I had to stop by Bambi's place the other day, and she was talking to this girl across the street, who moved to Lincoln during Christmas break. She's been a champion baton twirler for years in Iowa. She's even won events in Illinois. And now, because of her father's job, they moved here, and she's in your school. I mean, how lucky could you get?"

Linda covered her eyes with her hand. "Maybe she won't want to be one of four twirlers. She sounds like someone who likes the spotlight." *Much like you and Bambi.*

"Oh, I think she knows how it is set up at your school. Her parents talked to the principal and the music teacher. You'll probably just have to give your stamp of approval as a senior twirler."

"The girls have to come to practices and try out. Nothing is guaranteed. You had to try out for cheerleader, didn't you?"

"Of course. That was the rule. But everyone knew who was going to make it. I was a shoo-in, and so is this girl. I guess you haven't met her."

"No, but if she tries out, I will. I hope she isn't stuck up."

"Oh, no! She's as sweet as pie. Bambi said there have already been boys over there trying to impress her, and she's barely gotten unpacked. Cute little thing, did I mention that? She will certainly dress up your twirler team."

Because we're all scuzzbuckets? Is that what you're saying?

"Well, thanks for trying to do some recruiting for me. I'm sure it will come in handy next week when we start practices."

"Oh, no problem, Lindy. You know I am always here to help. But listen, Rick is downstairs waiting for me, so I'd better go."

I haven't met Rick either. But he is probably the latest in her long, long line of boyfriends. I wonder if she has to keep a scorecard? I should ask her if she has had sex with any of them. If so, she might finally have some useful advice for me.

The following week, Dawn Gray showed up for twirler practice. Linda realized she had seen her; she played the piccolo in the band, but Linda didn't have a good view of her from the trombone section. Most piccolo players played the flute and added the piccolo if a piece of music called for it. But she'd overheard Dawn tell Yvonne that she liked playing piccolo because it was higher and she could be heard over the flute section.

Nothing like a prima donna.

Nancy Evans' cousin Marilyn was also trying out for twirler. Nancy wasn't pushing for her to be chosen, which was good because Linda didn't give her much hope. The other girl trying out that Linda didn't know was Randy Sparks' younger sister, Melissa. She seemed like a hard worker. Linda's old charm school pal,

Janet Sparks, was Melissa's cousin. Linda was rooting for Melissa. There were also three other girls auditioning who were current band members: Joselyn Cooper, Renee Carpenter, and Sandy Hemp.

But Dawn rubbed Linda the wrong way from the first day of practice. Debbie and Yvonne came to the first few practices and demonstrated several basic twirls that they wanted the contestants to learn and master. Dawn, of course, probably mastered these twirls at age twelve when she started her twirler competitions. So, she wasn't content to do them slowly and carefully. She'd start spinning the baton over her wrists or neck. It distracted the other girls and made them self-conscious that they were new to baton twirling.

Linda pulled Dawn aside after witnessing this. "You're intimidating some of the other girls with your fancy tricks. Obviously, you know how to do all the basics. Maybe you could help some of the others learn them."

"Am I intimidating you, Linda?"

Linda's eyes flashed. "No. I'm already a twirler. I'm going to be one of the judges who picks the next two twirlers."

Dawn smiled. "It is a competition, isn't it? Isn't it an advantage to intimidate the other hopefuls?"

"We're also a team. You have a chance to show that you are a team player."

"You want me to be a teacher? I didn't expect that."

"I want you to be considerate. Is that too much to ask of anyone?" Linda found her patience wearing thin and walked over to help some Sandy and Renee.

Dawn stopped showing off around the other girls, so that was a step forward. Linda was optimistic that she'd come around until she saw something in her last period study hall. Linda tried to complete as much homework as she could in study hall, so she'd have to haul fewer books home and have more free time in the evening. Some of the other kids wasted time, and the study hall monitors ignored them usually.

Linda looked across the cafeteria when she heard a noise. Nancy's boyfriend, Peter, was laughing. Linda's brows rose when she saw he was playing some sort of game with Dawn. She didn't know exactly what they were doing, but it appeared one of them put their hand down on the table and the other tried to grab it before they could snatch their hand back. They were making noise, and she expected a teacher to stop them. But no one did.

What is Peter doing? I don't think Nancy would like this. I thought he was head-over-heels for her.

Nancy had told her that things had gotten a little out of hand on Valentine's Day when Peter was accidentally handed a room key at the Cornhusker Hotel and they made out on the hotel bed. Nancy confessed that her willpower was eroding and she was avoiding being alone with Peter to resist temptation. Linda admired Nancy for adhering to her Catholic upbringing, even if Linda wasn't following suit. But was Peter looking for a more accommodating girl like Dawn?

Linda was wondering if she should mention this to Nancy an hour later when the twirler practices began.

"I think we can start them on a simple routine today, combining the twirls they have learned," Nancy said, consulting a spiral notebook where she'd been keeping notes. "Do you have anything you want to tell them before we start?"

Nancy had become her best friend since they'd been twirlers together. She opened her mouth to speak to her friend and it was suddenly flooded with saliva. Linda's eyes got big, and she dashed to the girls' bathroom down the hall. She made it to the first stall before she began to vomit into the toilet. Linda hadn't eaten much.

She'd skipped breakfast as usual and hadn't eaten since lunch. What had brought this on?

Am I getting the flu? Most people get the stomach flu in the winter; we're past that. I don't have time to be sick. Prom is coming up, and we have to finish these twirler practices.

She thought about her mother, Mary Jo. She was frequently throwing up. Linda thought she had a chronic stomach condition and couldn't tolerate some foods or alcohol. But she also wondered if Mary Jo forced herself to vomit sometimes to keep her slender figure.

But Linda hated to throw up. It was something gross that felt out of control. At least she'd managed to make it to the bathroom. Now she had vomit breath. Yuck.

When Linda got back to the twirler group, she was happy to see that Yvonne had joined them. At least there were two other twirlers here to take charge.

"I'm sorry. I think I'd better go home. I threw up and I don't want to make anyone else sick." Nancy and Yvonne nodded sympathetically, and Linda picked up her bookbag and purse and headed for her car.

In a few hours, she felt better and was able to eat some dinner. By the next morning, she felt normal.

Over the next few days, she was sick a couple of times during afterschool twirler practice. She'd brought her toothbrush and some mouthwash in her backpack, so she resumed her duties after vomiting.

By the next week, she felt queasy in the morning. She didn't vomit, didn't eat anything, and didn't tell her mother she was sick. At least she stopped throwing up in the afternoon. Her first assumption was that she'd inherited whatever her mother had, and she'd probably have to see her mother's specialist. Maybe she'd have to stop eating her favorite foods. She didn't like that idea.

She was watching television one night when one of the characters had morning sickness. That hadn't occurred to Linda. She'd been intimate with Tom nearly every weekend for the past two months, but he said he had the birth control handled. She'd seen him use the condoms herself. How could that go wrong? How could she find out?

She certainly wasn't going to ask her mother. But someone at school might be able to help her—the guidance counselor. *I mean, it was right in the title. I need some guidance.*

Linda knocked on Mrs. Baker's door during the last period. Mrs. Baker had been a guidance counselor at Capital High for many years. Linda had last spoken to her about her college plans last fall.

"Excuse me. Do you have a minute?" Linda asked.

Mrs. Baker looked up from the journal she was reading. "Linda! Of course. How can I help you?"

Linda eased into Mrs. Baker's small office and closed the door. "How do I find out if I'm pregnant? Without telling my parents, I mean."

Mrs. Baker nodded as though this was not a new question for her. "Why do you think you might be pregnant?"

"Well, um I've been nauseated in the morning. And for a few days, I threw up every afternoon."

"Have you missed any periods?"

"Oh. I guess I didn't think about that. I have always been sort of irregular. I don't think I've had a period since February."

"And you've been physically involved with a boy, I assume?"

"Yes, I have a boyfriend. He's in college. But he's been careful about contraception."

"You know condoms aren't foolproof."

128

Linda raised her eyebrows. "They aren't? Then what good are they?"

Mrs. Baker pulled out a pamphlet about different methods of contraception and showed Linda the statistics on various forms of birth control. "I'd like to get these in the hands of every junior and senior in the school, but the board of education won't allow it. Students are supposed to be scared to have sex after watching those videos in health class," she scoffed.

"I guess I don't remember the videos in health class," Linda admitted.

"But your question was, how to find out if you're pregnant. Your best bet is to go to Planned Parenthood. I don't think they charge much for a test, and it's confidential. Here, I think I have one of their brochures."

Linda left the afterschool practices early, claiming she had a doctor's appointment.

"Even if used completely correctly, two out of one hundred women will get pregnant if they rely on their partner using a condom. The percentage is much higher if the condom is expired or breaks, or comes off, for example," the young woman at the clinic told her.

Did Tom know this? He acted like there was no reason to be concerned about a pregnancy.

"If you wish, you can provide us with a urine sample, and we can test for a hormone that is present in pregnant women. Sometimes we suggest you come back in two weeks and repeat the test, as the hormone doesn't show up right away," the counselor said.

"I suppose I should take the test. But what if I am pregnant? I can't have a baby. I'm seventeen."

"It isn't legal to terminate a pregnancy in Nebraska, but we can give you some referrals in nearby states. We don't recommend you decide too quickly. You'll want to hear what your boyfriend and parents think."

No, I don't want to hear what any of them think. I don't want to think about this at all. This was not supposed to happen.

They gave her a test number and told her she could call them back in three days for the results. She could also come back in two weeks to repeat the test if it was negative.

Somehow, she felt more in control after going to Planned Parenthood. She was going to have to tell Tom those condoms weren't nearly as foolproof as he thought. Maybe she should have asked about getting birth control pills. She supposed she'd have to wait for the test results.

In the meantime, she vacillated between believing she was pregnant and that she was not. She threw up a few more times after school, and that was enough to convince her that she was likely pregnant. Nancy was looking at her suspiciously.

When she came out of the bathroom one afternoon, Yvonne, Debbie, and Nancy confronted her about her frequent stomach problem.

"Okay, I think I'm probably pregnant. I am waiting to hear the test results," Linda admitted. She didn't add that she could have called about the test results two days earlier, but she'd been too chicken.

Her friends made comforting sounds and started acting like she'd be welcoming a little bundle of joy.

No way that was happening. Telling anyone was a mistake. Getting pregnant was an even bigger mistake. I'm going to have to control what happens next.

She had trouble zipping her favorite miniskirt the next day and decided she shouldn't keep putting this off. After school, she called the clinic from a payphone. After she ended the call, she didn't walk down to the music alcove where they were expecting her to help with practice. She stumbled out to her pretty blue Camaro and cocooned herself inside. Then she began to cry.

Damn, damn, damn!

This is Tom's fault. Don't worry, he'd said. I've got condoms.

Like that did any good. Stupid boys with their stupid penises. Always wanting to poke you. Oh, I liked the kissing part and the touching, but I could have stopped there. I should have stopped there. I should have stuck with kissing girls. Then I wouldn't be in this fix.

What was she going to do now? She shouldn't have told her friends. It might be all over school by now. No, she trusted them. She shouldn't trust boys. Ever again.

Linda banged her fists on the steering wheel. She was going to have to tell her parents. She couldn't get out of this mess without their help, their money. God, they were going to be so disappointed in her. Sarah would never get in trouble like this. She would never sleep with a boy before marriage. She probably dumped them as soon as they made demands.

But prom was coming up at the end of the week. Linda had a pre-prom party all planned. She had a lovely navy dress that Nancy had embellished to make it more "Linda," encircling the neckline and waist with rhinestones. They were going to have soft drinks and hors d'oeuvres by the pool. Tom was renting a tuxedo. How could she even see Tom?

No, she had to be strategic about this now. She couldn't tell her parents before the prom party. They might cancel the party or prevent her from seeing Tom. And Tom was her prom date; it was too late to change that. After prom, she'd have to deal with her parents.

How was she going to keep this from Tom? Three of her best

friends knew. They might say something. How would he react if she told him? Would he want to have the baby? He might even want to get married! He was still trying to sort out his whole who's-my-daddy drama. She couldn't lay this on him even if she were angry that he'd got her into this mess.

She had a plan: pretend everything is normal until after prom. Then in a week or two, before school was out, she'd tell her parents. But not Tom. She was not telling Tom. She started her car and drove home.

CHAPTER TWENTY-ONE

Linda pinned the last curl in place for her formal updo for prom. She'd gotten skilled at creating fancy hairdos and makeup for special occasions. When she slipped on her form-fitting navy sheath dress, she wondered if she had a slight tummy bulge. It was probably her imagination; nothing should be showing this soon. But she could skip eating at the party and stick to ginger ale and cigarettes.

She thought she'd be excited about going to her prom with a boy she was crazy about. But tonight, she felt like she was an actress playing a part. She was the girl who knew too much playing the ingénue. In this dress, with this hair, she could be elegant and formal. She could be Holly Golightly in *Breakfast at Tiffany's*. Sleek and mysterious. Hiding her secrets. It might be fun for an evening.

Tom didn't seem to understand. He arrived before the party started at 5:30 p.m. Linda was already buzzing around the table of snacks they'd set out by the swimming pool. He came bounding down the stairs when her father let him in to find Mary Jo in the basement kitchenette and Linda arranging things outside on the pool deck.

He took Linda's hand. "Well, look at you. Ready for the party, I see. You look very beautiful and about ten years older."

It was hard to look him in the eye, but this was where the acting came in. "You are looking very dapper yourself, Mr. Case. Would you care for an hors d'oeuvres?"

"Why thank you, Miss Bridges. But I'd rather have a nibble of you." Since he had passed Linda's mother indoors, he pulled Linda close and ran his teeth over her ear. When he tried to kiss her mouth, she put her hand on his chin to stop him.

"Lipstick. You don't want red lipstick all over you, do you?"

Tom's lips parted like he wanted to answer but he didn't. He tried to study her expression, but she pulled her gaze away. Tom was tall, trim, and broad-shouldered. He looked good in a black tuxedo, freshly showered and shaved, with his dark hair neatly trimmed. Even his black glasses frames seemed to make the whole picture come together.

But Holly Golightly always kept them guessing. She breezed by him to greet the first guests who were descending into the recreation room. He was forced to stand next to her so she could introduce him to her high school friends.

He met Debbie Adams and Robert Washington. They were with Yvonne Edison and Gary White. Seven other couples came downstairs over the next fifteen minutes. They were soon sitting at glass tables near the swimming pool, and Linda was checking on everyone.

"Where did you find that dress, Linda? You look very svelte," Yvonne told her.

"I bought the dress at Hovland Swanson, but Nancy made it sparkle. She could be a fashion designer, you know."

"Where are Nancy and Peter? I haven't seen them," Debbie said.

"I don't know," Linda said. She glanced around at the area. Tom was sitting at the bar smoking with her father. She supposed she had left him to fend for himself. But Nancy and Peter were late.

The party only lasted about an hour, and then it was time to leave for the prom. Her parents watched her trying to get into Tom's Jeep in her long narrow dress.

"Do you want to take the Lincoln? I'm staying in tonight. You've gotta come back here anyway to bring Linda home." Linda's father, Michael, fished keys out of his pocket.

Tom looked dumbstruck. "You'd let me drive your new Lincoln Continental?"

"You seem to be a safe driver. Your Jeep isn't banged up. And I know you haven't been drinking."

Tom moved his car to the side of the driveway and went into the garage. He backed the wine-red sedan out very slowly. Then he took Linda's hand and helped her into the passenger seat.

"Thanks, Daddy," Linda called out after dropping the power window.

"You kids have fun," Mary Jo said.

Later, they were dancing slowly, and Tom pressed his lips to her hair. She stiffened slightly. "After the dance, are you coming over to my place?"

"Oh, I don't think I can. We've got my dad's car."

"We can still go to my apartment. It might be our last time together before I go back to Gordon. And I want to see what you've got under that amazing dress."

She hadn't considered that. But she couldn't have sex with him again. Not when she was already carrying his child. She'd never be able to hide her emotions.

"No, I'd better not."

"I don't understand," he said. "We always go back to my place." He had his hand on the small of her back and he pulled her a little tighter against him, as though she might mistake his intentions.

"I can't. It's bad timing. You know, um, wrong time of the month." She eased back away from his grip.

"Is that what's bothering you? You don't seem like yourself," he said.

135

What's bothering me? You got me pregnant and you don't even know it.

"I'm trying to be formal tonight. I'm sort of pretending to be sophisticated."

"Yeah, well, sophisticated is not my forte. I'm your Rancher Boy, Baby."

Linda started. "Don't call me Baby."

"What? You want me to call you Miss Bridges?"

Why did he have to pick that word? Now she was fighting back tears. Holly Golightly, keep it together.

"Linda? Something's wrong. Tell me." Tom pulled her face to meet his eyes. "What's upset you?"

She couldn't hold it back. She broke away from him and fled the dance floor. She thought the bathroom was the safest refuge. She hoped to find Nancy or one of her other friends in there, but she didn't see anyone she knew well.

Do not cry. She went into a stall for some privacy. *You are not a crier, Linda. Be strong. Stop thinking about the baby. He's going to keep asking questions.*

She went back to find Tom in a few minutes. He was standing watching the band.

"I'm sorry, Tom. I guess I don't feel that well. I think maybe I should sit down and have some punch and a cookie. I didn't eat earlier," Linda told him.

"Sure. You sit down here, and I'll go get us some refreshments." He led her to a table, and she took a seat.

In a few minutes, he returned with three cookies and two glasses of punch.

"What was your prom night like last year?" she asked.

136

He laughed. "You really want to know?"

She nodded and ate a cookie.

"Well, the gym was all decked out kinda like this. I went with my high school girlfriend, Jillian. We weren't the king and queen, but we were finalists. One of the other seniors had a kegger at his farm after prom. We drank a lot of beer, and then Jillian and I did it in my dad's pickup. That's how prom goes where I come from."

She suddenly felt nauseated again. Maybe it was the mention of beer. Had he admitted to having sex with some other girl a year ago? Did she get pregnant too? She would have preferred not to have heard that. "I see."

"You do look kinda pale, Linda. Do you want to leave?"

"No, no. It's prom. I've been looking forward to this. I want to see who's crowned king and queen."

"Are you upset with me because I am going back home soon? I told you I'd be spending most of the summer working on the ranch. I'll miss you like crazy. But we'll talk on the phone, and I'll come back every few weeks."

"You're giving up your apartment."

"Yeah, it seemed dumb to pay rent if I wasn't going to live there. Maybe your folks would let me bunk in the pool house if I come to visit you."

Her eyes widened. *I can't see them agreeing to that once they know about the pregnancy.*

"We'll see."

CHAPTER TWENTY-TWO

School would be out in ten days. She hadn't told her parents about the pregnancy. Many nights one or both of them were gone at dinner time. But tonight, Mary Jo and Michael were home. They were expecting another couple to join them for a cookout on the pool deck.

"Mom and Dad, I know the Schroeders are coming over, but I need to talk to you for a few minutes." Both of her parents were in the kitchen organizing the food for the meal.

"Of course, Lindy. What's up?" Michael said.

"Can we sit down?" Linda glanced at her watch and swirled it around her wrist.

Mary Jo and Michael took a seat at the small kitchen table.

"You must be missing Tom. He's been back home a week or so, hasn't he?" Mary Jo patted her hand.

Linda looked at her mother's beautifully manicured hand on top of her own. Her mother's nails shone with poppy nail polish, and she wore two sparkling rings that reflected the lights of the chandelier. She looked up at her mother's face quickly. "I'm pregnant."

Linda watched for signs that Mary Jo's pleasant countenance was cracking. She saw it now, a slight tremble to her lips, an eyelid twitching oh so faintly. But the control her mother had was impressive. To watch her, you'd think nothing ever bothered her.

"What did you say?" Michael made no effort to control his emotions. Linda had seen him angry but never violent, never excessively crude. She could see his face becoming flushed, and his nostrils began to flare.

She dropped her gaze to the tabletop. "I'm pregnant, and I need to have it taken care of."

"Tom knows about this?" Michael asked, his mouth forming a tight line.

Linda shook her head. "I decided it would be better not to tell him. The fact that he's not here should make that easier. I would like to have this done with as soon as school ends."

"He strikes me as a decent kid. Of course, this..." Michael gestured to Linda's abdomen, "this is pretty irresponsible. But he may have an opinion you need to hear."

"His opinion doesn't matter. And if he doesn't know, it won't hurt him." Linda sighed.

"She's right, Dear. A woman controls her own body. I don't know a lot about this, but first thing tomorrow morning, I will make some phone calls." Mary Jo stood up, smoothing her hair. "Leave everything to me, Lindy. Who else knows about this?"

"Um, the school guidance counselor, some people at Planned Parenthood, I told my friends, Nancy, Debbie, and Yvonne, but they will keep it quiet." Linda bit her lower lip. "I don't want Sarah to know."

"Then don't mention this to anyone else," her mother warned.

The doorbell rang. Michael stood up. Linda thought he was headed to the door, but he stopped, put his big hand between her shoulders, and rubbed her consolingly.

His voice hitched when he said, "It'll be okay, Kiddo. You'll see."

Mary Jo was true to her word. She had the abortion arranged within days. Linda and her mother made plans to go to a clinic in Overland Park, Kansas, where it could be performed legally. The clinic administrator assured Mary Jo that they had done this procedure numerous times and were well-prepared.

Mary Jo picked up Yvonne and Connie Edison for the trip to Kansas. The Edisons had offered to go along with Linda for moral support. It was a long ride to Kansas. Linda leaned her head back on the backseat of her mother's Oldsmobile Ninety-Eight Town Sedan.

Yvonne reached out and took Linda's hand.

She said she'd come along and hold my hand. I guess she meant that literally.

"How are you doing, Honey?" Yvonne asked. "Did you decide to tell Tom about this?"

Linda looked out the window and shook her head.

Should I have told him? Would he have come with me instead of Yvonne? Would he be holding my hand or would I be crying on his shoulder? Would he be racked with guilt or concerned about my welfare? I thought I was being thoughtful by shutting him out. But he might be angry if he knew I'd kept this secret. It doesn't matter now. I made my decision.

"I don't know where things are going with Tom," Linda said softly. "He went back home for the summer."

When they got to the clinic, Mary Jo seemed to know where to go. She and Linda were ushered into an office and greeted by a stern-looking woman wearing a white lab coat.

"We have some questionnaires and forms to complete. You had a telephone interview with Dr. Nutt yesterday, is that correct?" the lab assistant said.

"Yes. That's right," Linda said.

"And he reviewed the procedure? Have you changed your mind about terminating your pregnancy?"

"No, of course not. We drove for hours to get here. I haven't changed my mind." Linda shifted in her chair.

The woman looked at her form. "All right. Kansas law stipulates certain conditions be met to perform an abortion. Has a doctor indicated to you that your life is at risk if you continue with this pregnancy?"

"No."

"Is the pregnancy a result of incest or rape?"

"Yes," Mary Jo answered for her daughter. Linda looked at her mother with wide eyes. Mary Jo gave her a stern side-eye glance. "She was raped."

How could Mom tell a bald-faced lie with such aplomb?

The lab assistant looked at Linda for confirmation.

"Uh-huh," Linda tried to shudder convincingly.

"I know under the circumstances this next question may seem out of place. Does the father know about the pregnancy?"

Linda's mouth dropped open, then snapped shut. "No, he's in prison."

I may as well make this lie a whopper.

It was Mary Jo's turn to look at her daughter with surprise.

"I see." The lab assistant tapped her pen on the desk. "I have a brochure here that talks about how fathers are required to pay child support and what services are available to mothers during pregnancy and after giving birth. Would you like a chance to review that?"

Linda put her palm up to stop her. "No. I want to get this over with as quickly as possible."

They finished signing several forms and were sent back to the waiting room to join Yvonne and Connie.

"Everything okay?" Yvonne asked.

Linda nodded. "The story is that I was raped, and my rapist is in prison. In case anyone happens to ask you here."

Yvonne's brows shot up. "I see. I guess I missed that part."

Linda smirked and shook her head. Gallows humor may be all she had going for her today.

When a nurse came out and called Linda's name, Yvonne stood up to go with her.

"Can I go in to hold her hand?" she asked the nurse.

"No, we have someone here to do that sort of thing. Her patient advocate will be right next to her."

Linda started to follow the nurse through a door, then turned back to look at Yvonne and Mary Jo with tears in her eyes.

Now that I'm here, it's scary. I know this is the right thing to do, but I don't know if it is going to hurt.

She thought about Tom again as she changed into a hospital gown. She wished she could feel his arms around her.

A tall red-haired woman came into the room. "My name is Maggie. I will be your patient advocate. I'm going to go over the procedure with you now."

Linda nodded.

"You will find that I am not one to use euphemisms or slang. I want you to have accurate information. They will be doing a D & C, or dilation and curettage. They do this by enlarging the opening to your cervix and use a tool to scrape the lining of your uterus, which removes and destroys the implanted embryo."

Maggie led her into the next room and had her sit on the procedure table. She went on, "First, they will insert a speculum. You've had that done at the doctor's office, haven't you?"

"I don't think so," Linda said.

Maggie picked one up to show her. "This is so they can see

your cervix. Then they use these Hagar dilators to gradually stretch out your cervix so that they can induce a curette to remove tissue." She showed Linda the various Hagar dilators, a dozen metal rods that increased in diameter. Then she held up the curette, a metal rod with a handle on one end and a loop on the other.

Linda took a deep breath. Her head was getting woozy. And her arms and legs began shaking.

"You okay, Linda?" Maggie asked. "We're going to give you some local anesthesia; you won't feel that much."

"You're not going to knock me out? I had my tonsils out when I was eight, and they put me under."

"No, they don't like to do that. They can't keep you here overnight. Maybe they will give you some moderate sedation if you like."

Maggie told Linda to lie on the table. "Oh, and sometimes they use this." She picked up a tenaculum, which looked like a giant pair of scissors.

Linda gasped. Another nurse came in and said she would be putting an IV into Linda's arm. By that time, Linda was trembling uncontrollably. Maggie sighed and held Linda's arm down so that the nurse could tap her vein.

"It's the young ones who tend to get so nervous. How old are you, Honey?" Maggie asked.

"Seven-seventeen. Why is it so cold in here? Can you turn up the heat?" Linda's teeth were even chattering.

In a few minutes, several men came in wearing surgical scrubs and masks. One of them said he'd be giving her the anesthesia. Once he gave her that, she relaxed a little. She stopped shaking and closed her eyes.

I need to go somewhere else in my mind. If I can't sleep, I have to imagine.

She saw herself running in a field when she was twelve years old. Brian was with her. They were chasing Brian's dog, who was bounding toward a pheasant her father had shot. The dog found the pheasant, and Linda picked it up by its feet. She was running back to her father when the pheasant suddenly started flapping its wing. She gasped and opened her eyes.

Maggie was holding one of her hands. "It's okay, Linda. You're doing fine. They are making good progress. Just relax."

Linda took several big breaths. She saw the anesthesiologist do something to her IV, and she drifted off.

She was back in the field with Michael and Brian. Michael was helping her point the shotgun and look through the sight. She looked at the pheasant in flight, and when she thought she had it in the right position, she pulled the trigger. The bird fell to the ground. She beamed when her father praised her aim. She'd killed it. She and Brian laid their guns down in the grass and went to find their prey.

I haven't talked to Brian since last summer. What happened to him?

"Linda! Linda! You're in recovery. All done. You did great." Maggie was patting her hand when Linda opened her eyes.

"Mom. Where's my mom?" Linda said. The tears were threatening to come back again. Damnit. Why had she been so weepy lately?

"We'll let your mom come in once you're moved to another room. It'll be about fifteen minutes."

She was still groggy and felt like she'd had the stomach flu when they got her up and helped her dress. She'd worn loose clothes to make her more comfortable. She was vaguely aware of the medications that were handed to her mother and the instructions that followed.

144

By the time they took her out to the waiting room where Yvonne and Connie sat, Linda felt like she was strong enough to walk. She looked at Yvonne's face.

I must look a fright based on Yvonne's expression.

Mary Jo brought the car up to the door, and they let Linda lie down in the backseat with her head in Yvonne's lap. Mary Jo covered her with a blanket, and Linda fell asleep.

After about thirty minutes, she woke up enough to think about Tom. She needed to see Tom. She hadn't answered her phone, so she'd avoided talking to him after he'd left. He might never speak to her again. And now the tears were back. Yvonne patted Linda's head, and she heard music fading away.

CHAPTER TWENTY-THREE

Tom could not figure out what Linda was doing. He'd been home for more than a week and had tried calling her almost every evening. He had to share the telephone with his eighteen-year-old sister, Theresa, and fifteen-year-old sister, Susan. A couple of times, he'd even gone down to Chief's bungalow and tried to call Linda from his line. But she'd never answered the phone.

Why wasn't she in her room? She should have been studying for finals or writing papers until school was done. Now school was out but she still wasn't answering her phone. Was she deliberately ignoring his calls, trying to break up with him? He called directory assistance, hoping to find a number for Michael Bridges, but was informed that his number was nonpublished. He might try to reach one of Linda's friends, Debbie or Yvonne something, but he didn't know either of their last names. He should have paid more attention on prom night.

"Theresa, can I ask you something? I'm not trying to be a smart-ass." Tom sat down on his sister's bed where she was reading.

"Shoot."

"Do girls get like all weepy when they have their periods?"

Theresa snorted. "You mean do they cry over every little thing, every sappy commercial, every sentimental thing someone says? God yes, it is so annoying."

"I've never seen you do that."

"I have learned to hide it, but I can be a real drama queen during that week. You do not want to cross me."

"Okay, well, the last time I spoke to Linda was on pr...I mean was the weekend before I left. We had a date, and she kept getting upset for no reason. I thought it was because I was leaving for the summer. When I asked her what she was crying about, she said it

146

was that time of the month and to ignore it. That was also her excuse when I wanted to make out. And since I've been home, I've tried calling her lots of times in the evening, and she doesn't answer. I can't figure out what's wrong."

"Sounds to me like you are ancient history, Brother."

"No, I don't believe that. Linda loves me. I know she does."

"Did she tell you that?"

"Well, not in so many words."

"Did you tell her how you feel about her?"

"Sure, I told her I was crazy for her. I couldn't get enough of her. She is beautiful. Girls like to hear that stuff, right?"

"But did you say 'I love you?'"

Tom sighed. "No. I guess I didn't." He scratched his head. "She wouldn't blow me off just because…"

Theresa squinted. "It sounds like she's found someone a little closer. Maybe even someone else who is still in high school."

Tom frowned, "How did you know she's still in high school?"

"Oh, please. You are so unobservant. At Easter, she was wearing her high school ring."

"So, lots of kids wear their rings after high school."

"Her ring has her graduation year on it, plainly visible. It's 1970. Next year!"

"Jesus. I never thought of that. Do Mom and Dad know she's only seventeen?"

"Beats me. I am the soul of discretion."

Theresa was right about one thing. He should be more observant. The next night was Theresa's graduation party. Tom enjoyed seeing the kids from his sister's class, as he'd known most of them his whole life. But he challenged himself to stand back away from the crowd and do some people-watching. It was more educational than he expected.

There was one boy at the party named Hudson, Hud for short. Tom supposed he was nice-looking, not that Tom ever thought about it. Like most of the boys in their high school, he played multiple sports and was pretty athletic. Hud seemed to drift from group to group, talking to all of the boys and girls. When he talked to Theresa her face lit up like a high-wattage light bulb. *Huh.* Then he watched as Hud went to talk to another girl out on the porch. Theresa watched him closely. Even when other people came to speak to her, her gaze always drifted back to Hud, wherever he was. All right, little sister. I guess I have your number now.

This is kinda fun. I should have done this before.

Tom went out to sit on one of the rockers on the porch. Most of the kids were saying goodbye to Theresa now. She was getting ready to go to another party. Tom thought he heard his mother's voice, raised in anger. He got up and sat on the porch rail where he spotted his mother talking to one of his dad's friends, Buck Henderson. He couldn't see Buck, but he knew his pickup. Denise was talking to him through the driver's window. There didn't appear to be anyone else in the truck.

What's that all about? Is Mom pissed at Uncle Buck?

Buck wasn't actually his uncle, but he'd been around the family as long as Tom could remember. His dad told him that Buck used to work on their ranch full-time when Jake was in Canada, and he still helped out sometimes when there was a lot of work. The problem with Buck was that he was a chronic drunk. He'd lost his driver's license more than once, and then it was hard for him to work. He'd been married to a nice woman, Claudette. But the story was that he'd eaten up her savings in legal fees, and she'd had enough. She'd been a teacher at the elementary school, but she moved to North Platte after the divorce.

148

Jake had stood by Buck when he needed a friend. Maybe that was why Denise was mad; maybe Buck was drunk or owed Jake some money. He didn't hear what they were saying. Buck must have been talking. Then he heard Denise swear at him and slap her hand on the hood of his truck. She turned and walked in the other direction toward the garage. Neither of them seemed to notice Tom watching.

Tom decided it was none of his business and dismissed it. A couple of mornings later, he was in the barn feeding the calves when Buck came walking down the row of pens.

"I've got something for you, Tommy. I'm thinking about taking a trip but I have some things for you first."

"Taking a trip? Where are you going?" Tom walked over to meet him near the entrance to the barn.

"Montana. My sister lives in Montana. I might move there." Buck carried a canvas sack and pulled some papers out of it. "Can we sit down a minute?"

Tom sat on one of the hay bales near the barn door, and Buck sat on another. "Whadaya got there? Is that for my dad?"

"No, Tommy, it's for you. Listen, Denise talked to me. We don't exactly agree on this, but I thought you should have this information."

Tom felt a tightening in his gut and studied Buck's eyes.

He handed Tom a piece of paper from a yellow legal pad. Buck had written some names on it. Tom saw Buck's legal name, Thomas Benjamin Henderson Jr. Below that he'd written Thomas Benjamin Henderson Sr., and across from his name was written Alice Lisette Marks, presumably Buck's mother's name. The list continued for another generation showing Alice's parents too.

"What is this, Buck?" Tom frowned.

"It lists my parents and grandparents. I don't know the names

149

back further, but I think there may be more Hendersons in the cemetery on the edge of town. And this here," Buck handed Tom another sheet. "This shows the diseases I know they have had, including my brother and sister. My brother died of a heart attack at age 47. I thought you might need to know things like that."

Tom stared at him slack-jawed.

Buck fished into his bag, pulled out a large hunting knife in a leather sheath, and handed it to Tom. "This was supposedly my granddaddy's knife. A famous Sioux warrior stole it once, but he got it back. Well, that's the story anyway." He pulled out a mother-of-pearl ring. "And this ring was my mother's. I gave it to Claudette once, but she gave it back when she left. I thought you might have a girl to—"

Tom stood up. "What's this all about, Buck?" He let the papers flutter to the ground.

"Denise said she talked to you," Buck began.

"No! She did not. C'mon, let's go." He grabbed onto the back of Buck's shirt and pushed him toward the barn entrance, forcing him to walk with him to the house. Buck was about the same height as Tom but forty pounds heavier. Tom was determined and propelled by adrenaline.

They found Denise in the kitchen making a cake.

Tom didn't say anything. He looked at her with disgust and then side-eyed Buck.

"Buck? What's going on?" Denise said. She slammed down the rectangle cake pan she'd gotten out of the cupboard.

"I want the truth, Mother." Tom's jaw clenched.

Denise stared back at Tom, then at Buck. "Jake, you'd better come in here!" she hollered.

Jake had been in the front bedroom but came ambling into the kitchen buttoning his shirt. "Oh, hi Buck, didn't know you was comin' out today."

Tom fixed Jake with a steely stare too. "Somebody better start talking. Cuz it sure as hell looks like you've all been lying to me my whole life."

Jake sighed. "Look, Son. Let's calm down…"

"Son? Okay, let's get that straight right now. Am I your son? Or am I…" Tom crooked his thumb at Buck. Buck looked at the floor.

Denise lunged toward Buck, screaming. "What did you say? You had no right to—" Jake moved around the counter to hold onto his wife.

"Denise, no. Let's discuss this rationally. We'll answer Tom's questions."

Tom was still clutching the hunting knife in its sheath. He unsheathed it in a swift motion and thrust the tip into the butcher block countertop. "Ain't nothing calm here!"

"Tom! Put that away before someone gets hurt!" Jake wrenched out the knife when Tom made no move to do so.

"Before someone gets hurt? Is that supposed to be funny?" Tom began pacing the room. "Okay, well, no one is telling the story, so let me guess." He narrowed his stare to his mother's face. "You went to Canada to live while Jake worked on the Canadian pipeline. You got bored with the artic winter with a toddler at home and came back here to live with your parents. Buck shows up one day, not quite the worthless alcoholic he'd become later, and you decided a bird in the hand is better than two in the bush. Then Jake got tired of Canadian bacon and beat it back here to try to reclaim his birthright. Am I getting warm?"

"No!" Jake grumbled. "Let us explain. Don't blame your mother. I was living with another woman in Canada."

"Oh, well, that clears it up. What part of being true to you lawfully-wedded spouse did you two miss?"

Jake grimaced. "It was rough up there, especially during the winter. It was a high-paying job, but I had to stay with the crew. We worked very long hours. Your mother tried to stick it out, but it wasn't any place for a young wife with a small child. She was right to come back home."

Denise folded her arms over her chest. "We didn't know if our marriage would make it. I found out he was shacking up with another woman. I lived with my parents in Gordon for a few months. Then, Chief said I could live here and cook for the men. Grandma Millie was delighted to have little Jerry running around the house. Buck was the ranch foreman, running the cowhands. I didn't know if Jake was coming back."

"I know you must think I'm a loser like everyone else in this town, but I swear, I didn't drink back then. Chief wouldn't allow it," Buck said.

"Didn't they have divorce back in the olden days?" Tom snarled.

"We assumed that would happen once we got in the same country, but we had no time or money to hire an attorney," Jake said. "I called Denise. She told me she was expecting another child. I went a little crazy and came home as quick as I could. We were still married. I quit the job in Canada and moved back in with her. It was almost like we'd never separated."

Tom looked at Buck incredulously. "And what about this poor sucker? He was just shit outta luck? Sorry, Buddy. Thanks for the sperm donation?"

"God, no. You got it wrong, Tommy," Buck said. "Things were already going badly for me. By the time Jake returned, I was having some problems. I hurt my leg and started drinking to ease the pain. The leg got better. The drinking got worse. I had a car

152

accident. Two teenage girls were killed. They charged me with manslaughter."

"What?" Tom raked his hand over his face.

"By the time Jake moved back here, I was in jail awaiting trial. So how can I blame Denise for wanting to go back to him?" Buck shook his head. "They had a trial months later, and the jury couldn't reach a verdict. There were some technicalities. They didn't want to do a second trial, so I was released. I wasn't found innocent or guilty. By that time, you were two months old."

"So, you put Jake's name on my birth certificate and pretended he was my father? Didn't Chief and Millie have anything to say about this?"

"Chief wasn't happy about the deception. He figured the whole town would know the truth. But once Buck's drunkenness became known, he agreed with us treating you like a Case. You were a Case legally, in every way that mattered." Jake reached out to Tom, but he stepped back.

Tom shuddered. "You kept this man as your friend. You bailed him out of scrapes. Did you feel some weird sense of obligation to him? I could never see why you tolerated him." He gave Buck a sidelong look. "And did you keep drinking because your friend had stolen your woman and son? Did it ever occur to you to get sober and fight for what was yours?"

"Thomas Benjamin Case! You are being cruel." Denise fixed her son with a scowl. "You don't know the pain these two have gone through to protect you!"

Tom scoffed. "I'm being cruel? I'm not the one who's been lying for nineteen years."

Buck pursed his lips. "I've tried to stop drinking, Tommy. I've even been to treatment, taken that drug that makes you puke when you drink. None of it worked. I'm a hopeless alcoholic; you're right about that. That's why I'm leaving."

"Okay, I've heard enough. I can't look at any of you right now. I'm going back to Lincoln." He picked up the hunting knife Jake had laid on the counter and returned it to the sheath. "I'll keep this. It's cool. But you can take your papers about your family and their diseases and shove it, Buck. You all make me sick."

Tom turned on his heel and went to his room. Five minutes later, he returned with a couple of bags and went out to his Jeep and threw them in. He didn't say goodbye to anyone. He left in a cloud of dust.

It was after seven in the evening when he found Michael Bridges drinking on a chaise lounge by his swimming pool.

"Good evening, Mr. Bridges. I don't mean to startle you, but I rang the bell. The door was open."

"Hmmm? Who's that? Oh, Linda's friend? Tim? No, no, Tom. Sorry. I'm a little tipsy."

Tipsy? Oh no, I think you're shit-faced, Sir.

"May I join you? I've had a pretty rotten day myself." Tom sat down on the chair facing Michael and looked at the half-empty bottle of Scotch he had on the nearby table. He tilted the bottle asking permission to have some.

"Sure, why not? I'm sure you're pissed as hell too." Michael leaned back on the chair and closed his eyes.

Tom frowned and found a highball glass at the outdoor bar and ice in a bucket. He put ice in his glass, sloshed some Scotch on it, and sat back down facing Michael. "I don't know what you're referring to."

"My daughter. She didn't tell you, did she? Oh no, women can do whatever they want. Like men don't even count anymore. Damn women's lib."

"Linda's not here? I was hoping to see her." He let the alcohol burn his tongue.

"No, no. She's not back. She and her mother. Went off to Kansas. To have an abortion."

Tom choked. "What did you say?"

"Ha! I'm right. She didn't tell you. I told her you should know." Michael smirked.

Tom's brow furrowed. "Are you saying Linda's pregnant?"

"She was. I just said that, didn't I? They went to an abortion clinic."

"Oh my God!" Tom set his drink on the table and stood up. He looked skyward. "Are you freaking kidding me, Lord? You decided to screw up my whole life in one day?" He looked back at Michael. "Are you sure? I mean, you seem like you're three sheets to the wind, Mr. Bridges. Maybe you imagined this."

"No, I didn't imagine it. See, Mary Jo left this paper on the kitchen table. It's their appointment time, ten forty-five this morning. The clinic must have mailed it to her."

Tom read the paper. It was a little vague, but Linda had some sort of medical appointment that morning. The letter went on to describe how she'd feel after the "procedure" and how to treat her symptoms over the next few days. It was from a clinic located in Overland Park, Kansas.

Michael had left a packet of cigarettes and a gold lighter sitting on the table. Tom helped himself to a cigarette.

No, this is not possible. That's why she'd dodged my calls? She'd gotten pregnant? How could...oh shit. Shit, shit, shit. The broken condom. The expired condoms after that. I never told her. I never thought she'd ...oh God. Now what?

"Mr. Bridges, do you have another bottle of Scotch? I'm not

sure this is going to be enough."

Michael laughed and pointed back toward the bar.

CHAPTER TWENTY-FOUR

Mary Jo had her arm around Linda helping her into the house. When they got inside, they saw lights poolside and went downstairs. By then, Linda was more awake and walking gingerly.

"Michael!" Mary Jo said. "Wake up. You fell asleep on the lounge chair. God, are you drunk? I thought you could help Linda get upstairs."

Michael snorted as he opened his eyes and stared at them. The second bottle of Scotch had been left uncapped on the table, next to two empty glasses and an overflowing ashtray. An identical empty bottle was beneath the table.

"Dad, what's Tom doing here?"

Tom was lying on an adjacent chaise lounge wearing swimming trunks and his cowboy boots. He was scooted down to the end of the chaise so his feet were flat on the ground. His black Stetson covered his face.

Linda leaned over him and put a hand on his knee. At first, he didn't stir. Then slowly, he picked up his hat and put it on his head. His abdominal muscles rippled as he moved to sit, then stand when he saw Linda in front of him.

He put his hands on her upper arms and blinked several times as if to wake up. "You okay?"

Linda didn't answer. She wrapped her arms around his neck and pulled him close. This is what she had been missing all day. The feel of his arms as they wrapped around her back, pulling her into his big embrace. He smelled like Scotch and cigarettes, and chlorine clung to his hair. Why was he here? Had he somehow known she needed him?

"Mike, can you get yourself up to bed?" Mary Jo asked. "It's been a very tiring day for all of us."

157

Michael grumbled something but unfolded himself from the chaise lounge and started into the house.

Mary Jo recapped the Scotch. "I'll put Tom on the couch in the family room. He doesn't look like he's in any shape to drive. Then I'll tuck you in the pool house, Honey. Will that do?"

Linda pulled back from Tom and nodded. "Go with my mom. I'll see you tomorrow," she said to him. Then Linda picked up the sack her mother had dropped on the cement, went into the pool house, and crawled into the bed.

Linda awoke the next morning when sunlight streamed through the east window of the pool house. She groaned, remembering the previous day's events. She felt like she should head to the bathroom to check her bleeding. She started to lift the covers and felt something warm next to her. Something holding the comforter down. She turned to find Tom was asleep next to her with one hand under her back. On her skin under her shirt. And oh yes, when she lifted part of the sheet, she could see he was naked. That woke her up.

Linda eased herself out of the bed and into the bathroom, trying to be quiet. It wasn't a pretty sight that greeted her in the mirror. Her hair wasn't bedhead, more like monsoon head. She tried to smooth it with her fingers. There were bags under her eyes, and she looked pale. It's not like she'd spent yesterday at a spa. And now the cramps were beginning to set in. She took some aspirin she found in the medicine chest.

She went back to the bed and propped her pillow against the headboard so she could sit up. Tom ran his hand along her leg, then opened his eyes and looked up at her.

"What are you doing here?" she asked.

"Um," he pushed himself up to a sitting position. "In your bed or at your house?"

"Let's start with the bed. I thought my mother had you sleeping in the rec room."

He smiled, rubbing sleep from his eyes. "I guess I got lonely. I don't remember it too clearly. Your dad got me drunk."

"What happened to your clothes?"

"Hmm? Oh. I dunno. I remember coming in here and getting some swimming trunks. Your dad said kids leave swimwear here, so there are usually extras. I put on some trunks and got in the pool. It felt nice, but I didn't think I should swim and drink, so I got out."

"So, what happened to the swimming trunks?"

Tom shook his head. "Couldn't say. I don't usually wear anything to sleep in."

She smirked. "What were you doing here last night?"

Tom propped his pillow next to hers and scooted up in the bed to sit next to her, tugging the sheet up to his waist. "Yesterday was the day I found out everyone I cared about, everyone I trusted in the whole world, had been lying to me. It started yesterday morning back home on the ranch."

"Go on," she said.

He ran his hands through his hair. "Turns out you were right; my mom was lying. My actual father is the town drunk, who was in jail the day I was born. When my legal father, Jacob Case, found out his wife was pregnant by another man, he hightailed it back to Gordon and acted like nothing was amiss. They've been passing me off as his son ever since. They made sure to invite my real father to all their social gatherings over the years so he could see his child being raised by someone else. Oh, and I shouldn't blame my mother because her husband was shacking up with some other woman while he was in Canada. I was at a loss to decide which of them was the most contemptible. So, I basically told them all to go to hell and left."

"Oh, Tom. That's awful," Linda said.

"I drove all day to see you. To find out why I haven't been able to get you on the phone for over a week. Then your dad tells me you were also lying to me. You had gone to get an abortion and didn't even tell me you were pregnant. I was ready to yell at you, but by the time you got home I was too drunk and tired."

"I'm glad you didn't yell at me last night. My day was terrible too."

Tom sighed. "Why didn't you tell me? You tried to shut me out." He wove his fingers through hers.

"I was trying to shut the whole thing out. If I'd talked to you, I was afraid I'd tell you."

"You didn't want me to tell you what I thought."

"No, I didn't."

"You still don't want to hear it. You're afraid I would have tried to stop you from ending the pregnancy."

"Are you saying you would have agreed with me?"

Tom dropped her hand and leaned back. "I dunno. We could have talked it through at least. The thing is, this whole thing was my fault."

"Oh, it was absolutely your—" Linda glanced toward the window. "Are those your clothes on the chair over there?"

Tom followed her gaze. "Oh, maybe so. I can't see them clearly without my glasses. I guess I took them off in here to put on the swimming trunks."

Linda got out of the bed and brought his clothes to him. "Get dressed. You shouldn't have tried to sneak in here naked after the ordeal I went through yesterday."

160

"It's not like you haven't seen me naked before." Tom pulled on his shorts and jeans while Linda turned her back toy him.

"Yes, but we shouldn't have ever gotten naked. That's where this whole thing went wrong. I think I'm too young for this kind of relationship. I should have said no. But I didn't understand that at the time."

"You're sorry we had sex?" He stood pulling on his shirt and buckling his belt.

"I'm sorry I got in over my head without thinking about the consequences." Linda turned back to face him. "The consequences these past few weeks have been horrible. I was so angry with you when they told me I was pregnant. Then I was throwing up, and I had to tell my friends. Two of them were acting gushy like I was going to have a sweet little baby. I knew right away I couldn't do that. Not in the middle of high school. I wanted it over with.

"My parents were surprisingly great when I told them. My mom said she'd find out where to go, and she'd handle everything. And she did. If there was one bright spot in this whole fiasco, it was that I realized how lucky I was to have my mom helping me. I always thought I was so different than my mother, but she's been a rock. Even yesterday, she knew what to do at the clinic and how to take care of me. And she didn't fall apart once. Can you imagine what this has done to my parents? This was their first grandchild!"

"Your dad seemed pretty broken up—"

Linda put her hand up to silence him. "Trying to hide my pregnancy was bad enough. Trying to forget about it so that I could take my semester tests and finish my junior year was majorly stressful. But that was nothing compared to yesterday. Apparently, they want to make sure you don't come back for a second abortion. They do their best to scare the dickens out of you, showing you the tools they will use on you. They showed me these metal rods they use to stretch you out so they can insert this thing that looks like a small shovel to remove the fetus. I was terrified! My whole body was shaking, and I thought I'd pass out. And that was before they'd even started."

"You were traumatized," Tom said, his eyes filling. "I wish you'd let me come with you."

"They wouldn't have let you in for that part. Traumatized, yes, that's what I was. It seemed like they were telling me how they were going to torture me under 'moderate sedation.' I don't know how I will be able to forget that whole experience. I'll probably have nightmares."

Tom walked around to her side of the bed and tried to embrace her, but she stepped back. "You're still angry with me. Your parents must hate me."

Linda shook her head. "I don't know why neither of them told you to get the hell out and stay away from me. But they didn't. I guess their good manners won out."

"Baby, I don't know how to —" Tom scratched the back of his neck.

"So, I have to say 'get the hell out and stay away from me.'"

Tom's chin jerked up and he searched her face. "You want me to leave?"

"Get the hell out and stay away from me!" Linda's eyes narrowed as her voice rose.

Tom pressed his lips together tightly and backed up. "I have to find my glasses. I think I left them out by the pool." He waited for a beat, then turned and went out the door. She could see him through the window as he picked up his glasses from the table where he'd sat with Michael the night before. He grabbed his Stetson from the chair. Then he straightened up, put his glasses and hat on, and strode into the main house. Linda put her arms out to her sides and fell back onto the bed.

CHAPTER TWENTY-FIVE

She didn't want to talk to Tom. After three days, Linda felt like it was safe to answer her phone in the evening. She and some of her friends had a code. If one of them wasn't answering their phone, the caller would hang up and call back, letting it ring only three times. Then the third time they called back, the other person would know it was one of them, not a boy they were trying to dodge.

She didn't know if Tom had tried to reach her. Other than calls from Nancy, her phone had been eerily silent. By the fifth night, she didn't even hesitate when her teen line rang.

An unfamiliar deep voice responded to her greeting. "May I speak with Linda?"

"This is Linda."

"Oh. This is Charles Case, Tom's grandfather."

Linda's mind flew in different directions. Charles? Who was Charles? Had something bad happened to Tom?

"Yes?"

"Chief. I think Tom probably referred to me as Chief. The family all calls me that."

"Oh, sure. I remember meeting you, Sir."

"I found your phone number on my bill. I'm trying to get in touch with Tom. He left here about a week ago, and no one has heard from him. Have you been in touch with him?"

"Oh." She breathed a little easier. "Well, I did see him. I think it was the night he left the ranch. He told me he'd had a problem at home."

"Well, yes, I guess you could call it that."

163

"But, you see, Tom and I had our own little fallout, and I haven't talked to him since."

"Oh, I am sorry to hear that. I was hoping you might help bridge the divide. You don't know where he is staying or have a phone number?"

"No. I don't have any idea where he is. I assumed he might have gone back to the ranch by now. I mean, I thought he was supposed to be working there."

"That's right. And he'd already worked a couple of weeks." Chief's cough rattled in his lungs. "His dad owes him wages, and I am concerned he might need the money if he is renting a room. I wanted to try to get some money to him. I guess I'm an old man who worries when he doesn't know that all his kin are safe and sound."

"I doubt Tom wants you to worry. Should I take your number? If he does contact me, I would tell him to call you."

"I think Tom knows my number, but I'll give it to you. Would you call me to let me know he's okay even if he is too stubborn to call home?"

She wrote down Chief's telephone number and wondered if she would get to use it. *Will I ever talk to Tom again?*

Linda went back to working at the Runza drive-in at the end of June. She hadn't been available for several weeks in the spring, so they only had a few shifts per week to give her. Lots of students were vying for summer hours.

It was around the Fourth of July when she spotted a familiar Jeep in the parking area. Linda tried to put on her most professional demeanor when she approached his car. The Jeep's doors were gone since it was hot weather.

"What can I get for you today?" Linda pressed her lips

164

together.

Tom stared at her, then looked down at his hands in his lap. "I'll try to make this quick. There are two things I should have told you, but I didn't get the chance the last time we spoke."

She should tell him to stick to business, but she wanted to hear what he had to say.

His eyes locked on hers again. "The first thing is I love you. I should have told you that months ago, I know. I'm sorry I didn't."

Linda glanced back at the restaurant; afraid they would know she wasn't taking his order. "You mean you loved me, past tense."

"No, I don't think that will ever be past tense. I love you, Linda. I think I fell in love with you the first time I saw you in that Pinocchio getup." He cleared his throat, took a breath, and lowered his voice. "The other thing is, um, the first time we ever had sex, the condom ripped. Not just a little. It was pretty much worthless. So, I threw that batch of condoms away and started using the ones I had gotten for graduation. Later I read the packaging and realized those had expired and they might not have been effective. But this was all after the fact; it was too late by then. And I suppose you were already, well, you know. I guess I was afraid to tell you. Denial. I was in denial. But you deserved to know." Tom squinted and looked back out through the windshield. "I'm sorry, Linda. I know I screwed this up."

Do not make me cry, dammit. Why are you doing this now when I am finally feeling in control? I thought I could stop loving you if you left me alone.

"Tom," she whispered, not trusting her voice.

"I know. I'll let you go. I wanted to tell you—"

"I'm off work in fifteen minutes. I have something I need to tell you too. Can you wait or come back?'

His brows winged up. "Yeah, of course. Why don't you bring

165

me a coke? I can wait."

He met her behind the restaurant when her shift ended. It seemed odd to get into his car again, especially in her uniform. She hadn't ridden in the Jeep without the doors.

Tom rapped his fingers on the steering wheel. "Where do you want to go? The park? We could talk there."

She nodded. There was a park about six blocks away and he pulled into the lot.

Tom took off his cowboy hat and threw it in the backseat. He ran his fingers through his damp hair. "It's good to see you."

"Have you spoken to your family? Your grandpa called me." Linda scooted forward on the seat and turned to face him.

He frowned. "Chief called you? When?"

She pursed her lips. "I dunno. A week or so ago. About a week after I last saw you. He was worried and didn't know where you were or how to reach you."

Tom propped one boot on the dash. "I haven't talked to any of them. I don't know what to say. Not sure I belong there anymore."

"You can't mean that. I saw how your family was. You can't throw away something that important. Not everyone has a family like that."

Tom stuck out his chin. "I'm not even related to the Case side of the family."

She waved her hands. "No one cares. What if you were adopted? You'd still be as much in the family as those with blood connections."

"They lied to me. Not once but every day of my whole life."

"I lied to you too. And you just told me you loved me. Don't try to tell me you don't love them."

166

He sighed. "It's not the same. I hate that you lied to me, but I understand why you were mad. I'm to blame for that mess. With my parents, it feels wrong now." He crinkled his nose. "Like I am suddenly the bastard child."

"You're being stubborn, just like Chief said."

Tom scoffed. "Sounds like Chief."

"You need to start talking to them. Maybe a phone call to let them know what you're doing. What are you doing?"

Tom put his foot back down and sat straighter. "I decided to try to find a job here—something with landscaping or lawn care. I checked with a bunch of people who mow lawns in the summer and came up empty until I got together with a friend from one of my botany classes, Trey Hansen. His dad works on East Campus. I think we're going to start our own little business. He knows a lot about plants, and his parents have a greenhouse. We're going to start advertising to do mowing and landscaping, trimming bushes, fertilizing, sowing grass, going beyond what most services offer for people who want fancy landscapes but don't have the vision or time to care for them. I've already got a few mowing gigs lined up. I'm thinking of trying to find customers in your neighborhood since the lots are so large."

"You're starting a business? What about school?" Linda watched a butterfly land on the dashboard, then rise through the open roof.

"That's the nice thing about this. It's mostly seasonal. We might do some snow removal, but only if it makes sense. I'm planning to go back to school in September and try to work this around classes."

"Where are you living?"

"I'm staying in Trey's basement right now. But when I have some money ahead, I'll get an apartment again. His mom is answering our phones. Tom and Trey's Lawnscapes. That's what we're calling it so far. And you know what? I'm not cleaning cow manure off my boots."

"Wow. I'm impressed. You're becoming a businessman."

He shrugged. "It's a start. It's the kind of job I think I would like. And the idea of being my own boss, well that's hard to beat."

"You should share this good news with your parents. And your grandpa."

"I'll tell you what. I'll call home on one condition."

She squinted at him. "What?"

"You let me buy you dinner."

"Pizza?"

"Whatever you want."

Linda tucked one leg under her and leaned toward him, stopping inches from his face. Her voice was soft and low. "I want pizza. Pepperoni with extra cheese."

He shifted his gaze back and forth between her eyes. "You know what I want?" He moved closer so that their lips nearly touched.

"Pizza first. Maybe you'll get dessert." She leaned back away from him.

He smiled.

God, how I missed that smile. But this time, we're taking it slowly. Very slowly.

CHAPTER TWENTY-SIX

Linda was surprised to see Debbie on her doorstep. Debbie had always been a little heavier than the other twirlers, but now Linda could see her face was fuller than usual.

"Debbie! I wasn't expecting anyone. I've been sitting out by the pool working on my tan. Come on back."

Debbie was wearing shorts and a matching shirt, over-dressed for lounging by the pool in the midday July heat, but she followed Linda through the house and down the wooden stairs from the second-story deck to the pool area.

Linda was wearing only a skimpy two-piece red swimming suit and had her hair pulled into a top knot. Baby oil covered and accentuated her tanned skin.

"You look like you've recovered," Debbie said.

Linda glanced down at her abdomen and ran her tongue over her bottom teeth before meeting Debbie's eyes. "I guess you heard about my trip to Kansas from Yvonne."

Debbie pursed her lips. "I think Yvonne told my brother. They're dating again. Daniel told me when I said I didn't know the status of your pregnancy."

Linda looked away, "Well, it's, you know, over."

"I told you I was getting married and having a baby, right?" Debbie asked.

Linda nodded. "This shouldn't have to be weird between us. I can see you're doing what is right for you. You're a year older than me; you already graduated. It's different." She perched on a chaise lounge.

Debbie reached into her purse and pulled out a wedding invitation in an envelope addressed to Linda. She held it out to her.

"I decided to save postage and hand-deliver some of these. You can bring Tom if you want to. It's going to be a pretty simple wedding, with the ceremony at Robert's church and a reception at Bethany Park."

Was she trying to decide if she wanted me to come to her wedding? She could have handed this to me at the door.

Linda set the invitation on a table by the chaise lounge. "Debbie, are you ready to be married and have children?"

Debbie sighed and sat down in one of the chairs under an umbrella. "I don't know, to tell you the truth. Robert and I fought for the right to be married and keep our child. But I do sometimes wonder if we are growing up too fast. Maybe someday I'll miss being able to be wild and free at eighteen or nineteen."

Linda jumped up. "You want some pop? There's Coke and 7-Up in the little fridge by the bar."

"I'd take a 7-Up."

Linda got one for her and a Coke for herself. "I told you I was having sex with Tom last spring. At the time, I thought I was okay with it, but after everything that has happened, I think I made a mistake. I feel like Tom kind of convinced me it was a good idea. I suppose that's how boys are. But I told him last week that I wasn't sure I ever wanted to have sex again. And he still wanted to date me. So, I might have misjudged him."

"He didn't believe you."

Linda chuckled. "About never having sex? Yeah, you're probably right." Linda picked up a pair of sunglasses from the table and stretched out on her chair. "Maybe I am taking a long sabbatical from sex."

Two nights later, Linda was getting off work when she spotted Peter walking toward her as she left the restaurant.

"Linda, are you through working? Can I talk to you?"

"Sure. What's going on?"

He ushered her into his Pontiac Catalina but made no move to start the car. "Nancy is mad at me and won't talk to me. I need to know how to apologize if she won't listen."

Linda smirked. "She's freezing you out, huh? What stupid thing did you do?"

Pete leaned back on the seat and closed his eyes. "I guess she thought I was going out with Dawn Gray. I'm not. I went to get ice cream with her once. Then Nancy went out with Chad. You remember Chad Duncan from band?" Peter gave her a sidelong look.

Of course, I remember Chad. I told Chad to call Nancy.

"Last night, I called Nancy's house and her mother said she was out. I went over there and waited on her street to see who she was with. I was hoping she had been out with you or one of her other girlfriends. No such luck. Chad pulled into the driveway. I just saw red. I yanked him right out of the car as soon as he opened the door."

Linda's eyes rounded. "Oh no, then what happened?"

Peter waved his hand. "Chad was fine. He landed on his butt. But Nancy got all defensive and started in on me. I told her we needed to talk. We were walking to my car parked on the street. But that idiot Chad calls me out, even after I'd told him to go home. I didn't even think about it. I punched him right in the schnoz. I guess that training I've been doing in the ring sort of kicked in."

"You punched Chad? In Nancy's driveway?"

"Yeah, and he started bleeding like a stuck pig. It was beautiful. But, of course, Nancy was pissed as hell. And it was a dumb move, now that I think more about it. I was only trying to get a chance to talk to her and straighten things out. But now she thinks I'm out of control or something. She won't talk to me. I need her to forgive me." Peter sniffed and turned to look at Linda. "So, how do I fix this?"

What would it be like to have boys fighting over you? To watch them going to blows? It probably only happens to sweet little girls like Nancy. Boys probably assume they should defend her honor. Kind of romantic. Kind of ridiculous.

"This just happened last night? You might want to give her a few days to get over it."

Peter shook his head. "I don't want to give Chad a chance to move in on her."

"Nancy can think for herself. She'd not going to let anyone talk her into being with them if she doesn't want it. You mean a lot to her, Pete."

Peter raked his hand over his face. "You have no idea what she's done for me. I can't lose her. I just can't."

"You probably scared her. I know you scared me a little last winter when you almost got into a fight with Chad in the school parking lot. Boys who show they're not afraid to fight can be intimidating," Linda wiggled her eyebrows. "But also, a turn-on."

He raised one brow. "Which is it? Scary or sexy?"

Linda smiled. "Sometimes one, sometimes the other. Depends on the situation. Depends on a girl's mood. Maybe you'll have to convince her. She has confessed that she finds you somewhat irresistible."

"Maybe not after last night. But do I keep calling her every day and hope she'll get over it?"

"Let me talk to her. I'll take her pulse, then I'll let you know."

He nodded, "Thanks, Linda. I owe you one."

She chuckled. "If I want you to punch someone in the nose, I'll call you."

"My knuckles are still sore. Punching is better if you're wearing boxing gloves."

After Linda had tried to patch things up between Nancy and Peter, she was surprised when Nancy continued to date Chad. She was even more annoyed when she'd heard Peter started dating Dawn Gray. Linda had reluctantly agreed with Nancy to select Dawn as a twirler for next year. The other new twirler for the coming year was Melissa Sparks.

But now Linda's previous mistrust of Dawn was rearing its ugly head. *I have to find another way to save Nancy and Pete's relationship. I know they belong together.* She invited herself to Dawn's house on the pretext of working on twirling routines.

"Dawn, I thought it would be nice if we spent some time together. I was hoping you could help me figure out how to integrate some gymnastic moves into a twirling routine."

"Sure, Linda. Come on over this evening, and we can work in my backyard," Dawn said.

When they got ready to try some moves, Linda asked, "Have you ever taken gymnastics lessons?"

"Gee, I'm trying to remember. I think I did for about six months when I was eight or so. I wasn't as good at that as some of the girls. Twirling came easier for me. But I can do cartwheels and a front and back walkover still. I learned some of that from my twirling instructor. She had me every summer for six years and most Saturdays during school."

"No wonder you're so good. You've put a lot of time into this." Linda figured it might help to flatter Dawn, and she couldn't deny her skill. They needed to become teammates, if not buddies, to make the football season bearable.

"What moves are you thinking you could incorporate?"

"Well, I have narrowed it down to a cartwheel, a roundoff, a scissors leap, and a split leap. Where I need help is trying to figure out if any twirls work with these movements."

They worked for about ninety minutes, trying different things. Dawn showed Linda how to do some passes she'd never tried. She worked on trying to do an aerial cartwheel while tossing her baton. Next, they both worked on illusion turns, which looked like a cartwheel in place while also twirling the baton in a circle.

"I think we are going to feel that in our hips tomorrow. I haven't done some of those moves in years," Linda said.

"I know. I wish I had a hot tub. That would help."

Linda smoothed her hair back in her ponytail and stretched. "I've got one. Go grab your swimsuit."

Dawn didn't hesitate and followed Linda back to Piedmont in her little red convertible. Before she got into the hot tub, Linda poured them two Cokes on ice and added a little splash of rum, to help them relax. Then she grabbed the aspirin bottle and took it to the hot tub with her.

"Have you ever tried putting aspirin in Coca-Cola? I've heard it makes you high," Dawn giggled.

"Let's find out," Linda said, dropping two tablets into her drink. Dawn shrugged and did the same.

After taking a sip, Linda asked, "Are you meeting a lot of people here? This must be a change from Cedar Rapids."

"It is, but I like it now. I miss my friends back home, but the kids I've met are nice enough."

"Have you been dating much? You went to prom, didn't you?"

"Yes, I went with Bill Edwards. He just graduated. I didn't

174

know him very well, but he seems very intelligent. I only dated him twice."

"Interesting. Any other boys catch your eye?"

"I must admit, Peter Thompson and I have had some moments. I don't know if he is still with Nancy or not, but he's come by to talk to me. And I can usually get him to go get ice cream or something if I let him drive my car."

"I don't know what to tell you about Pete and Nancy. They were pretty hot and heavy last year. I remember he practically swept her off her feet when they came over here before homecoming. I'm not even sure why he kissed her like that, but John Anthony, who was my date, and I were standing there with our jaws dropping. It was like something you see in a movie."

"But isn't that over now?"

Linda shrugged. "Who knows if it is ever over?" She took a big sip of her pop and leaned back into the bubbles. "This feels so good. Glad you thought of it."

Dawn took a big gulp, then hiccupped. "Oh my, I'm sorry. You'd think we were drinking alcohol."

Linda grinned. "Aren't there any other boys you're interested in? When my sister told me she met you, it sounded like you had boys at your house all the time."

"Oh, they weren't there for me. My father works for the university athletic department. He's starting some sort of big brother program. I'm not sure how it works, but he's had lots of college athletes come over to our house. Most of those guys are eighteen or nineteen, and my dad wants me to stay away from them. It could cause a conflict if I started dating one of his protégés. I've spoken to some of them, but I can't date them."

"That seems like a waste. College boys are more worldly. But you have to be careful." Linda pursed her lips.

"Yeah, I heard about your little situation," Dawn said, studying Linda's reaction.

Linda sniffed. "Who told you?"

"Peter. But don't worry. I haven't told anyone. I figured we twirlers should stick together."

"You already know about the biggest mistake of my life. What's yours?" Linda leaned forward hoping for some enticing tidbit. It was time to find out what made Dawn tick.

"Hmmm. I'm not sure. I probably haven't made it yet." Dawn's smile portrayed the cat who swallowed the canary. "But back in Iowa, there was this one boy…"

"Yeah? What happened?"

"He was fine, he really was. But he was pinned to my best friend."

"So naturally you treated each other with the proper deference." Linda rolled her eyes.

"No," Dawn sighed. "We got naked."

Linda chortled. "What? I have to hear the rest of that story!"

Dawn laughed. "My best friend, Daisy, was a cheerleader. She went to cheer camp for a week. I went out for a coke with her boyfriend, Johnny, and another guy. Then we went skinny-dipping at the lake. I believe there was some beer involved."

"Did you and Johnny…"

"Have sex? No. But there was some horsing around, making out. A risqué photo was taken of us by the other guy. Daisy was not amused. Somehow this became my fault even though none of it was my idea. Johnny was blameless."

"Let me guess. She patched things up with Johnny, and they both treated you like dirt."

176

"Exactly. What about your love life, Linda? Are you still dating that older fella?" Dawn stretched out her legs to float on the warm water.

As if on cue, Tom walked down the steps to the pool deck.

"Your dad said to come on back. I brought your red sweater; you left it in my car last night," Tom said. "I didn't know you had company."

Linda put one arm around Dawn and pulled her next to her on the hot tub seat. "Dawn's my secret girlfriend. Sorry that you had to find out this way, Tom."

Dawn giggled and hiccupped again.

He shrugged. "You want me to join you? I might have left my swimming trunks in the pool house."

Linda pushed out of the hot tub and walked up to him. He was wearing cut-off jeans and one of his new "T&T Lawnscapes" T-shirts. She embraced him, trying to get his clothes wet.

Tom slid an arm around her waist holding her close. "If you think that's going to annoy me, you're crazy. The water feels nice on a hot night."

"Dawn, this is Tom Case. I don't think you've met. We've been doing gymnastics and we are going to be sore tomorrow. Dawn said 'hot tub,' and I said 'aspirin' and 'coke and rum,' so here we are."

Dawn pulled herself onto the ladder of the hot tub but was wobbling slightly. Her long black hair poured over the front of her two-piece flowered suit. "Golly, Linda. Your boyfriend's a hunk."

Linda ran her hand down Tom's chest. She couldn't argue the point. That T-shirt showed off his bronze biceps. She hadn't missed how buff he was getting from all that outdoor physical labor.

She shifted her attention back to Dawn. Maybe Linda had given Dawn a little more rum than she could handle. "Tom, help me get Dawn out of the hot tub. I'm not sure she's okay."

Tom took Dawn's arms, and she stumbled around on the cement before he set her down on a redwood loveseat. Tom sat down next to her to study her.

Linda leaned over her. "How do you feel?"

"You got a towel? I'm a little cold." Dawn said, with a goofy smile.

Linda grabbed a nearby beach towel and put it in Dawn's lap. Dawn pulled it to her like a blanket, then toppled over, landing her wet hair in Tom's lap.

He gasped. "Okay, now that's pretty cold. Come here." He motioned for Linda to sit on the other side of him. She could barely squeeze in. Tom put his arm around her and kissed her.

Linda left one arm around his shoulders. "I guess this means Dawn is spending the night. When did my pool house turn into the refuge for drunken friends?"

"Maybe you should stop plying your friends with booze. You want me to help you get her undressed?"

"No! I'll see if I have a nightgown or something for her. I'd better have her call home before it's too late."

CHAPTER TWENTY-SEVEN

Tom was settling into his second year of college. He'd managed to change his major to landscape design and management. His business with Trey Hansen was going pretty well, although it had slowed down as soon as classes began. He'd found a one-bedroom apartment that was newer and fairly close to his classes.

Then there was Linda. He wasn't sure anymore where that was headed. Over the summer, Linda had helped him get lawn work. She'd taken photographs of Tom and Trey and made up a colored flyer listing their services. Then she'd ridden her bicycle around Piedmont and talked to some of her neighbors or left flyers in their doors. He'd picked up a few customers that way and paid her a commission. But he'd had high hopes they'd be skinny-dipping in that swimming pool of hers when her parents went to bed, and that hadn't come to pass.

Now she was busier than ever, in her senior year of high school. She'd informed him that she needed to practice a lot for the homecoming football game halftime performance. She was doing a solo, and she was trying to make it as complicated as only Linda could: some gymnastics and dance, combined with fancy twirling moves. Her perfectionism was front and center, and she didn't seem to have a lot of time for him.

Enter Jillian. He wasn't sure he would ever set eyes on his high school sweetheart after she moved to Colorado. So, he was shocked when he walked right past her in Love Library.

"Tom?" Jillian called out. She'd been sitting at a table and stood up when she spotted him.

Tom whirled around and squinted at her. "Jillian? What are you doing here?"

It looked like the old Jillian. Her cherubic face and long dark hair were the same. But he remembered how she was always complaining in high school that she was too fat. He hadn't agreed with her, he found her comfortably curvy, but he suspected that was part of the reason he could never get her naked. But now, no one would consider her fat. She was wearing a slinky green sweater and jeans that hugged her thighs and hips. When she stood, he noticed other boys eyeing her.

"I transferred to NU this semester. What are you doing right now? Do you have time to get some coffee?" She picked up her knapsack and slipped her arm in his, almost as if she'd been waiting for him to walk by.

Tom set down his tray at a table at the Student Union and unloaded their coffee cups and a sweet roll for himself. "Okay, what happened in Fort Collins? I thought you were sold on Colorado State."

"I was. The school was fine. I liked living in Colorado. I started running and hiking with some of my girlfriends and finally got in shape. But when I got involved in some of the student protests, my parents thought I was being corrupted by liberal extremists. Just because my boyfriend was working with the Black Student Alliance, who had some connections with the Black Panthers. I did get in trouble once when we took over the Ag Building to protest Dow Chemical recruiting students. But we got some good publicity. Anyway, they made me transfer to old NU where they thought I would have fewer distractions as they called them."

"Jesus, Jill. That doesn't sound like you at all. I'm surprised you weren't scared." Tom studied her over the rim of his coffee cup.

"I kind of surprised myself. But once I stood on the top of a few mountains and looked down, I gained some perspective. We're all insignificant; we're here for a finite amount of time. Do what you want, and don't let fear stop you." Jillian flipped her hair behind her shoulder. "Are you letting fear stop you, Tom?"

He shrugged one shoulder and broke off a bite of Danish. "I don't think so. I started a landscaping business this summer."

"You're kidding! You used to talk about that in high school. You mean lawn mowing or something else?"

"Well, mowing was part of it, to get started. But my business partner has access to a greenhouse, and we did some plantings and trimming. We're trying to plan what to concentrate on for next summer."

"Your parents must be thrilled," she said.

"Yeah." Tom's jaw tightened as he glanced away toward the windows lining the open second-floor space. "They probably would have preferred to have me working on the ranch."

Jillian seemed to be trying to read between the lines. "Where are you living?"

"Oh, I have an apartment not too far away. It's closer to East Campus, where I have about half of my classes. Do you want to see it?"

Why had I said that? It sounded like a come-on. She might be dating someone or even engaged by now.

Jillian smiled. "Sure, I'd love to see it sometime. I'm afraid my room is pretty small at the sorority house. I was lucky they had a Phi Mu chapter here so I could transfer. You don't think your girlfriend would mind if I came by?"

How did she know about my girlfriend? Had she talked to my sister, Theresa? Maybe she's fishing.

"My girlfriend's been pretty busy since school started. We haven't seen each other a lot. I don't see why she'd care."

They exchanged phone numbers, and Jillian came to visit him on Saturday afternoon.

Now that he didn't have to worry about a messy roommate, Tom liked to keep his space neat. His furniture was still pretty sparse, but he had a couch and coffee table in the living area and a bed, dresser, and nightstand in his bedroom. Things that he didn't have room for were organized in a few boxes or his closet. He had an old television that his parents no longer used sitting on a wooden crate.

Tom had no idea what he and Jillian were going to do. When Linda came over, it was usually after they'd gone to dinner. They watched TV and made out on the couch. More making out than TV watching, although Linda still insisted on keeping their clothes on. But he hadn't been around Jillian for more than a year.

After he'd given her the tour, he sat on the couch. "I don't know what you want to do. Are you in a hurry? I've got some pop in the fridge or coffee if you're thirsty. Do you want to see what's on TV?

Jillian sat next to him on the couch and looked into his eyes. "No, I don't want anything to drink. I assumed you wanted to pick up where we left off. I don't remember you being this shy."

Tom gulped. Was he crazy, or had girls gotten more forward? "Shy? No, it's that we don't know each other anymore."

Jill leaned close enough to give him a whiff of her perfume. "Should we get to know each other, Tom?"

God, she smelled good. Musky or something. It smelled like sex. He supposed that was the idea. He thought about Linda for about half a second before he pulled Jillian's mouth to his.

How long has it been since I've been with a girl? Months and months. Maybe early May, before Linda's prom.

All that pent-up need hit him like a freight train. In a moment, he had Jillian on her feet again, and they were stumbling into the bedroom. The condoms were now conveniently stored in the nightstand, and he pulled a packet out before he even started taking

182

clothes off.

"You don't need that, Tom," Jillian said, slowly unbuttoning the front of her dress. "I've been on the pill for a long time."

"I'd rather not take any chances," Tom said before he took over the job of unfastening her buttons. He was shocked to discover she wasn't wearing anything underneath.

Hello Jillian.

Although she had gotten thinner, she was as stacked as he remembered, and today she wasn't hiding the goods under bulky sweatshirts. It wasn't long before they were under the covers.

A couple of hours later, Tom was still in a daze. He'd been debating whether to order a pizza for dinner. Jillian was certainly a lot more adventurous than he remembered, but she'd claimed to have a previous engagement that evening and left. He had no idea what to think about her. Would they see each other again?

When he heard a knock on the door, he thought maybe Jillian's plans had fallen through. But there was Linda, and right on her heels came a powerful dose of guilt.

That's stupid. It's not like Linda and I have some sort of agreement we can't see other people, just because we haven't since we met. She can't expect me to be celibate forever. You should go with the flow. Be free. Let the sunshine in. Hell.

"What's wrong, Tom?" Linda studied his expression. "Did I catch you at a bad time?"

"Oh no. Everything is a-okay. I was thinking about getting a pizza. Are you hungry?"

Linda walked around his apartment like she was a bloodhound. He would swear she was sniffing for another girl's scent. She was wearing one of her short flirty skirts that wafted around her long legs when she took a step. And a white tank top that was snug enough to outline her bra.

"I haven't seen you all week," Linda said, her gaze surveying the room. "Or even talked to you for a while. What's been going on?"

"Nothing is going on. Absolutely nothing."

She squinted at him. "No classes? I thought you were writing a paper."

Tom took a big breath. "Oh, yeah. I finished my paper. That was hard." He rolled his eyes. Then he noticed she was drifting toward the bedroom. "Come back in here and sit down. Tell me about your twirler routine. How's it going?"

"You been studying in here today? Usually, your bed is so neatly made, but it is a little messy—" Linda was in his bedroom now, and she'd stopped talking. This was not a good sign.

He slowly went to the bedroom to see what she was doing. He froze when he saw she had a condom package in her hand. The one he'd ripped open a few hours earlier.

"You are such a neat person, Tom, but you always miss the wastebasket with these packages. Maybe they are too lightweight, or you are in such a rush. Looks like you had a visitor, huh?"

"Shit."

She threw the package in the wastebasket. "Don't try to lie about it. You are not a good liar."

"I'm not. That is, maybe we should talk about um the parameters of our uh relationship." He nodded. "It's not like we ever said we couldn't go out with anyone else."

"You're having sex with someone else. That's not the same as having a coffee date."

"I don't know what this other thing is. You and I haven't

184

exactly been seeing each other much lately, and we haven't been …you haven't wanted to go to bed with me for a long time."

Her blue eyes flashed. He was caught off guard when she practically leaped on him, wrapping her arms around his neck and kissing him hard. He put his hands under her hips when she entwined her legs around his waist. He nearly toppled into the wall behind him.

Far out! Is this my lucky day or what?

He kissed her back with equal gusto. He liked how competitive Linda was sometimes. When he pulled back, she dropped her legs as she slid her hands up his T-shirt from the bottom, signaling he should pull it overhead. Then she ripped her tank top off, revealing another one of her cute little lace bras. He had missed this kind of contact with her.

Their tongues were dancing, and his hands were stroking, grabbing, and tugging off her clothes wherever he could. He sank to his knees and unzipped the back of her skirt so it eased toward the floor and slipped his fingers under the band of her bra.

Then when he felt his temperature peaking, Linda shoved back, landing him on his backside. She pulled her straps back in place and rezipped her skirt. In a flash, that tank top concealed her pretty bosom again.

"What's going on? We were just—"

"I wanted to remind you what you've been missing. If you'd held out a little longer, I was beginning to think it might be time to get it on again. But since you've found someone else to …well, it doesn't matter. I'm outta here."

"Linda, wait. Let's talk about this. Don't be ticked off." Tom scrambled up. "You've still got another year of high school. You should be enjoying high school activities, like homecoming. I'm a little beyond that stage. I'm ready for other things, college-type relationships."

"Oh, that's your excuse. You're no longer interested in going to high school events. It would have been nice to know that more than a week before the homecoming dance. You're interested in college stuff, like free love? Well, have a good time. I can't believe I ever cared about you."

"Linda, stop." He put a hand on her arm as she pushed out the bedroom doorway.

"Let me go, Tom. You're right. I think you've gotten too old for me."

He closed his eyes and leaned on the doorframe. He jumped when she slammed the apartment door as she left.

CHAPTER TWENTY-EIGHT

As if she didn't have enough on her mind, Linda had a wonderful but challenging performance to do at the next football game. Her first real solo, so all eyes would be on her. It might be spectacular. But if she made a mistake, she might never live it down.

Then her best friend and twirler co-captain, Nancy, had confided that she was pregnant and was about to drop that bomb on her ex-boyfriend, Peter. Why hadn't the two of them listened when she tried to keep them together last summer? And this little calamity was going to have ripple effects when Dawn found out. Linda was beginning to like Dawn and didn't want to see her heartbroken, even if she shouldn't have gone out with Peter in the first place.

And now, Linda had to find a new date for the homecoming dance. That is if she wanted to go to the homecoming dance. She considered skipping it, but it was her senior year. She might look back and regret it if she missed it.

It isn't merely one dance. I've taken myself out of circulation at school. It's common knowledge I've been dating a college boy. How do I get the word out that I'm available again? It's going to be a long year if I can't find someone new.

She turned to a clean page in one of her spiral notebooks. Who had she been attracted to that might be available? Hmmm. There was Madeline's old beau, Gus. She thought his real name was Wally. Madeline and Gus had broken up. He'd kind of given Linda the eye, but she didn't know how to contact him except through Madeline. And she'd blown off Madeline, without meaning to. There was a boy in her calculus class who'd been watching her. What was his name? Felipe Gomez, she thought. But she hadn't even spoken to him. God, she'd been a snob. She made a note to talk to Felipe. That was a start.

This is hard. I can't be such a loser that no boy in school would want to dance with me. Isn't there a single guy who tried to flirt with me in the past nine months? Maybe I shot someone down—big mistake. Oh, wait! That's it. Larry. My trombone buddy. He sits right by me. Well, not lately because we spend all our band classes out on the field practicing for the Friday night performances. So, I've been practicing twirling while he's rehearsing formations. I wonder if he still likes me. Or if he ever liked me.

Larry Bonner. He was a viable option. He seemed to have changed somewhat over the summer. He was always a funny guy and made band period more enjoyable. She liked a guy who made her laugh. But junior year, she pictured him as a little chubbier, and he wore a kind of old-style glasses. She hadn't seen him wearing glasses. She heard he'd gotten contacts. And he looked like he'd grown a few inches and was well, maybe not as trim and well-built as Tom, but less chunky, more average. She thought he liked her. He acted like he was interested. At least six months ago he was. Larry was a top contender. Or at least a specimen she needed to take a close look at.

Linda needed to pay more attention to the boys in her grade. That was her goal now. She'd focused too much of her energy on Tom. Even now, she had trouble not thinking about him. *Who was that slut he'd been ...NO, not my problem anymore!*

"Larry!" Linda called out when the band was returning to the building on Monday morning. Larry turned back and waited for her to catch up to him.

I was right. He had gotten taller and leaner. He might even be taller than Tom.

Larry's hair was reddish-brown and curly. He blinked at her expectantly. "Did you want something, Linda?"

"Oh, yes, I do. I'm hoping you can help me. I don't mean to

impose on you, but I thought we were friends."

"I would consider you my friend; what is it?"

"I'm trying to fix any little things that might be off on my solo routine. I know you're marching on the side of the field nearest to me for that song. I wonder if you could tell if I am lined up parallel to the hash marks on the field when I come out of the aerial cartwheel. I'm worried that I might be crooked and that won't look good from the stands."

"What?"

Linda sighed and tried to elaborate on what she needed to know.

"I can't say I noticed that particular thing, but I can try to look tomorrow. What part of the song does that come in on?"

After talking more about the routine, she thought she might be wasting time. She probably should have stuck to simple flirting, like "my goodness, look how big and strong you've gotten" but that felt so fake to her. At least this way, he'd have to look at her.

In calculus class, she made a point of glancing behind her and to the right where Felipe was sitting. The first time, he seemed to be intent on taking notes or working on a problem and didn't look up. When the teacher was talking, she felt his stare on her and gawked at him through lowered lashes. He quickly looked back at the teacher. Later, when they were working on their assignment, she gave him the side-eye. This time he smiled, looked down at his paper, then looked back at her.

Progress. If only I had more time.

She'd nearly forgotten what she asked Larry Bonner to do the next morning when she rehearsed her solo in band class. Larry didn't forget. He was so intent on watching how well she lined up her landing that he ran right into the band member in front of him while playing his trombone. A poor little sophomore girl named

Missy was knocked to the ground while playing her clarinet.

Linda watched in horror as Mr. Humphreys, the band director, helped her up.

"What in tarnation are you looking at, Bonner? You're supposed to be marking time, not running over the person in front of you!"

Larry turned fifty shades of red amid twitters of laughter from some of the boys in the back of the band formation.

"It's not funny!" Mr. Humphreys shouted. "Poor Missy could have been seriously hurt or broken her instrument. Let's do this song from the top. Get in your starting positions."

Linda was glad to have a second run-through of her song but felt bad for Larry and Missy. Maybe she should suggest he take Missy to homecoming instead. She didn't even get a chance to talk to Larry after class, as he hurried off the field and out of the band room before she could catch up.

Things started looking up before her second-period calculus class. Felipe sidled up next to her in the hallway. "Hey, Twirler Girl. *¿Cómo estás?*"

"I'm fine, I guess." Linda looked up at him. His ebony eyes seem to smolder at close range, and his dark hair framed his seriously sensuous eyebrows. "I didn't know you spoke Spanish. Felipe, right?"

"*Aye, Chica.* I was born and raised in Mexico. What else would I speak, Pig Latin?"

"You're Mexican? I didn't know that. How did you get to Lincoln?"

He shrugged. "*Mi familia.* Always on the move. My uncle works here as a janitor. That's why I ended up in this school. And most of my friends call me Phil."

"All right, Phil," Linda stopped outside the classroom and let others pass.

"You know, in Spanish, Linda means beautiful. Your parents must have been thinking of that when they named you."

Linda grinned. "That's very sweet. Why have you and I never spoken before?"

Felipe leaned on a locker next to the door. "Today the stars aligned. The time was right."

Linda was surprised when she saw him again at lunch. He was already sitting at a table when she left the lunch line. He motioned with his head that she could join him. She hoped her usual lunchmates, Nancy and Janet, would see where she was going and not wonder what had happened to her.

When she slid onto the bench across from Felipe, he slid down a little way to give them more privacy.

"You're ready to dine with me already? This must be serious," he joked.

"I didn't realize you had lunch at this time. You've been looking at me in class, haven't you?" Linda tried to remember how to flirt with a boy she didn't know. She tried to channel Sarah, who'd developed flirting into an art form.

"Is there something wrong with looking at beautiful women? If that is so, every Latin man in the world is in trouble."

"Oh, so this is built into your DNA? To be a voyeur?"

He chuckled. "Not only to watch. To act when we like what we see. You must have heard about Latin lovers. Why else would you be sitting here?"

Linda felt the flush creeping up her neck. He wasn't messing around. Or was he merely messing with her? She cleared her throat. "Do you like to dance, Felipe?"

He smiled, then looked away. "Of course, I dance. And I would love to take you to the homecoming dance on Saturday. But I'm afraid there is a problem."

Linda couldn't believe she'd been so obvious. But maybe that was saving them both time. "What problem?"

"I see how you are, what you wear. Expensive things. You have money. I have no money. I have no car. It is hard for me to date a girl such as you."

"Oh." Linda stopped to try to look at it from his viewpoint. "I mean, that's not a problem as far as I'm concerned. I do have a car. I could pay for the dance tickets. But maybe this would not suit you."

"You're generous as well as beautiful. Give me your phone number. Let's think about this, and I will call you later."

She wasn't at all sure how things stood after eating lunch with Felipe. He seemed to be weighing his options. What was that about? But she supposed she was doing the same thing. And she liked the way he spoke. She hadn't heard it when they were in class, but he tended to pronounce all his vowels as long ones. It must be his Mexican heritage. Like he said bee-you-tee-fool instead of beautiful. It was sexy.

After school, she and the other twirlers were practicing their halftime show on the nearby football field. It wasn't unusual for other students to walk or run on the track at that time of day. But when Linda stopped to pick up her dropped baton, she saw Larry watching her.

She immediately walked up to him. "That incident this morning. That was my fault, wasn't it? I am so sorry!"

"No, no, I should've been concentrating on my steps. I lost track of where I was in the program. But I wanted to tell you that your landing looked pretty straight to me. Do you want to do it a few times now? I can watch without worrying about my marching."

"You are so sweet, Larry. As long as you're here, I could use your help."

And that was laying it on a little thick. Why did this seem so easy with Tom? I guess because he was already eighteen and had the hots for me.

Linda went through the parts of her routine where she did the cartwheel, the split leap, and the illusion turn and had him watch if she kept her alignment straight. He even came out to talk to her after each run-through. He took this more seriously than she expected. Or maybe he wanted an excuse to get closer to her.

"You about have this perfectly now, Linda. I guess I'll take off."

"Thank you so much, Larry. How can I ever repay you?" Linda wrapped her arms and baton around his neck and gave him a firm hug. A friendly hug.

But Larry was a little quicker than she'd given him credit for. He took the sides of her head in his hands and pushed back her hair. Then he glanced around and hesitated.

We don't have privacy here. He's probably more of a private guy.

Larry kissed her forehead and then turned and walked away quickly.

How had I managed to embarrass the poor guy twice in one day?

Project Homecoming Date was not going so well. One guy was trying to uphold the reputation of his entire culture, while the other one was trying to figure out how to kiss a girl for the first time. Heaven help them!

She got a call from Felipe that evening.

"I've thought about how this might work, and I think I can go to the homecoming dance with you. But I would have to meet you there," he told her.

She wasn't sure what it was he was trying to work out on his end. "I could pick you up. It wouldn't be any trouble."

"No. I am not going to subject you to the inquiring eyes and mouths of my family. There are a lot of them living with me. I will buy the tickets, I already checked the price; it's not too much. But I have to meet you at the school."

"Okay, if that's what you want. But can we meet in the parking lot somewhere? I'd rather not have to wander around the cafeteria looking for you in the dark."

And I don't want to be in full view of the whole school if you don't show up.

"Sure. We could meet at eight o'clock by the cat statue."

"You mean the cougar, don't you? We're the Capital High Cougars."

Felipe snickered. "I heard the football team all pats the head of that cougar on the way to the field each week for luck. Hasn't done much good."

"Well, I give them credit for trying at least. Have you played any sports?"

"Wrestling. I am a very good wrestler. Maybe you will find this out."

Linda didn't know what to make of that remark. She was beginning to see his snarky side. She wasn't sure she liked it, but it was hard to fault someone else when she made plenty of sarcastic comments herself. "Did you wrestle last year?"

"I did. But that was in L.A. I didn't get to finish the season before we moved to Idaho."

"Los Angeles? Idaho? How many places have you lived?"

"You mean altogether? I don't think I ever counted. Maybe twenty, could be thirty, just since I was eight. Before that, we were in Mexico."

"You're kidding. Is your father in the service?"

"No. My father is Mexican. When he says it's time to leave, we go." He laughed. "Don't worry. I'll probably still be here on Saturday."

By the next day, she wasn't sure if she'd made the right choice agreeing to go to homecoming with Felipe. Why had Tom put her in this position anyway?

It rained that morning, so they practiced marching in the gym, which didn't work as well for her routine, as there wasn't enough space. Mr. Humphreys told both Linda and Dawn that they could use the gym by themselves that day during their study hall periods to rehearse their solos.

After class, Larry caught up with her.

"I know this is late notice, but I heard you broke up with your boyfriend."

Linda sighed. "Yeah, you heard correctly."

"The thing is, I wondered if you would go to the homecoming dance with me."

Linda's eyes widened. "Oh wow. Darn it." They'd been walking back to the classroom, but she pulled him out of the flow of traffic. "I would like to go with you, but I accepted another invitation last night. But maybe we can go out another weekend. I would like to get to know you better, Larry."

"You ain't just saying that, are you? To let me down easy?" Larry narrowed his eyes.

"No! In fact, we can set up a date for another time right now if

195

you want to." She grinned at him. Maybe she hadn't lost her touch after all.

"Well, we'll have to go to the basketball games in a few weeks. Next Friday night the football game is out of town. We could see a movie."

"That's good. Let's plan on it." She nodded. She was going to enlarge her circle of friends if it killed her.

And maybe it is going to kill me, cuz I'm still thinking about kissing Tom.

CHAPTER TWENTY-NINE

Linda was ready. She'd practiced, she'd perfected. It wasn't going to get any better. Her hair was swept into a tight bun. The last time she wore this much makeup, her sister, Sarah, had tissued it off.

Right before the twirlers headed to the football field for the pregame show, Linda, Nancy, Dawn, and Melissa gathered in the music alcove bathroom. They'd carefully stretched gold sequin headbands around each other's heads and topped it off with a burst of glitter and hairspray. It was time to shine.

When halftime arrived, Linda and Nancy started the fire baton routine as the band played the first strains of "Light My Fire." The field lights were killed right before they took the field so every eye in the stadium was on them. It was a real power trip. A few measures later, Dawn and Melissa joined them with their fire batons, and they weaved in and out of the band formation without a glitch.

Next up was Dawn's solo. For the first sixteen measures, the other three twirlers stood at attention in front of the band, then they joined in the band's formations. It was during that first interlude that Linda thought she spotted Tom. He was sitting in the front row where the band usually sat, except they were on the field. Had he moved there during halftime? Linda didn't recognize the dark-haired girl sulking next to him. He seemed to be looking right at Linda.

It couldn't be Tom. Why would he come now? I must be imagining it; another guy who looks like him. But he's wearing that damn black Stetson.

She blinked away tears, took a deep breath, and snapped back to her performance. Then she moved when their cue came up.

Her solo was next. Her hands were sweating, her pulse was

racing. But she could do this. She plastered on her biggest smile. On an impulse, she winked at the stands. Her parents planned to be there, so they would think that was for them.

The band started playing "I Got Rhythm." She did her routine like she had a hundred times. She counted and grinned her way through all of it, sometimes not even hearing the music, just listening to the beat of her thumping heart. She got slightly ahead at one point but slowed herself down. The aerial cartwheel went off without a hitch and she landed exactly right, the baton spiraling down from a high toss precisely where she wanted it. The split jump and baton pass-through were executed nearly perfectly. But she brought down the house at the end where the drumline played alone and she did a funky dance incorporating the illusion turn multiple times. Her heart swelled when she heard the crowd's roar. Although it looked like she was rotating her leg 360 degrees, it was not much different than a magic trick.

And then it was over. She felt her pulse drop and she thought the sweat running down her temples must be caked with gold dust. She glanced one more time at where she thought she'd seen Tom, but no one was there. She'd imagined it. Imagined he cared.

All that was left were the hugs and congratulations from other band members. Her parents came over to congratulate her before the third quarter of the game began. Even Yvonne and Debbie had come to the game and told the twirlers it was even better than last year. Linda was happy it was over. She didn't know how Dawn did solos over and over. The stress was exhausting.

The twirlers planned to go out after the game, but Melissa bowed out with an upset stomach. When Linda looked for Nancy after the game, she saw her talking to Peter. She wasn't sure where things stood between them, but she guessed Nancy was not going out with the girls. So, Linda went home and took a very long shower.

She was lying on her bed in her robe trying to find the energy

198

to put her pajamas on when her phone rang. Who was calling her teen line this late? It must be Nancy updating her. She rolled and scooted on her bed until she could reach her phone.

"We were great tonight, weren't we?" she said when she answered.

"You were spectacular," Tom told her.

Linda sat up. "You were there?"

"I wouldn't miss it. I thought you saw me. You winked."

"I-I wasn't sure. But your hat. I thought I saw your hat."

"That was me, under the hat. We're often a set. But I was blown away. No wonder you were practicing like a maniac. Seriously, it was stunning. And that thing you did with your leg. It hurt me watching you. I guess I never got to watch the twirlers when I was in school, but I'm sure they were nothing like…not like what you did."

"You never watched the twirlers in high school? Why? Were you sneaking beer under the bleachers?"

Tom scoffed. "Of course not. I was on the football team. We were in the locker room at halftime. You know some people pay to watch football. But now I know, that's not the best part."

"Tom," she said softly. "It means a lot to me that you came to watch me. Even after, you know, I was kind of a bitch to you."

"Kind of? Jesus. You got me all revved up and then you knocked me on my ass. That was heartless. But I suppose I deserved it."

"You deserved it." Linda cleared her throat. "Who was your date tonight? The same girl from last week?"

"Uh, yeah. Jillian. I went to high school with her, and she transferred to NU this fall."

"Jillian? The girl-you-screwed-drunk-in-Daddy's-truck-after-prom Jillian?"

"Oh, I must have told you that, huh? The only Jillian I know."

"I'm surprised she wanted to come to a local high school football game."

"When I told her why I wanted to see your performance, she agreed to come. She thought you were cute."

Linda felt a growl forming in her throat. "Cute? Hmmm. I don't get cute much. But you know what? I'd better get some sleep. I have a date tomorrow for the dance with a new guy. He told me the other day that my name, Linda, means beautiful in Spanish. I think I like that more than 'cute.' But I thank you for calling." She pulled the towel off her hair. "It was nice of you to watch my performance, if only for old times' sake." It felt like her lungs were constricting and it was harder to breathe.

"Linda, I thought you wanted me to be honest with you. Didn't we agree to that after we got back together in July?"

"That pact didn't seem to last very long, did it? But you want honesty? I've been trying very hard to forget about you, and I've failed miserably so far. I was happy to see you tonight, but now it feels like one more blow, one step backward in trying to move on. So don't call me again, Tom. It hurts too much." Before he could respond, she hung up the phone and went to brush her teeth vigorously.

CHAPTER THIRTY

Linda had her head on Felipe's shoulder as they rotated around the dance floor. It was nice being in his arms, even if they weren't the arms she wanted. But her attention was focused about twenty feet away, where Peter and Nancy were alternately beaming and laughing with each other while trying to dance. Sometimes he'd kiss her fingers or her ear and she'd try to make him stop. It was glorious to see them back together. Their love was palpable. It was like a homecoming; they found their way back, even with a baby on the way. Linda was both happy and sad watching their joy.

Felipe was trying to be a gentleman. He had on a nice sports jacket and dressy pants. He used good manners. He even smelled like he'd used an aftershave. When she got close, she realized he had shaved; his beard was dark and thick. More so than most of her classmates.

"Phil," she said softly. "I know you mentioned you moved a lot. It must have been hard for you to keep up with school. How old are you?"

He smiled. "That obvious? Do you think I am past my prime? I am nineteen, turned nineteen last month."

"No, it's not important." He was only a few months younger than Tom.

Stop thinking about Tom! I am being crazy!

"You keep looking at that couple over there. Is that your ex-boyfriend?" He glanced over at Nancy and Peter.

"No. Nancy is my best friend. She and Peter broke up and they got back together last night. I'm happy because they are so happy with each other."

"Huh," he said, pulling her closer to his mouth. "Thees ease boolsheet."

She giggled. She was beginning to appreciate Phil's humor. "Well, okay, maybe I am also a little jealous."

Felipe nodded.

"Because how can anyone look so happy? Still, I know they deserve it."

"And you don't think you deserve happiness?" His brows rose.

"Yes, of course. I'll be that happy. Someday."

The next song was more upbeat, and she had fun dancing with Felipe. He was right. He could dance.

"It's too bad they don't play any Latin music. It's better for dancing. Have you ever done the tango or salsa?"

"I don't think so. I don't know how."

"Would you like to learn?"

"Sure."

"We can't do it here. Wrong band, wrong style. But c'mon, I know a way."

"We're leaving?" Linda looked at her watch. The dance would be over within the hour. "Where are we going?"

"You have a car, yes? I'll show you where to go."

Linda frowned. She didn't know why this worried her when he got in the car with her. After all, she'd offered to give him a ride before and this was no different. He directed her to a small shopping center in the north-central part of town.

"Pull your car around to the back. There is parking back there and we won't be seen."

Linda frowned, not sure this was safe. But he had been a perfect gentleman up to this point. So, she followed his directions. There were no cars parked in the area he indicated.

"Okay, now we need music." He turned her radio to a station she didn't even know existed. And strains of a distinctly Latin tune poured from the car speakers. He turned up the volume and rolled down the windows.

They got out of the car. Felipe removed his jacket and left it on the passenger seat. Then he held out his hand to guide her through the steps for her first salsa lesson. The Camaro's headlights simulated a spotlight dance.

She never would have guessed the evening would end like this. It was tricky learning parts of it, and she didn't get the hip-swaying completely, but he was a good teacher and it was fun. Certainly, more sensual than doing the mashed potato. After the salsa, they tried the tango. She liked that too, especially when he let her wrap one leg around his and dragged her across the cement.

"Some of these things are easier on a wooden floor," he assured her.

"How did you get so good at this?"

"Lots of *Quinceañeras*."

"What's that?"

"In Mexico, when a girl turns fifteen years old, '*quince años*,' her family throws her a big party. There is also a special mass associated with it. And always at the party, there is dancing. A boy who learns to dance well is likely to dance with the guest of honor."

"You were trying to impress fifteen-year-old girls?"

"Fifteen-year-old girls become sixteen-year-old girls who later become...But alas. I had to start with the older ones, as I was never there to see the little ones get bigger."

"I'm sure you were a hit with the ladies of any age group."

"Yes. There were many secrets behind the walls at a

Quinceañera."

Linda wasn't sure what he meant by that, but she could imagine Felipe wooing the ladies in more ways than one. "I think it's time to go home. Looks like the homecoming dance ended about an hour ago, so we are very late."

When she got into the car, she noticed the music had stopped. She turned the key, but there was only a click.

"Oh no! We ran the battery down! I didn't even think of that."

"No worries, senorita. I'll get help."

"Help? Where are you going to get help after midnight on a Saturday night?"

Felipe shrugged. "I live across the street. I'll get my uncle's car and we'll jump you. Happens a lot."

Linda's mouth flew open. "You live across the street?"

But Felipe was already walking away in the direction he'd pointed. She sat and waited. Ten minutes later, he was back driving an older Buick and brought jumper cables. She was more relieved when he seemed to know how to hook them up.

"We have to wait a few minutes to make sure your battery is charged," Felipe said. "Not every girl can say that they got jumped after the homecoming dance, can they?"

Linda squinted at him. "You know, sometimes I can't tell if you realize you're saying something dirty."

He smiled. "I know. But I think you would be fun to jump."

She pursed her lips. "Is my car ready yet?"

"We'll see." He motioned for her to turn the key. Her car started. "Don't turn it off for about twenty minutes to charge it well."

"Okay. Thank you for fixing it."

"Aren't you going to pay the mechanic?" He leaned in through the open window.

"You're the one who turned on the radio and lights—"

Linda couldn't finish when he covered her mouth with his. Only then did she remember what he'd implied about the Latin lovers. He did dance like a Latin lover might. And she guessed this kiss was heading in the same direction, hot and spicy. The confines of the driver's seat made it hard to pull away. When she did, it was hard to breathe. "Uhm goodnight then, Phil. See you in church. School. See you in school." She shook her head and put the car in reverse. The last look she had of him; he was laughing.

CHAPTER THIRTY-ONE

Linda picked Yvonne up on a snowy morning in December to make the nearly two-hour trip to Marysville, Kansas for Nancy and Peter's wedding. Their initial conversation was limited to Yvonne studying the map and giving Linda directions for heading south out of town. But once they were on the highway, they began catching up. Linda hadn't seen Yvonne since she'd come to the twirlers' homecoming show. As always, Yvonne looked stunning, her mahogany hair in generous curls resting on a trim ski jacket, tight jeans, and stylish boots.

"How do you like college, Yvonne? You're living on campus, aren't you?"

"Yes. I like living close to my classes. It's like being where the action is. But sometimes I feel like I am still missing the action." Yvonne folded the map in her lap.

"What do you mean?"

"I guess I expected the dating scene to be better in college. There are twenty thousand students at NU. About ten thousand young men. Why haven't I found a good guy to date yet? I've had a few blind dates and been to frat parties, but all I've found there is entitled drunk boys who don't even remember your name the next day."

Look at you, Yvonne. You should be beating boys off with a stick. I guess you never know.

Linda nodded. "I do know how you feel. I've been looking for the next Tom. You know I thought he was too old for me, and I should date some boys in my class or even junior boys, but it's just not the same. I've been seeing this guy named Felipe. He's good-looking, but he told me right up front that he has no money and his family is likely to move away. It didn't bother me at first. He's been to my house and he's always ready to make out on the couch

206

downstairs. But if I want to go out for burgers or pizza, I have to drive and I have to pay. That feels a little weird."

"I could see how that might make things awkward."

"Then I started dating this other guy, a friend from band. You remember Larry Bonner?"

"Mr. Chunky four-eyes with the red hair?"

Linda laughed. "He's not so chunky anymore. He sort of grew into his weight, and he wears contacts now. But any time we're outside, he blinks like crazy. That's annoying. I still enjoy his company though, and he does take me places and pays for the dates. But he's only kissed me a few times, and I like him better as a friend. Pretty much zero chemistry. Am I crazy to want to fall in love again?"

"I think it's easy to romanticize past relationships." Yvonne sighed. "I still wish I was with Daniel. But he's in another state, and I haven't heard from him. I don't want to ask Debbie what he's doing because I'm afraid she'll tell me he's found another girl."

"That's what happened with Tom. He brought another girl to our homecoming football game. His old high school girlfriend, who I guess is his new college girlfriend. Maybe I was his fill-in until she came back into his life."

"Don't say that, Linda. I saw you two at prom. He was devoted to you. And if that whole pregnancy thing didn't break you two up, you had a pretty strong bond."

"We did survive that, but it made sense for us to break up this fall. Yet I can't seem to get my heart on board with it."

"You know what Tennyson said: 'tis better to have loved and lost than never to have loved at all.'"

Linda scoffed. "To quote my new friend Felipe: Thees ease boolsheet."

Yvonne laughed, and when she couldn't stop, Linda laughed with her. It was nice to know she had company. Especially someone she admired as much as Yvonne.

A few days into the second semester, Linda got a note from Mrs. Baker, asking her to stop by the guidance counselor's office when she had study hall. Linda assumed it was related to her college applications or test scores.

"Hi, Mrs. Baker. Did you ask to speak to me?" Linda took a chair in front of her desk.

"Oh, yes, Linda. Thank you for coming in. Another student mentioned that you were friends with Felipe Gomez."

Linda's brows came together and she blinked twice. "Is Felipe in trouble?"

"He's truant, I'm afraid. He hasn't been to school since the new semester began on Monday. His locker is empty."

"We had calculus together last semester. I assumed we didn't have any classes together this time. I haven't talked to him since last week, I guess."

"Of course, we called his phone number but got no answer. The truancy officer went to his apartment but found no one there. It appears he may have left but we'd like to know for certain. We ask parents to inform the office of any address change."

"He told me his family moves often. Something to do with his father's work, I think. Wait, Phil said his uncle is a janitor here."

"At this school? No one named Gomez, but I can do more checking. That might help, thank you. You don't know where he is?"

Linda shook her head, thankful she hadn't gotten more involved. "He told me his family had moved twenty or thirty times since he came to the United States when he was eight."

"Oooh. That sounds like it might be an immigration situation. In that case, Gomez probably isn't even the family's name. You've been helpful, Linda. It does sound like he's gone."

Linda walked back to study hall feeling a cloud descending on her. He said he was only here for a short time, but she wasn't quite ready to say *adios*.

CHAPTER THIRTY-TWO

If her senior year had not gone well romantically, there were other highlights at least. She'd made the all-city band playing her trombone. She was particularly proud of that since she hadn't played regularly while she was twirling. She'd done well in all her classes and got pretty good scores on her S.A.T.s. She'd applied to the University of Nebraska, Nebraska Wesleyan, and the University of Missouri and been accepted by all three schools.

Her parents had been getting along better, and they were pleased with her focus on school work and preparation for next year. Why had she spent so much time wallowing over her love life when there were other things to enjoy?

Art class had always been a favorite. Linda enjoyed drawing and painting and had made batik decorations that were hanging on her bedroom walls. Unfortunately, in the first class of the second semester, she learned that her favorite teacher, Mrs. Wiggins, had taken a leave to care for one of her parents on the East Coast. Her replacement was a recent college graduate, Miss Destiny Radcliffe.

The teacher wrote her name on the chalkboard with a flourish. "I am anxious to get to know each of you in this class. But I want to learn about you through your work. This is an advanced class and I expect you are all familiar with charcoal sketching. We will get right to your first assignment, which will let me know where everyone stands. I am going to be your first model."

Miss Radcliffe had arranged the room so that they could sketch a subject situated on a stool in the center. She was wearing a blouse buttoned to her collarbone, but she unbuttoned the top two buttons and flattened her blouse against her body. "What you will be working on is three separate busts, in other words, a sketch of my head and neck down to the top of my shoulders. You will need to move around throughout the first two classes so that you can sketch my left profile, my right profile, and from straight on."

The students all picked up sketch pads, charcoal sticks, and pencils for the assignment and situated their chairs and easels to begin. Miss Radcliffe settled on a stool in the center focusing her gaze on the classroom door.

Before Linda began, she studied the teacher's features. She could have been a professional model. She had shoulder-length strawberry blonde hair that she had pushed behind her ears and shoulders to provide a better view of her neck. Her large hazel eyes were wide-set. Her nose was more prominent in profile, thin and pointed with an upward slope at the tip. Her lips were neither full nor thin, but her upper lip was straight across, not bowed, and they rested peacefully as if in slumber. Her neck might have been her best feature, if one was assessing her beauty, long and graceful, flaring out to narrow shoulders, much like Vermeer's *Girl with The Pearl Earring.*

Still, the overall combination was not completely symmetrical. She wasn't classically beautiful; she was intriguing. What was the reason her features were disruptive? Part of the effect was her bushy eyebrows one slightly higher than the other, and both accented and detracted from her eyes. She wore no eye makeup highlighting her pale lashes, and her lips were coated with only a pale pink sheen. Her prominent cheekbones begged to be kissed by the sun, but in mid-winter were as delicate as the rest of her ivory complexion. When Linda walked around for a different view, she noticed that her ears were slightly different, one more pointed than its mate, but both slender and with free lobes. Her jaw was strong but receded in profile below her nose and mouth.

Only when she was satisfied that she had understood her facial structure, Linda began to capture the image on paper. Nearly everyone else was well into creating their sketches before Linda started. Although Miss Radcliffe's eyes appeared frozen in place, it was clear that she had not missed anything that had gone on as her students worked.

The class was half over, when Linda suddenly flipped her sketchbook to the next page, making more noise than she intended. She wasn't unhappy with her initial renderings. She decided she wanted to sketch the whole body to understand the subject further. It seemed more complicated to sketch clothing. Her skirt was knee-length and stretched from the angle Miss Radcliffe was perched on the stool. Because she'd unbuttoned her neckline, the cuffs of her blouse languished on the backs of her hands. Linda didn't even get to her flat shoes before the bell rang.

I think I made a good start. I have the image I want in my head and I can begin to fill in more details.

Sometimes Linda found her quest for perfection annoying. It was hard for her to get those images that she forged into her mind's eye to leave her alone. She chalked it up to her brain telling her the project was half complete. That night, she took her sketchbook home and filled in some of the details, especially in the full figure. She had another classroom session to finish the three bust drawings.

In her sleep, she saw her. Destiny was walking, half running ahead of her, that hair streaming from her face exposing her neck and clavicle. But she was wearing something old-fashioned and diaphanous, as though she belonged in another era. Linda was trying to keep up, but she didn't know why. Perhaps she still needed her to pose to finish her sketches.

When she awakened, she remembered the dream, but it did little to help her sketching.

I don't think I have ever dreamt about a teacher before. Very weird.

Two days later, Miss Radcliffe posed for the second sitting. The class noted that she had placed a piece of tape on the floor to indicate the position of the stool and her feet, as well as a mark on the door where she returned her gaze.

Before finishing the assignment, Linda sketched in her feet and shoes in the full figure drawing. She squinted. There was something odd about her foot. Had it been that way before? Miss Radcliffe wore the same blouse, but her skirt was different, and her shoes were not the same either. And her shoes did not match each other. They were the same color and style, but one shoe had a thicker sole. Linda's eyes bounced from the unusual shoe to Miss Radcliffe's face. A slight tremor of recognition flitted across her eyes.

If her sole is thicker, that must mean one leg is shorter or one hip is higher. Something is a bit off.

Linda walked behind the subject and studied her hips and back and how she perched on the stool. Her classmates frowned at Linda because the assignment did not involve a rearview. The curve of her spine was not pronounced but evident when you were looking for it. When Linda returned to a frontal view, she felt rather than saw a minuscule grimace cross Miss Radcliffe's mouth.

She's in pain. Sitting in one position may be hard for her, but she's suffering for her art.

Linda flipped back to her sketches of the subject's face from three angles. They are a little off. One shoulder is dipped slightly, and I corrected it to make it more even. But it's not accurate. She erased and made corrections. Better.

When the class was over, the teacher asked them to place their work on a back table and apply a spray to protect the charcoal from smearing when handled. Linda thought she could have added more details, but was happy with her result.

"Linda, would you stay a moment?" the teacher asked.

Linda stood hoping for some artistic advice.

"Why did you walk behind me when my back was not included in the assignment?"

Linda stiffened. "You were hiding something. I was trying to uncover it. I try to create truth in my art."

Miss Radcliffe's gaze seemed to consider her answer. "We're all hiding something, don't you think? Art can also correct and memorialize life without flaws."

"But flaws make us who we are." The teacher nodded and Linda went to her next class. She was optimistic that she would learn a lot about art this semester.

By the time the school day ended, it was snowing. The twirlers had a meeting after school with Mr. Humphreys about auditions, but he cut it short due to the weather. He said the teachers were told to leave by four o'clock.

Linda cleaned the snow off her car and started it to get the defroster working. She sat for a few minutes letting the engine warm up, and shook the snow off her gloves and hat. She glanced over and saw Miss Radcliffe coming to the parking lot, carrying a bag. She didn't go to one of the snow-covered cars, she went to the passenger side of a car parked right in Linda's line of vision. The light went on when she opened the door. Linda saw her lean over and kiss the driver, who was wearing a hat.

I guess she has a boyfriend. Or maybe she's married even though she's not going by Mrs. Radcliffe.

Linda started to ease her car along the snow-packed road. She had to wait at the edge of the lot to enter the main road, and the car that her teacher had entered passed in front of her. The driver had momentarily rolled down the window for better visibility. Linda squinted when she saw a woman with long dark hair covered by a faux fur headband laughing and rolling the window back up. She looked again. She was sure it was the car she'd seen earlier; it had a heart decal on the bumper. What had she seen exactly?

Her teacher, Destiny Radcliffe, got into that car and kissed the driver. The driver was a young woman, probably the same age as

Miss Radcliffe. It wasn't one of those pecks on the cheeks you might greet a friend or relative with, especially in some countries. It looked like the kind of smooch you'd lay on your boyfriend. What was going on?

Her teacher was becoming more of an enigma by the minute. Some people, Linda knew, might be upset by what she saw. She merely found it fascinating.

A few nights later, Destiny Radcliffe appeared in her dream again. This time the dark-haired woman was chasing her. Snow was falling around them and they both slipped and fell into an embrace and tumbled together like lovers. Linda jolted up in bed. Maybe she shouldn't eat pizza so late.

The boys' basketball team was having a winning season, and the pep band was one of the biggest boosters. She and Larry sat side by side at the games and competed over who could cheer the loudest.

It was the Friday before her February birthday, and the Capital Cougars had barely defeated the Beatrice Orangeman in a rousing home basketball game. The whole gym at Capital High was rocking with excitement. The band members were practically jumping in the air when they left the gym to return to the band room for their instrument cases and coats.

Linda and Larry were walking toward the main hall when she saw him. Tom was standing in front of her, people milling all around him. He was holding a single red rose and waiting for her.

"You go ahead, Larry. I'll be right there," Linda said.

She stood in front of Tom, studied his face, and rocked back on her heels.

"Nice trombone," he began. She merely stared. "It's almost your birthday again. I thought I'd um…" he looked down. "Can we go somewhere to talk?"

"Like where? Your place? Probably not a good idea."

"Then your house. Let me take you home."

"I drove."

"I can follow you. Please." She took the rose he held out to her and tapped it between her thumb and forefinger as though she feared its thorns.

She wished she were stronger. She wished she wasn't happy to see him. But his face was the sun that had come out after months of gray skies. She caved.

Linda put a pan of milk on the small stove in the kitchenette in the basement recreation room to make hot cocoa.

"Why are you here, Tom?" She sat on the couch and he sat on the coffee table facing her.

"It's sort of obvious. I want you back. I want us back."

Linda looked down at her hands and he took them in his. "Didn't we both decide it wasn't working before?"

"It may not be practical, but I don't care. No one else makes me happy. I haven't been able to forget you."

"You didn't want to be stuck with a high school girl."

"I didn't say that, I said—it doesn't matter. I want to be stuck with you."

"Something happen with what's-her-face?"

"We were a flash in the pan. I think she was dating me just to appease her parents. I don't know, but Jillian and I are done. I never meant for that to hurt you."

You're saying all the right things, but can I believe you? Should I trust you again?

Linda shook her head. "You're back here because it's convenient. We know each other. You don't have to work hard like you do dating someone new."

"I'm here because I still love you. And since you haven't kicked me out, I think the feeling might be mutual."

She bit her lip. Why did he make her want to cry and scream? She took his face in her hands. "You're wrong. I hate you." Then she took his mouth with hers and he wrapped her in a tight embrace, pulling her into his lap.

"You have no idea how much that turns me on when you kiss me first," he gasped.

And just like that, it was on again. He picked her up and laid her on the couch, pulling her V-neck pep club sweater over her head. He unbuttoned the first few buttons of her white shirt and kissed her neck and cleavage. Then he pulled her face back to his and ravaged her mouth and his tongue rolled over hers again. Linda gasped and closed her eyes tightly, craving the sensation of his familiar taste and smell, the feel of his warm hands caressing her. Her fingers ran over his jaw and she saw Destiny's. No, it was Tom's jaw with a hint of stubble. She trailed her fingertips over the rough texture.

She closed her eyes again when he kissed her, but it was hazel eyes staring back at her, not his blue ones. Destiny's lips were on hers, exactly the way she'd drawn them, as she had dreamt, had imagined.

No! That's not right. That's not real.

Linda pushed back, struggling to sit up.

"What's wrong? You don't want this?

"Yes, but. Wow. Something odd…" Linda wrinkled her nose and brow. "Have you ever had some strange thought or image pop into your head and you have no idea why?"

He laughed. "All the time. Right now, I have all sorts of strange thoughts about what I'd like to do to you. I don't even know where to begin." He leaned off her and sniffed. "But if you don't want to scorch that milk, you'd better take it off the burner."

Linda gasped and slid off the couch. She got to the stove in time to stir in the chocolate mixture and pour the hot drink into two mugs. Then she added a generous handful of marshmallows. She smoothed out her shirt where he'd tugged on it, and buttoned one of the buttons. Then she took the cocoa to the table and put the mugs on coasters.

"I guess maybe we should stop attacking each other and drink our hot chocolate."

Tom smiled, "Are you sure?"

She nodded.

"What was it that popped into your head that scared you?"

Linda's eyes grew wide. What could she tell him? "It happened in a dream too. I see this woman. She looks like she's from a long time ago from her clothes. But I can see her eyes, her mouth, her whole face. And I saw her now, when we were kissing. It's like she's haunting me."

"She pretty?"

"Oh yes. In a mysterious way."

"I want your dreams."

"I think it has something to do with my art class. We had to draw faces. Oh, and then I saw my art teacher kissing a woman in her car in the school parking lot."

"You have a man for an art teacher now?"

Linda shook her head and blew on her hot drink.

"Wait. You have a lady art teacher, and she kissed another chick? This isn't that old gal you said had been there for decades?"

218

Linda snorted. "No, she's gone, at least this semester. This is a young art teacher and her girlfriend." She took a hesitant sip, getting mostly marshmallows.

"Oh, now there is a whole porn movie playing in my head. Chick on chick making out in the school parking lot? You saw this for real?"

"Yeah. I doubt they realized I saw them. But I don't know what to think."

"I guess you haven't had anyone kissing you enough lately. Your imagination has gotten away from you." He reached up and took her chin in his hand. "You have some marshmallow on your lip right—"

Before she could wipe her mouth, he stuck his fingertip into her mug, scooped up more marshmallow foam, and spread it on her lower lip. Then his teasing tongue came out and he slowly began tasting it.

Linda chuckled and pulled away. "I've been kissing people. High school boys, as you suggested. Some of them are decent kissers."

Tom frowned. "Well, you see, that's what you don't want. Kissing should always be at least a little indecent. Let me demonstrate."

He set both mugs back down and pushed her onto her back again and took her mouth. She could taste the marshmallow on his tongue. Then he chuckled and flipped her pleated skirt up and kissed her on her thigh, and started working his way up to her panties.

"Stop!" She laughed. "You are being naughty already and I haven't even decided if I want to go out with you again."

"Oh, you want to go out with me again. And you like it when I'm naughty, tell the truth."

"Drink your cocoa. Then you'd better leave. I will consider dating you."

"All right. Do you want to go out on your birthday, Tuesday night, or Saturday, on Valentine's Day? I thought we could go to a nice restaurant in Omaha."

"I already have a date for Valentine's Day. It's the Sweetheart Dance."

"The what? You're going to a dance with someone else?"

"I went to the homecoming dance with someone else. I missed the Sweetheart Dance last year since I was seeing you. I didn't think you'd want to go."

Tom pursed his lips and knit his eyebrows. He took a few sips of his drink. "Let's plan on Tuesday then. I'll make a reservation."

That was the thing about dating an older guy. He kept trying to take control. But sometimes, it was a pleasant change of pace.

CHAPTER THIRTY-THREE

"How do you feel about prom this year?" Linda sat with Nancy on the sidelines watching Dawn and Melissa go through the basics with the next crop of twirler hopefuls.

"Pete and I have talked about it," Nancy said. "It will be very strange to go to prom now that we're married and have a baby. We'd have to get a sitter."

"But you have that prom dress from last year you didn't get to wear."

"True, but it might be a little tight."

"I think your tummy is already pretty flat. You're an inspiration to new mothers everywhere."

"It's not my tummy I'm worried about. I don't want to fall out of the top."

"Oh, I forgot, the milk machines. How long do you plan to keep that up?"

"I don't know yet. Sometimes they say babies stop on their own. I figured I might keep breastfeeding for six months as long as she seems to be gaining weight. Pete thinks it's a good idea."

"I'll bet he does. But back to prom, do you think you two will go?"

"Who are you going with?"

"Um, Larry? Or Tom."

"What are you saying? They both think you're going with them?"

"Maybe. I'm still dating Larry. I need to keep Tom guessing."

"But you and Tom are…" Nancy looked back toward the other students, "intimate again?"

Linda shook her head. "Not yet. I keep putting that off. Maybe after prom. Maybe after graduation. It's driving Tom nuts."

"I can't believe you. You've got willpower."

"I'm a little afraid, to tell you the truth."

"Of sex?"

"Of another pregnancy."

"Aren't you on the pill?"

"Yes, I have been all year. But nothing is one hundred percent effective. Except for what I've been doing."

"Prom is earlier this year. You'd better decide who your escort is soon."

"You should go, Nancy. Both you and Pete missed it last year, and I had a fabulous party."

"No pre-prom party this year?"

"No, I didn't feel like going to all that trouble. But what if just you and Pete came over? I could recreate what we did last year but it would only be the four of us. We could put on records and dance around the pool. Then we could still go to the real prom for the last hour, to see who gets king and queen."

"That sounds like more fun. I think Pete would rather do that than go to the real thing. But would he have to rent a tux?"

"That's up to you two."

Two days later, Larry took the decision out of her hands. Melissa Sparks came up to her after school.

"Linda, I don't know what to do. Larry Bonner asked me to go to prom with him. Aren't you still dating him?"

Linda chuckled. "If he asked you to go to prom, then I'm not

222

dating him. Larry and I are good friends."

"But isn't this one of those, don't date your friend's ex-boyfriend kind of situations?"

"If I was in love with Larry, I would tell you not to accept. But I want Larry to be happy. He's a nice guy. You'll have fun."

When Tom called that night, he asked about prom. "I know you probably still think I don't want to take you to prom because it's a high school thing, but I hate the idea of you going with some other guy. If you still want to go to prom, you need to go with me."

Thank you, Universe. Since when are you on my side?

"All right, I'll go with you. I guess I should find a dress. Or maybe Sarah has something hidden in her closet I can wear." Linda sat back in one of the overstuffed chairs in her room. "Nancy and I were thinking about having a little private party before prom. Like we did last year but with only Nancy and Peter and the two of us. Maybe we'll even have dinner catered instead of appetizers. We could enjoy the pool. Dance a little. Then go to the actual prom late. You remember that they missed last year's prom because of his car accident?"

"Yeah. But now they're married and have a kid. Still going to prom?"

"Everyone should go to prom once."

"Whatever you want to do, Baby. It's your night. I'm just the good-looking guy on your arm."

"That's exactly right. Leave everything to me. I'll make sure you'll have a good time."

He laughed. "I'm counting on it."

The next afternoon, Nancy and Linda went through Sarah's closet. Sarah hadn't lived at home at all for two years and had her current wardrobe at her apartment, but she'd left most of her fancy dresses. Nancy brought baby Jennifer with her, but she was asleep in her infant carrier.

"You might as well try some of these dresses on too, Nance, even if it is merely for kicks. I know Sarah is bigger than you are, but she might let us alter one if she no longer wants it."

"I thought I was going to wear the peach blossom dress I made a year ago, but I tried it on and it just screams 'virgin.' I don't know that I can wear that in good conscience."

The first dress Linda tried on was the green silk V-neck with the back slit. It had been big on Linda when Sarah first got it, but now it fit her better, especially in the hips.

"Oh yeah, that's a winner. Can't imagine you'd find something cooler than that." Nancy rotated Linda around facing the closet door mirror so she got the view from the back. "It's pretty from the front, but downright dangerous from the back. When did you get a tush?"

Nancy tried on one of Sarah's older dresses. The bodice was gathered, so it flattered Nancy's bust and accented her waist without being too young-looking. It was about two inches too long, but that was an easy fix if Sarah would part with the dress.

"I never wear red clothes with my red hair, but this looks okay. I'm surprised." Nancy spun around trying to get the effect.

"Oh, you look much better than okay, Honey. You're going to sizzle in that."

They tried on a few more. Nancy liked a pale-yellow dress that was more ingénue, but it dipped too low in the front and made her self-conscious. Linda looked good in a purple dress with a long full skirt, but it was modest compared to the green silk. She decided to live dangerously.

"Gosh, I wish I could shop in my sister's closet," Nancy said.

224

"I thought the only things in your sister's closet were habits," Linda smirked.

"You mean my older sister, the nun. She never did wear anything very flashy even in high school. My second sister had a few nice things. But not nearly as stylish as these. Thank you for letting me play."

"It's fine if Nancy wants that red dress and you can wear the green silk. You're not altering that one, are you? I might wear it again," Sarah told Linda that evening on the phone. "But we need to set aside a time this summer to go look for bridesmaids' dresses. I have two of my sorority sisters in the wedding party too, plus Gavin's sister. The wedding is in November, you know, so there's not much time to waste."

"I'll go whenever you want, Sarah. I only need enough notice to get off work."

Sarah was set to marry Gavin Parker Jr. He'd graduated from business school two years earlier and was already a successful investment banker. Their wedding was the day after Thanksgiving, and Sarah was planning to graduate in December.

Linda let her mother help her plan the pre-prom dinner for four. Mary Jo hired a caterer to prepare and serve a fancy meal next to the pool, with candles everywhere, nice table linens, crystal, and china.

Peter whistled when he and Nancy came out of the recreation room door. "You went all out, Linda. This is fancier than a restaurant."

Linda beamed. "My mom always says, if you're going to do something, do it right."

"It's beautiful all right," Tom agreed. "And you ladies look like you are much too sophisticated to go to a high school prom."

Linda was wearing the green silk sheath with her hair in a loose pageboy around her shoulders. She wore a sparkly rhinestone headband and emerald earrings. Nancy had shortened Sarah's flowing dress, but it swirled around her like a red storm when she walked. And the gathered bodice dipped low enough to attract attention. Nancy had gathered her hair into a tight bun with embellished hairpins catching the light. She'd left a thin tendril of ginger curls cascading in front of each ear, tumbling onto her chest.

It was a little cool outdoors in May for their sleeveless dresses, but Linda had turned on the gas patio heaters to keep their dining area cozy.

When the four of them were seated, the caterer set bowls of salad greens atop their dinner plates. "Would you care for parmesan cheese on your salad?" the caterer asked.

Tom raised his brows. "I think I'm good, thanks."

"I hope you all like steak and lobster. My mother called it surf and turf," Linda said.

"Well, I certainly like steak. Never tried lobster," Peter said.

"Me neither," Tom said.

Nancy smiled and shook her head.

"Oh my, then you are all in for a treat!" Linda said. "I think I was eating lobster in my high chair. Of course, my parents met in Georgia, and they say lobster is much better on the coast."

"I'm seeing a whole new side of you, tonight, Miss Fancy Pants." Tom helped himself to a hot crusty roll from a silver basket that the caterer had slipped onto their table.

"A true lady can find herself at home in any environment. That's what I learned in charm school."

"Charm school?" Tom and Peter both hooted.

"What the hell is charm school?" Peter asked.

"Well, you would flunk out, clearly," Nancy laughed. She ran her hand over her husband's forearm. He picked up her hand and kissed the back of it.

Linda huffed out a chuckle. "My mother insisted I attend. My older sister loved it. The teachers didn't know what to do with me, I kept telling them how outdated the class was. Part of it was how to get a boy to talk to you." Linda took on a breathy voice. "Like, 'can you tell me why my car is making that awful noise? Cuz it is a complete mystery to me once I turn the key.' I couldn't figure out why any self-respecting girl would act dumb."

"What's that building over there?" Peter asked, looking toward the pool house.

"It's the pool house. It has a bathroom and bedroom inside so guests can change clothes."

Pete's brows winged up. "There's a bed in there? Does the door lock?"

Linda laughed. "Yes. Don't be getting any funny ideas, Peter."

"Too late for that. Are you girls sure you want to go to the school event tonight? I'm having a nice time right here. I'll bet your parents even have a fully-stocked bar over there." Peter leaned back in his chair. "Wada you think, Thomas? Should we have our own party here? We could put on some music."

Tom shrugged. "It's up to the girls. I'm flexible."

Peter narrowed his gaze at Tom then shifted it to Linda. "You two ever try out the pool house bed?"

Tom laughed, then looked toward the pool house.

"Yes, but not in the way you mean." Linda turned to signal the caterer to bring the main course.

The conversation died when the food was presented.

227

"We'll be back tomorrow for the leftovers," Pete suggested.

"I won't be leaving any leftovers," Tom said.

Once dinner was over, Linda put on some records and turned off some of the overhead lights. They danced under the stars around the pool.

"When do you want to go to the school prom?" Nancy asked.

"In about an hour," Linda said. "Does that work?"

"It works for me," Peter said. "I think my wife and I are going to take a tour of the pool house. You know we rarely have a babysitter."

Linda stared at the two of them. Nancy smiled sweetly giving her the side-eye as she was led through the door.

Tom pulled her back into a dance. "Don't be too hard on them. I can't even imagine being married and living apart. Add a baby into the mix and they probably have very little privacy."

"I thought the four of us were going to have a nice time," Linda complained.

"Looks like it's down to you and me, Babe." Tom began kissing her as they swayed to some Three Dog Night. "Maybe one of these days you'll let me take you back into that pool house."

They made it to the prom for the last thirty minutes.

CHAPTER THIRTY-FOUR

May 4, 1970

"Tom, we have to go join the protestors." Linda had knocked on his apartment door around six in the evening. "This is supposed to be a National Day of Protest against the president's escalation of the war into Cambodia. They're doing this all over the country. I heard that something is happening at the university. I called Yvonne since she lives on campus, and she said there were protestors outside the union."

"And this involves us how?" Tom said, stepping back to admit her. "Maybe we could watch it on television." He turned on the TV.

Both Linda and Tom stood transfixed to the events being replayed of Ohio National Guardsmen shooting student protestors at Kent State University. David Brinkley, the NBC news anchor, described how four students who were protesting the war were killed.

"This can't be right. These kids were unarmed," Tom said. They watched in horror as the news video showed the guardsmen throwing tear gas canisters.

"Then a formation of guardsmen marched up the hill and fired their rifles at the students," Brinkley reported.

Linda grabbed Tom's arm when they heard rifle shots ring out on the video.

"Two young men and two young women were killed and at least a dozen others were wounded." The report went on to say that classes were canceled at Kent State University for the week, and the area was sealed off by police. There were claims that snipers had fired on the guard.

"This is insane. We have to go down to the campus now." Linda picked up her purse that she'd dropped on the sofa.

"Are you nuts? You want to be one of those kids shot by a policeman? This is the kind of craziness that gets people killed."

"It's the war that gets people killed, Tom! Maybe you lucked out with a high draft number but young men your age are dying in Vietnam. Peter Thompson is going into the army next month. And now Nixon wants to go into Cambodia. We have to try to stop this."

"You think you can stop the war? That's a lot of idealistic bullshit! You need to look out for yourself, and not get mixed up in something where people are acting irresponsibly. You're not even a student at the university yet. But I am. You want me to get suspended?"

"I'm doing what my conscience tells me is right. Are you coming or not?" Linda stormed out of his apartment.

"Dammit Girl, you can't go without me. You'll get lost." Tom grabbed his sweatshirt and keys and followed her.

There was a lot of waiting around once they found their way to the campus square. There seemed to be some unorganized activity happening outside the Student Union. Linda got in line to purchase supplies to make a protest sign. Tom queued up to buy sandwiches and coffee.

"I should be working on my assignments tonight. Don't you have any homework, Linda?" Tom asked as they found a spot on the grass outside of the Teacher's College building. He offered her a sandwich. "Ham or roast beef?"

"I decided to stop eating dead animals," she said.

"You do realize my family raises beef for food consumption, don't you?" Tom narrowed his eyes at her and unwrapped the beef sandwich.

"I don't mind if you eat it. I have peanut butter." She pulled

230

out a somewhat squished sandwich wrapped in foil from her big purse. "And an apple. If you're nice, I'll let you have a bite."

"I'm being nice by coming with you. I still think this is potentially dangerous."

"You can leave anytime. No one is forcing you to be here."

"I'm the one with the student parking sticker. And I'm not leaving you here alone. Look at these kids. A bunch of long-haired hippies who probably haven't bathed in weeks. I smelled someone smoking weed over by the fountain."

Linda laughed. "Sometimes I forget you were born in the heart of conservatism. I think this is exciting. It's like being a part of a rebellion."

"I don't think much is happening—" Tom started to say when they noticed the crowd moving toward the library square.

"On to the Military Science Building!" Someone shouted' into a bullhorn.

They got up and fell in with the others moving en masse.

"Didn't they say on the news that the ROTC building was burned at Kent State? If this starts to get risky, we're leaving," Tom said.

Linda wrapped her arm around his. "Said like a true revolutionary. Don't worry."

When they arrived at the Military Science Building about fifteen minutes later, they entered a large gymnasium area where students usually performed drills. There were no officer training cadets in evidence now. They joined other students sitting cross-legged on the floor of the large room.

"Now what?" Tom asked.

"I think this is it," Linda said. They watched as some students stood before the crowd and began to talk about the events at Kent

231

State. There were jeers and shouts of "stop the war" and similar slogans heard around them.

One of the speakers at the front said, "We are here to enact a silent protest. We are occupying this building to stop the fascist government from training more military men. This is a sit-in. We won't leave until we have the attention of the university leaders. However, if it looks like the police are here to arrest us, I urge you to ditch all of your identification. Throw away anything in your possession with your name on it so they won't know who you are."

"What good would that do?" Tom asked. "They start arresting people, we're leaving. I don't think your parents would like that."

"Relax. It's a peaceful sit-in." Linda patted his leg.

"I'm going use the john before the line is out the door. You coming?"

"No, I'll save our places here," Linda said.

When Tom got back, Linda was laughing with a guy wearing a bandana around his long unkempt hair, and taking a drag on a joint.

Tom squatted beside her. "Linda, what are you doing? You know that's illegal."

"We're at a sit-in. I think smoking a little grass is part of it. You wanna hit?"

"No, I'm good. I'll stick to my Marlboro's." He settled close to her, and the other guy took the hint and moved on.

"Don't be a sour puss," Linda laughed when he gave her a stern look. She put her hands around his neck and kissed him. And kept kissing him.

He pushed her back. "Okay, so smoking pot makes you horny. Good to know. I may revise my thinking."

Nothing new seemed to be happening until 10:00 p.m. when

the word was passed around the crowd that they might attend a meeting back at the Student Union to discuss further plans.

"It's a school night, you're going home."

Linda yawned. "All right, but you have to tell me what happens here tomorrow. You might be on strike."

CHAPTER THIRTY-FIVE

Linda no longer worked at Runza, but tonight she'd craved one, and drove across town to treat herself. She supposed she could have waited until the next day when Tom came back to town, but sometimes you want what you want when you want it. It had been a nice day. Nancy, Debbie, and Yvonne had been over for a pool party bringing little André and Jennifer.

The lazy summer still stretched out before her. She'd been helping Tom's business partner, Trey, transplant seedlings yesterday. She'd also been doing odd jobs for T&T Lawnscaping: helping them design a new logo, placing ads, and returning calls to schedule their services. But mostly she thought she'd take it easy before she started pre-dental studies at the university in September.

Linda was walking down the hall to the bathroom when she heard voices. She thought her mother had the TV on, but when she glanced into her parents' bedroom, it was empty.

That's right. Mom left this morning to go visit her sister in Atlanta. Guess Dad and I are on our own this week. Maybe I should have brought him a Runza.

She heard voices again. It sounded like laughter. She hadn't turned on the television anywhere. She went down to the main level of the house and looked around. No one there. Then she glanced out the big window overlooking the deck and saw some movement down in the hot tub. Was her dad in the hot tub? How odd. She didn't think he'd used it in years. There was music now, kind of jazzy older generation music. Maybe that was what she'd heard.

She opened the sliding door to the deck overlooking the pool and hot tub. She'd ask if he wanted her to try to make him some dinner. It was starting to get dark and her father didn't notice her when she approached the railing to call to him. Linda squinted.

234

Michael Bridges was in the hot tub but he wasn't alone. She couldn't identify the woman he was with, the one he was kissing. But she had long blonde hair. Linda felt like she was frozen in place watching this strange scene. And it gave her time to notice the woman's two-piece gold bathing suit was strewn near the hot tub. And her father's plaid trunks were a good five feet away, on a chair. From her perch almost directly above them, she didn't see much more than bare shoulders, but as they were jostling around in the water's turbulence, it was obvious what was happening.

Oh my God.

Linda screamed. Two heads whipped up instantly. And now she saw things she'd wished they'd kept hidden. Her father stood up.

God no! He must be drunk if he thinks that's okay.

Her first thought was to bolt back into the house. But as her head started to pound, the puzzle pieces clicked into place. Her father had gone out so often at night alone, especially on Saturdays. The many disagreements her parents had. The time he'd had a flat tire outside a strange apartment building. Her mother's vague responses when Sarah or Linda asked why their father was missing for dinner. This was nothing new.

She charged down the stairs like a snarling pit bull, striding right up to the hot tub. Michael dropped back down in the water.

"Get me my swimming trunks, Linda. They're on that chaise."

Linda snatched up his trunks, and then impulsively grabbed the woman's bathing suit too. She marched over to the brick fence that separated their property from the neighbors and threw all of them over the fence. The neighbor's dog barked.

"Well, that was dumb! Now you'll have to get me a towel unless you want me to come out of here naked!" Michael roared. His companion seemed to sink deeper under the cover of the bubbles.

"What are doing in the hot tub naked, Daddy? With a blonde bimbo no less! Of course, I know what you're doing. You're cheating on your wife! Could you be any more of a cliché?"

"Now see here, she is not a bimbo. Suzette works at my company as—"

"I don't care what she does!" Linda screamed. "It's what she does with you that matters. She's blonde, much, much too young for you, and has big bazookas. That's the definition of a bimbo!"

"Get Suzette a towel, so she can go inside. You and I can talk about this," Michael pleaded.

"NO! If she's embarrassed, good. She should be. I ought to get the movie camera so I can share this little scene with Mother when she gets back."

"Your mother knows."

"What?"

"She knows about Suzette. She's met Suzette," Michael said taking a big breath. "Mary Jo and I have an arrangement."

"An arrangement! What does that mean?"

"It's called an open marriage. Both partners can see and sleep with other people."

"Why the hell would anyone agree to that?"

"Language, Young Lady!" was Michael's automatic response.

Linda scoffed and paced between the pool and hot tub. "I don't believe you. Mom would never go along with this. She's probably waiting for you to come to your senses. And you obviously have not done that yet!"

"Lindy. You are old enough to understand these things. As I remember, it was a year ago that we were untangling you from ill-timed pregnancy. So don't try to pretend that you're still an innocent child. This is reality."

"Don't you dare throw that in my face! All I know is that I used to look up to you. I wanted to do anything I could to get your attention; hunting, fishing, going to the gun range, watching baseball. But this, this is not the father I adored! You're a cheat and a liar!"

"Lindy! Come back here!" Michael called.

But Linda was already running to the sliding door of the walkout basement, swiping angry tears away. She locked the door from the inside, then pounded up the stairs to the main floor and locked the sliding door off the upstairs deck. By then she could see her father had a beach towel wrapped around his waist and was holding one up for Suzette. They might find some type of clothing in the pool house. She supposed it didn't matter.

Linda went to her room and pulled a large backpack out of her closet. She threw jeans, shorts, and T-shirts inside. She emptied half of her underwear drawer into the backpack, socks, and an extra pair of sneakers. She took the cash she had in her purse and her ID but left her keys to the Camaro on her dresser. She scrawled a hasty note and left it on the desk. She added two hundred dollars her mother hid in her drawer with the feminine hygiene products. She grabbed a sweatshirt she'd worn home from Tom's a few weeks ago and threw that on top of the shirt and shorts she had on. She pulled on heavy socks and good walking shoes. She'd need them.

As she went out the front door, she could hear Michael cursing and pounding on the glass door in the back. That was her last memory of home the rest of the summer.

237

CHAPTER THIRTY-SIX

Tom toweled himself off after taking an early morning shower. He'd gotten back around nine the previous evening, and tried to call Linda, but she didn't answer. She might have been taking a late-night swim. That would be a nice way to end the day.

He checked the clock as he got dressed. Seven a.m. Maybe too early to try Linda now, but she did say she was available to work with the landscaping business, and the earlier you could start that in the day, the better. He'd try her after breakfast.

After eating eggs and toast, he called Trey to see what was on the schedule that day. Then he dialed Linda's number.

"Hello!" a man's gruff voice answered. It didn't sound like her dad, but he couldn't be certain.

"Oh, sorry. I must have dialed the wrong number," Tom said.

"Who are you calling?" the man asked.

"Uh, Linda Bridges. I'll try again."

"Who is this?" the man demanded.

Tom hung up. What the hell? Had he reached a wrong number? He shook his head and checked his phone list where he had Linda's number. Maybe he transposed two numbers and reached someone's jealous husband.

The same man answered the second call.

"Look, is Linda there? This is her boyfriend, Tom." He heard the man speak to someone else. Another man's voice came on the line. This one was familiar.

"Tom, is that you? This is her father. Is Linda with you?" Michael asked.

"No, of course not. I'm calling to speak to her. Isn't she home?"

Michael blew out his breath. "No. I don't know where she went. Do you think you can come over here? I could use some help."

Tom frowned at the phone. "I was going to head to work, but all right. I'll stop by."

The front door to the Bridges house was open beyond the glass storm door when he got there. "Hello?" Tom called.

"Upstairs," Michael answered.

Tom found Linda's father and another man in what he assumed was Linda's room by the girly flowered wallpaper and bedding. His gaze drifted between the two men.

"Tom, this is Investigator Harold Hopkins. He works with the state patrol and he's an old friend, here to try to help me out. He said it's too soon to report a missing person. This is Linda's boyfriend, Tom Case."

"Missing person? You think Linda is missing?"

"When was the last time you saw Linda, Tom?" Investigator Hopkins asked.

"Last week, Saturday, I guess. I've been at my parents' ranch near Gordon since then. Got back to Lincoln last night."

"When did you last speak to her?"

"Uh, not last night. The night before last. I couldn't reach her after nine last night."

"Did she say anything about going somewhere last night or today?"

"No, I expected to see her today. I thought she was coming by work. She was supposed to make some calls for my lawn service." Tom crossed his arms. "I don't understand what's going on."

"We're all trying to figure it out," Michael sighed. "Linda got upset last night. She was gone when I got home from work. I assumed she was out with you and would be late. She came home and found me in the hot tub with a woman and she got very upset. I tried to reason with her, but I couldn't. She locked the door to the house, and by the time I got in, she was gone."

Tom sat down on the bed. "She got upset because you were entertaining a woman? Are you sure there's not more to it than that? I mean, did she let you explain?"

Michael snorted. "I already went through this with Harry here. We were naked. Linda thought I was cheat—"

"Eeeww," Tom said. "Now I see why she was upset."

"I want to make sure she's safe. She'll get over being mad," Michael said. "Now Harry asked me if anything in this room looks different. What do you think?"

Tom shrugged. "I've never been in this room. Never even been on this floor of your house. How would I know?"

"You've never been in her bedroom? I thought you two had…"

"Not here. And not lately actually."

"Well, a couple of things look strange to me," Hopkins said. "When I looked in the closet, there is a space in the center where there are empty hangers and no clothes as if she removed the clothes and packed them. Same with the closet floor, two spaces near the front where a couple of pairs of shoes might fit. Then there are the car keys. She left her car keys right in plain sight and her car is in the garage."

Tom walked over to the dresser and picked up the keys. "Why would she go anywhere at all without driving?"

"She left you a note," Michael said and handed him an unfolded piece of paper.

Tom read it: "Tom, I will call you when I can." He shook his

240

head slightly, frowning, and glanced up at the two men.

"But she hasn't called you?" Hopkins reiterated.

"No, but I'm starting to get worried. Especially if she's not driving."

"Did she ever talk about taking a trip this summer?" Hopkins asked.

"No. I mean we talked about her coming back to Gordon before school started, but she wouldn't go without me. How would she even go anywhere without her car?" Tom studied the contents of her closet.

"Oh, there are other ways," the investigator said. "A car on a highway can be found by law enforcement. There're buses, trains, planes. Someone else could drive. She could hitchhike."

Tom whirled back. "Hitchhike? Jesus. She wouldn't do that, would she, Mr. Bridges?"

"I don't know. Linda has been known to do the unexpected," her father said. "Do you see anything in her closet that is missing?"

Tom shook his head. "How could I tell? I never saw a girl with so many clothes. When we first started dating, I think I saw her a dozen times before she repeated any item of clothing. She even had different underwear every time we um…she has a lot of clothes."

He moved over to the dresser and opened some of the drawers. One drawer had earrings, one had necklaces, one for bras, another for panties.

"This looks odd," Tom said. The other two men looked over his shoulder.

"What?" Michael asked.

"The front of this drawer is empty, but there are a few bras still in the back. Same way with the panties. Like she took the whole front half of the drawer but left the back alone."

"Just like the closet, spaces where things were removed," Hopkins said.

"Or maybe the clothes are in the laundry," Tom suggested. "Did you check to see if there is a hamper full or if her clothes are in the laundry room?"

"We looked there earlier. But you have a knack for this, Son. Maybe you should think about studying law enforcement." Hopkins opened the rest of the drawers but they were items such as scarves, gloves, and knit hats not for summer wear.

"Tom, Harry and I were hoping you could go talk to some of Linda's friends. I found the addresses and phone numbers in Linda's book. I believe she said Nancy, Yvonne, and Debbie were all coming over yesterday afternoon. She might have told them something useful."

Tom took the list of names and addresses and started driving through Eastridge looking for the addresses. He found Debbie Washington's address on Mulder Drive first.

Debbie was putting baby André into a stroller for an early morning walk.

Tom walked up the driveway before she got underway. "Good morning, Debbie. I need to talk to you for a minute. Can I walk along?"

"Tom? My goodness. I didn't expect to see you here. Is everything okay?" Debbie squinted into the eastern sun.

"I'm not sure. I came from Linda's house. She left last night and her father doesn't know where she went. So, I have been asked to talk to her friends to see if she said anything to you about going somewhere." Tom fell in step with Debbie as they headed up the street.

"We were over there yesterday for a pool party. Even the kids were there. Everyone seemed to be in a good mood. I thought Linda said you were coming back to Lincoln today. Why would she leave now?"

"I dunno. Her father said they had a fight or something and then she left."

"Her father? Uh-oh. What did they fight about?"

Tom wasn't sure he should divulge that information. "Well, um Mr. Bridges said something about another woman being at their house." Tom let his gaze shift to the neighboring houses.

"Linda found out about her father cheating?"

Tom looked back at Debbie. "How did you know about that? Did Linda mention it?"

"No. Robert and I ran into him last summer, on our wedding night. Robert talked to him in the bar of the Clayton House where we were staying. Then we saw him with a woman the next morning. Robert didn't think I should say anything to Linda."

"Well, that's interesting. Yeah, I think that is what they fought about. But you have no idea where she might have gone?"

"No, sorry." André began to fuss, so Debbie stopped and picked him up and put a pacifier in his mouth.

"May I hold him?" Tom asked. She passed him over to Tom who bounced him and made him giggle.

"You know, Linda and I were both pregnant at the same time. She told us she was pregnant and then I found out I was about two weeks later."

"Well, you knew before I did."

"Right, but if she'd had the baby, he or she would be about the same age as André."

Tom gave Debbie a tight smile and handed André back to her. "That's a little hard to imagine. Neither one of us was ready to have a child."

"It's possible Linda's having some sort of anniversary reaction. I've seen people go through that on the anniversary of something bad that happens to them. Like my grandma and my mom always commemorate the day of my uncle's death, and it's a sad time of year for them. Wasn't the abortion about a year ago?"

Tom frowned. He felt a prickling along the back of his neck. "Yeah, I suppose. Hey, I guess I should try to find Yvonne. Doesn't she live nearby?"

"Sure, her house is right there. The yellow one."

Tom was glad to have an excuse to shift gears and walk toward Yvonne's. He inhaled and pressed his lips together. He hadn't allowed himself to think about the baby that never was. That was too damned sad.

Yvonne was coming out of her house with a beach bag heading toward the carport.

"Yvonne, may I speak with you for a moment?"

"Oh, Tom. Hello. I was about to get on my bicycle. I'm supposed to be lifeguarding in about twenty minutes." Yvonne was wearing a midriff-baring top and short shorts.

"I can give you a lift. This won't take long."

Yvonne shrugged and followed him to the Jeep.

"I'll get to the point. Linda fought with her dad last night and took off. I'm trying to find out if she told any of her friends where she might have gone." Tom put the car in gear.

"We all saw her yesterday. She seemed happy then. Turn left on Randolph to get to the pool."

"She has never mentioned where she'd go if she wanted to get away?"

"Oh, well sure. In an offhand way. She said she'd love to

244

backpack through Europe. But that takes some planning. And once she said she should hitchhike to California and join a hippie commune."

"What?" Tom turned to look at Yvonne. They were nearing the pool by then.

"I assumed she was kidding. Linda says a lot of crazy things to get a reaction. She even kissed me once to piss me off."

Tom's eyebrows winged. He might like to kiss Yvonne. All that lovely summer skin she was showing shouldn't go to waste. But why would Linda find her attractive? Yvonne had a point. Linda liked to shock people.

"Thanks, Yvonne. If you think of anything else, would you call me or Mr. Bridges? Here, I wrote down the phone numbers." He handed her a notecard with the two numbers on it, and Yvonne disappeared into the pool office.

Linda talked about hitchhiking. Did she have any idea how dangerous that could be?

One more stop. Nancy lived on Sunrise Road. He checked the street sign and realized he was already on Sunrise Road. He followed the curve up to her address.

Nancy's mother let him in. Nancy was sitting on the couch nursing baby Jennifer. She'd put a blanket over the baby when she heard him come in, but the baby kept trying to push it away.

Tom had never been exposed to this before. He wasn't sure where to look. Neither Nancy nor her mother seemed to think this was nearly as awkward as he did. He sat on a chair facing the couch and averted his eyes. His shoes seemed to be the safest place to cast his eyes

"Would you like some iced tea?" Nancy's mother asked. "It's already getting warm out there."

"Sure, if it's not too much trouble." He could feel the heat rising to his face. "Nancy, I know you and Linda are pretty tight. Have you talked to her today or last night by any chance?" Tom fidgeted with the paper he had pulled out with the twirlers' addresses on it.

"No, we talked yesterday at her house. We all had fun. I was afraid Jenny might have gotten too much sun, but she seems fine now. What's going on?"

"Linda and her dad argued last night before I'd even gotten back to town. Mr. Bridges said she took off, and we don't know where she went."

"Her mother doesn't know?"

"Uh, her mom is out of town. Went to Georgia or somewhere I think." He sipped tea when Nancy's mother handed him a cool glass, then set it on a coaster.

"Maybe Sarah knows. What did she say?"

"Sarah? Oh, Linda's sister, Sarah. Gosh, I dunno. Maybe no one checked with her." Tom let out a sigh. "That's probably where she went. Good thinking."

"Linda said she was supposed to go shopping for bridesmaids' dresses with Sarah sometime this week. Her sister's wedding is in the fall. Linda was trying to come up with some sort of prank to pull at the wedding or the rehearsal dinner."

Nancy pulled the baby out from under the blanket. She looked like she was sleeping. She laid Jenny on the couch on her back, then Nancy put her hands back under the blanket, apparently fastening something. Nancy wrapped the blanket around the baby and put her on her shoulder, patting her back.

"You seem to be a pro at that," Tom said, daring to meet Nancy's eyes now.

"You learn."

Tom stood up. "I'm hoping you're right about Linda's sister. But in case that's a dead-end, call me if you have any more ideas about where Linda went or if you hear from her." He handed Nancy a notecard matching the one he'd given Yvonne.

Tom was glad to get out of there. Those babies were making him itchy.

He swung by Trey's house and did some work in the greenhouse. Trey's parents were letting them use half of their greenhouse space for T&T Lawnscaping now, and the Hansens were building a second one.

After lunch, he went back to check on Mr. Bridges. This time, Michael opened the door and motioned him in. He'd no sooner entered the foyer when someone started shouting behind him.

"Daddy! What in the world is going on? There was a detective at my door this morning asking about Linda!" Sarah stormed in behind Tom, her blonde ponytail whipping around her head. She was wearing a pink halter dress that looked expensive. Maybe it was how well it fit, as though she'd been poured into it.

Tom had trouble yanking his gaze away from her dress. She was not as thin as Linda. No doubt Sarah was used to men looking at her curves. She seemed too preoccupied to notice him ogling her.

"Do you know where Linda is, Sarah?" Michael asked.

"No. Why would I? It's your turn to watch her! Mom left her home in your care. And you lost her? Is that what you're telling me?" Sarah crossed her arms over her chest. Tom found the effect a little startling and looked away. That was when Sarah seemed to notice he was standing there.

"Linda disappeared Monday night after we disagreed," Michael said. "You know Tom Case, Linda's boyfriend?"

"Tom? I think we met once. Linda's mentioned you. You

attend the university, right?"

Tom nodded. "You haven't seen or heard from Linda, then?"

"No. I didn't know anything was wrong until Inspector Hopalong started giving me the third degree."

"Tom, did you learn anything from Linda's friends this morning?" Michael asked.

"Not much. Nancy thought she might be with Sarah. Yvonne said she mentioned hitchhiking to California once. Debbie thought she might be having some sort of anniversary reaction from, you know, what happened a year ago." Tom scratched the back of his head.

"Hitchhiking? Even Linda isn't insane enough to do that," Sarah said. "And I thought anniversary reactions were for people who have suffered some sort of trauma. You've kept her so sheltered, the most trauma she's probably ever had is a broken fingernail. This is clearly a cry for attention! What did Mom say about this when you called her?"

Tom cleared his throat. "I think I'll go back up to Linda's room and see if I can find anything else relevant." He started up the stairs while Michael explained why he hadn't called Mary Jo yet.

His own family secrets were bad enough. But at least they were buried under twenty years of denial. Linda's family's issues were bubbling out of the ground like trapped methane. Sarah didn't know her little sister had been pregnant or had an abortion. She probably didn't know about her father's extramarital affair. Sarah's pretty protected herself.

Linda's room looked as it had earlier. He studied it more closely now. It didn't look like Linda decorated it, more like her mother had. All those cabbage roses. And lace curtains on the dormer windows. But there were a few posters of rock stars on the wall and some striking batiks that Linda had probably created. Her

248

double bed was carefully made with a half-dozen small pillows arranged symmetrically. Amid the pillows stood a stuffed lion. A lioness, he realized, there was no wild mane. He picked it up. On the underside, in a child's hand, was written "Linda the Lion."

Tom chuckled and hugged the stuffed toy to his face. That's how she saw herself, a fierce female warrior. If not King of the Jungle, a close second. Something smelled in this lioness though. He looked more closely and found a small pocket in its chest. Inside was a half-smoked joint. He laughed aloud and put it back. She must have left in a hurry.

God, is she really gone? What would happen to her? There was no end to danger out in the world. And Sarah was right when she said Linda had been sheltered. This room, this mansion she lived in is proof of that. Could she be the fierce fighter if she had to be? I want her back, home, and safe. If not that, she has to survive. What if I never see her again? My heart wouldn't be the same.

He walked around her room once more. The car keys were still sitting in the same spot. Her car! Had anyone searched her car? He took the keys and went to the garage. He didn't see Michael on the first floor and Sarah's Firebird was no longer in the driveway.

He opened the trunk of her car, but it was empty save the spare tire and tools for road emergencies. The backseat was empty too. He sat in the driver's seat. The car smelled like Linda. *Emeraude*, he thought it was. Wrapped around the rearview mirror was the tassel from her graduation a few weeks earlier. In the glove compartment, he found a small plastic figurine of Pinocchio that he'd given her. He squeezed it until his palm hurt and hot tears filled his eyes.

Where the hell are you, Linda?

Tom tried to keep his mind on his growing business. He had to hire more workers and their customer list tripled in the second year. Word had spread around Piedmont and similar areas that T&T was creating interesting and attractive spaces. But every little milestone they reached, wearing the new T-shirts Linda had designed, the ads she'd run that started paying off, it all reminded him of her.

He spoke to one of Linda's parents at least once a week. A truck driver had reported seeing a young woman in a brown South Dakota sweatshirt hitchhiking on Nebraska Highway 34 the same night Linda left. Tom remembered he'd lent Linda a sweatshirt like that a few weeks earlier and it hadn't been found in her room. But that was the last sighting they'd heard about.

About three weeks after Linda left, two men came to Tom's door about eight in the evening.

"Can I help you?" Tom asked.

The men pulled out badges. "I'm Agent Dulles and this is Agent Sweeney with the Federal Bureau of Investigation. May we come in and talk to you?"

Tom grimaced. "This is about Linda? Has she been seen?"

The two men came in and took a seat on his sofa. Tom remained standing, tapping his foot.

"Nothing solid yet. You are the only lead we can follow. She left a note saying she'd call you. Has she done that?" Agent Dulles asked.

Tom shook his head. "But I work from about eight until seven or so."

"We're gonna tap your phone, record any incoming calls. If you're not here to answer, by the third ring, it goes to an answering service. Maybe we'll catch a break." Dulles walked up to Tom's phone visible on the kitchen wall. He removed the receiver and noted the phone number written on the dial.

250

Agent Sweeney leaned forward. "If you do hear from her, keep her talking so we can do a trace. Ask where she is. Say anything to keep her on the line."

Tom paced and put his thumbs in his pockets. "How long is that going to go on?"

"Look, Kid. If you're not involved in this thing, you have nothing to hide." Agent Sweeney took out a cigarette. "Mind if I light this?"

Tom handed him an ashtray. "What do you mean involved?"

"You watch TV. Girl disappears, it's always the husband or the lover," Sweeney grinned. "Are the two of you lovers?"

Tom scowled. "Not recently. But you can't think I had something to do with her disappearance. I was just arriving in Lincoln when this happened. I want her to come back."

Dulles sat on the arm of the sofa. "Yeah, we did some checking. Your mom told us when you left her house."

"You talked to my mother? I haven't even told her about this!"

Sweeney shrugged. "We saved you the trouble. Part of our service. We wanted to let you know about the phone thing. When you're home, try to answer before three rings. Here's the answering service's number." Sweeney laid a business card on the coffee table with his contact information and wrote another phone number on the back. "They can tell you about calls you missed."

The two agents went to the door. Dulles stopped and turned back. "Oh, and the outgoing calls will be recorded too. So be nice when you call your mommy back tonight."

Tom heard them laughing as the door closed. He sank to the couch staring at the card.

CHAPTER THIRTY-SEVEN

June 20, 1988

Nancy was organizing the papers on her desk. It wasn't a big space, and easily became a catchall for clutter, especially with a family of five. One of the items she found that she had to file was Peter's birth certificate. Terry and Nancy's son, Peter Mark Thompson, had been born on January 15, 1982, but unlike the girls, she had never gotten around to getting a baby book to catalog his milestones. She had some of them listed on a paper and baby snapshots buried deeper in the desk.

Then she stumbled onto Linda's invitation. That was coming up soon. What was it that Linda planned to spring on them? And was there anything that Nancy had not shared with her high school best friend? There was one incident. The birth certificate triggered a memory.

It was one of those beautiful autumn days in 1986, nearly two years ago, where the temperature was just about perfect. Nancy had been outside raking leaves with the radio tuned to KFOR listening to the Nebraska Cornhuskers' football game. The third-ranked Huskers were playing a tough matchup against South Carolina. Four-year-old towhead Petey was jumping in the piles of leaves about as fast as she could rake. Terry was changing the oil in his Chevy pickup in the driveway.

Glenda Parker, Terry's sister, pulled up at the end of the driveway, and a sulking Jenny bailed out of the passenger seat. She lit into Nancy as soon as Glenda pulled away.

"Where's Allie?" Jenny demanded.

"She's in her room, reading a book." Nancy frowned at Jenny's outburst. Had she been such a moody teenager? "We told her to bring it out here, but she wanted—"

"Why have you two been lying to her? Why did you lie to me?" Jenny flung her arms out.

Terry shot his creeper out from under the truck to see what was going on.

Nancy felt an eerie reflection of her father at times when she butted heads with her teenager. "I don't know what you're talking about, Young Lady. Maybe we should take this inside if you're going to raise your voice."

Jenny took the hint and stormed into the house. Nancy shot a glance at Terry, then shrugged. Terry got up and put one grease-stained hand on the rake Nancy was holding.

"I'll keep the little one out of the street. You see what's eating her," Terry sighed.

When Nancy reached the kitchen, Jenny was pacing and making noises as she'd seen in cartoons where steam blew out of the character's ears.

"Enough theatrics! What happened at Glenda's house?" Nancy sat on a kitchen chair and picked up her forgotten glass of tea.

Jenny planted her palms on the tabletop. "Glenda finally told me the truth. She didn't want to, she said it was only speculation, but she's been suspicious for years."

Nancy rolled her eyes. "About what? Glenda has been known to believe the craziest gossip."

"About Allison!" Jenny's voice suddenly dropped in volume several notches.

"Allison?" Nancy studied Jenny's face before reacting.

"Grandma has a copy of her birth certificate. Terry is listed as her father. I thought my father, Peter, was Allie's father."

Nancy tried to slow her breathing. "When Allison was born, Peter was already dead. Terry was at the hospital with me, and the nurses assumed he was her father."

"But why wouldn't you correct them? It's okay to list a dead person as the father, isn't it? That must happen to other people."

"It seemed easier to let it go."

"I did the calculation. Peter died July 1, 1974. He would have been alive when Allie was conceived. Glenda said you went to be with him a few weeks before that in Hawaii."

"That's all true."

"I get that Allie will never know her father, and that's too bad. I barely remember my dad. The pictures you took in Germany are the only tangible evidence I have of him and me together."

"We have a few baby pictures of you with Pete," Nancy said. "They're in your baby book."

"But I don't remember being a baby. I remember a few things from when I was three. I remember the carousel he took me on that's in a photograph."

"You loved riding the horse on that carousel," Nancy smiled.

"But I remember I was scared at first. He held me on and told me he was there to protect me, I wouldn't fall. I always hoped he was still protecting me, even after he died."

Nancy's eyes filled at the memory. "He loved you in his own way."

"You loved each other, didn't you, Mom?"

"Yes, of course. Your father was my first love. He was bold and charming and had an enormous sense of duty, to his country, to his family. We grew up together. I'd hoped we grow old together."

"You never talk about him anymore."

"You can ask me anything about Peter, you know that."

"The two of you were still in high school when I was born?"

"Yes, I'm sure I mentioned that before."

"But now, I'm in high school. I know there are pregnant girls in my school. The administration still tries to expel them. It must have been so strange to be pregnant and go to school back then."

Nancy sighed. "I had to hide my pregnancy. I was lucky that you were born when spring break started. Your father was very excited to see you. I remember him kissing your forehead when you were about fifteen minutes old."

Jenny sat down at the table across from Nancy. "If you loved my father, how could you not put his name on his second child's birth certificate? It feels like you are taking away half of his legacy on earth."

Nancy studied her hands wrapped around the glass. Jenny deserved to know the truth.

"You are his legacy, Darling. The only child he had."

Terry appeared in the kitchen doorway then. The sound of a four-year-old could be heard running noisily to the bathroom.

"What's going on?" Terry said.

"You're saying Terry is Allison's father? Glenda was right?" Jenny's scowl bounced from Nancy's face to Terry's.

Terry furrowed his brows and took another seat at the table. "Yes, I am Allison's father. I thought you knew this."

"You let her call you Uncle Terry!"

"She called me that when she was little because you did. Once we got married, and I adopted you, you both called me Dad."

"But this doesn't add up. Weren't you married to my father when Allie was conceived?"

Terry drummed his fingers on the table. "They were separated.

I know you want to idolize your dad, but the truth is he chose to go back to Vietnam when he could have come back to the states and stayed with your mom and you. He could have been assigned to an army base, and he probably would have lived."

Jenny folded her arms. "You think it's his fault he died in the war? You showed me his last letter. He wanted us to be a family again. He even talked about another child. He still loved us."

"I know what that letter said," Nancy began. "But it isn't what he said to me in person in Hawaii. You have to understand what had been going on for the year before that. Peter decided before we left Germany that he was going to take another tour in Vietnam. He wanted to help with what he thought was a transition for the South Vietnamese to take over their struggle against the north, which was largely backed by the Chinese. The South Vietnamese lost their fight within a year or so.

"But I was unhappy that he chose to do that over returning to the states with us. I took you and left Germany to come home. We didn't communicate very much during that year until he asked me to meet him in Hawaii. I had been building a life here for myself and you. And Terry was someone I leaned on a lot. He filled in for Pete, trying to be a father to you. Terry and I fell in love. I still cared for your father, but we had drifted apart and our reunion didn't do much to help that. By the time I came back from Hawaii, I knew I had to divorce him."

"You were going to divorce him while he was in Vietnam? How cruel is that?"

Nancy got up and leaned on the sink with her back to Jenny.

Terry put his hand on Jennifer's shoulder but she pushed him away. "Jenny! It wasn't cruel. We both loved Peter very much. I grew up with him, and I knew how pigheaded he could be. He wasn't giving Nancy what she needed."

"So, you moved in on your brother's wife? You were sleeping

together while she was married to my father. Did you know that Glenda suspected the two of you were involved before that trip to Hawaii?"

"This isn't Glenda's business," Terry said. "We were only together once after Nancy came back from Hawaii and wrote to Peter to say she was going to divorce him. Then we got word that he'd been killed and we weren't together like that again for many months. I didn't even know about the pregnancy until Christmas."

"You let everybody think the baby was my father's. How were you planning on explaining this to him when he returned from the war?"

Nancy turned. "He was gone before I knew I was pregnant."

"I guess I inherited the pigheadedness. Cuz, I think what you both did was rotten." Jenny got up and went to her room. They heard a chirp indicating she picked up the phone extension in her room.

"Who is she calling?" Terry asked. Little Petey came in and sat on his father's lap.

Nancy shook her head. "Your sister, I suppose. Why would Glenda even discuss this with her?"

"Glenda's going through her own marital problems. Jeremy has been seeing that Darby woman again. She's probably angry about that."

"She should be angry about that. Not about something that happened twelve years ago to her brothers."

"I'm hungry!" Petey announced.

It was two days later before Jenny seemed willing to reopen the topic. Nancy went to her room in the evening while she was studying. She sat on the bed next to her daughter.

"You know your father and I did have some very good times.

Our first date was right about this time of year; homecoming when we were juniors. We were the same age as you, sixteen. He was tall, handsome, and so sweet to me. And before we could go on a date, he had to help your grandpa milk cows."

"I'm glad they don't have cows anymore. But Mom…how did you deal with it? You were pregnant with me as a teenager. You must have been six months pregnant when you got married. Then when you got pregnant with Allison, you were widowed. You could have married Terry right away but you didn't."

"No, it didn't feel right to do that. I don't think I can explain that, but everyone was still grieving for your dad. I wanted to wait. Then after a few years, getting married seemed less important."

"And even the third time you got pregnant, you hadn't married Terry yet. Didn't you always tell me not to put the cart before the horse?"

Nancy stroked Jenny's hair. "I know. My timing has been bad sometimes. But I have been really lucky to have three such awesome children. Are you gonna be okay?"

"I guess so. Glenda said I must be the most important person in the Thompson family because I belonged twice. Hardly anyone has two dads who were brothers. You are going to explain this to Allison though, aren't you? I don't want her to be confused."

"We will when she's a little older. Maybe you can be there to help us."

Jenny nodded. "I can if you want. You know sometimes I pretend that Terry is my real dad. They must have been alike in some ways."

"They were alike in all the ways that are good."

CHAPTER THIRTY-EIGHT

Tom awoke at five in the morning. It was raining hard. But he thought he heard another noise. Someone in the hall coming home drunk? It was the start of the Labor Day weekend and he had plenty to do before classes started next week. There was that noise again. Someone was knocking on his door.

He fumbled into his shorts and staggered to the door, hitting the living room light switch. If he'd been more awake, he wouldn't have flung the door open without wearing pants.

Linda stood before him, soaking wet. She wore his brown South Dakota sweatshirt over a long drab cotton dress, all of it drenched by the rain. Her dishwater blonde hair flowed in streaks down her shoulders. Even her knapsack was dripping.

At first, he thought he was dreaming. He hadn't plucked his glasses off the nightstand. Ten weeks with no word from her, no trace, no hope, no sign of life. But those delicate blue eyes pierced his consciousness. He pulled her to his body. Not only was she wet, but cold as ice. He closed the door as she slid her arms around him in a watery embrace.

"Thank God," he said, burying his face in her sodden hair. "You need a hot shower."

She complied when he began peeling off her clothes right there in front of the door where a puddle on the doormat was already seeping onto the linoleum. The sweatshirt landed atop the knapsack, the shapeless dress was so large on her, it came easily over her head. The color of the dress must have been lost on the color wheel between beige and khaki. Her panties were nothing like he'd seen on her before, or anyone really, too oversized to stay upright under her navel. He removed it all, even her soaked to squeaky tennis shoes.

He saw at once how thin she looked. Where her formerly trim

athletic body displayed muscle tone, her ribs and hips now protruded defiantly. She wasn't wearing a bra and her sternum seemed prominent between her smaller breasts.

"Have you eaten anything in the last few weeks?" Tom asked as he helped her to the bathroom.

"Food was scarce. I had no money."

He turned the shower on full blast to a hot setting, then tested the water before easing her in. He dropped his shorts on the floor and joined her.

Linda lifted her face to the spray and shivered. "I'm so cold and tired."

She made no move to reach for the soap or shampoo, so he took over. His sister had slept on his couch for two nights a month earlier and left some girly-smelling soap that he'd put on a higher shelf than his usual products. He used a washcloth to lather her back and worked his way down her body. He told himself this was like caring for a child but his libido was not easily fooled. She was too vulnerable to engage in any kind of sexual encounter, but his body was still reacting, and that was hard to hide.

When he turned her around to soap her front side, her eyes dropped to acknowledge his attraction. He poured shampoo into his hands and rubbed it into her hair. She closed her eyes and moaned slightly as if her hair had nerve endings. When she lifted her neck to rinse, her lips parted and the water formed a stream down her eyelashes and bottom lip. He'd never seen anything so sensuous. He ran his thumb over her mouth.

Desire ripped through him as his pelvis pushed her against the wall. His mouth found hers and his tongue searched for answers. She draped her arms around his back and gripped him tightly. When his hands slid down to grab her bottom, he was painfully aware that it had been more than a year since they'd been skin to skin.

260

Stop, stop, stop! This is a bad idea. She hasn't even told me where she's been. I have every right to be pissed as hell at her.

"I walked all the way from the bus depot," Linda whispered.

Tom nodded. He turned off the water and stepped out to gather towels. He wrapped one around each of them as they stood on the bathmat. "Do you want a towel for your hair?"

She didn't answer but took the towel he offered and wrapped her hair in a turban as he'd seen his sisters do. Then he dried himself off and when she stood there with water beading on her arms and legs, he dried her off too. He wasn't sure if she was playing a game to force him to keep touching her, but it was getting uncomfortable.

When he opened the bathroom door, she shuffled to the bedroom.

"Can I sleep in your bed?"

That was unexpected. It was nearly six by then, most people would be rising, not going to sleep.

"Sure. Here, do you want something to sleep in?" He grabbed one of the T-shirts she'd designed from his drawer. "Or maybe you have something in your bag?"

She slipped on the T-shirt, dropping the towel on the floor. "No. They stole my money and clothes, except that sweatshirt."

As if that explained everything. I don't know if I can stand to hear the rest.

She climbed into his bed and pulled the covers up around her tightly. Her hair was still encased in the towel. He moved toward the bed.

"I want to sleep in your bed by myself. It's been so long since I've been able to be in bed alone."

Tom stopped and frowned. What does that mean? She needed

261

to start explaining. But he took out clean shorts and another T-shirt from the drawer and put them on, settling onto a beanbag chair in the corner.

She closed her eyes and snuggled into the bed. After about a minute she looked at him again.

"What are you doing?" she asked.

"Watching."

She sat up and rubbed the towel over her hair, then finger-combed it. She folded the towel on top of the pillow and laid her head back on it. Then she smiled coyly and opened the bedding beckoning him in.

He got up slowly and climbed into bed with her. Within minutes, her wet hair was spread over his shoulder and chest, and Linda was asleep.

Tom must have dozed off too. When he looked at the bedside clock, it was almost eight. He carefully slid out from under her and grabbed his jeans. He was lucky he'd taken the day off.

After making instant coffee, he debated what his duty was regarding Linda's case. As far as he knew, the FBI was still tapping his phone. Should he reach out to them? They might charge in here and wake her up. No, her parents or that investigator at the police department should handle that. He wanted to tell her parents she was safe though. This whole ordeal had been at least as hard on them as it was on him. He'd even started feeling bad for her father.

He looked out the window, drinking his coffee. The storm had passed and the sun was emerging. He should make some breakfast. He watched someone using a payphone across the street in front of a gas station. Of course. He could call Linda's house from there.

On his way out, he put all of Linda's wet things in a trash bag to keep them from soaking his floors. He opened the knapsack, and it was empty.

"Good morning, Mrs. Bridges," Tom said when Mary Jo answered.

"Where are you, Tom? I hear traffic."

"I'm at a payphone. Listen, Linda showed up at my door a few hours ago."

"What? Oh, my goodness. That's wonderful. She made it back for school, didn't she? Is she okay? Can I talk to her?"

"Um, she seems to be fine but she's thin as a rail. She said they stole her money and clothes. I don't know who she was talking about. I let her take a shower and sleep at my apartment. I don't know how she got here or where she's been. I think we should let her sleep a couple of hours, then maybe you could bring her something to wear. I suppose she'll want to go home."

"Okay, right. I'll find something for her to put on. Give me directions to your apartment. Then I'll call before we leave."

"No, I don't think you should call my apartment today. Not until the FBI removes the phone tap. I assumed you'd want to talk to her before they did."

"Oh, you're right. Plan on us coming over at eleven thirty."

When Linda was still out at ten thirty, Tom made pancakes and bacon. The aroma brought her out to the kitchen in time to enjoy them. She still was only wearing the T-shirt which barely covered her bottom.

"Do you want something else to put on? I might have some long johns that would fit you."

She laughed. Man, it had been so long since he'd heard her laugh.

"Long johns? Who wears long johns? Aren't those the things with the drop bottom?"

"No. Well, maybe I am calling these the wrong name. I'm talking about thermal pants that are knit, and you wear them under your jeans when it is especially cold outdoors. Like when you have to feed the livestock and it's twenty below."

"Okay, let me see 'em. I guess you don't want to look at my legs."

He returned to his room for a pair of navy-blue thermal pants and tossed them to her. "It isn't that. Your parents will be here in a little while." He set a plate with pancakes and bacon in front of her.

She smiled and pulled on the pants. They were large but covered her. "You called my folks?"

"They've been sick with worry. So have I. Where did you disappear to?" Tom had already finished half of his breakfast but brought it to the coffee table.

She sighed. "I went to the Haight. Always thought that would be cool." She poured syrup on her food and started eating.

"The Haight?"

"Haight-Ashbury. It's in San Francisco. Right near the Golden Gate bridge. It was an interesting mix of people. Hippies mostly, but lots of tourists. I thought about asking a tourist to give me a ride back home."

"How did you get there?"

"I hitchhiked. The first guy who gave a ride was nice, but he was only going to Laramie. The next guy was creepy and I had to hide from him in the ladies' room at a truck stop. He stayed there for ten hours, sleeping in his truck. He wanted me to go to bed with him. I finally got a ride with someone else."

Tom frowned. "That's why hitchhiking is dangerous especially for young girls alone."

264

She waved away his concern. "I was so happy when I finally got to Haight-Ashbury. I had a little money but the hotel rooms were exorbitant. I had to find a room to rent. Then I met these young people who said they lived in a commune. They came to the park near the bridge every day and entertained people for donations. I went to stay with them. It wasn't as perfect as they made it sound.

"I tried to keep an open mind. I was there to experience new things. There were four men and five girls living there. And three young kids who were mostly in a bedroom in the back of the house. They had four mattresses on the floor in the main living area, all lined up together. All of the adults slept there. They called it a love-in. The first night, they passed a pipe around, some sort of drug. I don't know what it was, but I started seeing things that weren't there. They had grass too. I remember lying on the mattress, and everyone kissing me and you know, stuff. I didn't know what was real. But it didn't take long to discover that the men went with men and women and so did the women."

"What? The men were homosexuals?"

"They were all you know, with everyone. I don't know what you'd call it. An orgy maybe? They all seemed to not care who they were kissing or where."

Tom shuddered. "This didn't freak you out? Didn't you try to escape?"

"When I was under the drugs, no, it didn't. But then the next morning, I wasn't sure this was for me. Especially when I discovered they'd stolen my money and my clothes. When I asked for them back, one of the men said I had to work to support the commune. I was lucky I brought my baton. They had me perform and tourists would throw money in a hat."

"Why didn't you call home or call me? We would have gotten you home."

"At first they watched me all the time. There was this one guy with long hair and a dark beard, Charley. Everyone seemed afraid of him. He never let me out of his sight for the first few weeks. After that, I did try calling you twice. The first time, no one answered. The second time, a woman answered and it sounded like she said a company name so I hung up. I thought you changed your number. I could only call during the daytime."

"The FBI tapped my phone, hoping you'd call and they could trace you."

"The FBI? I haven't broken any laws." She waved her fork around with a bite of pancake on it.

"No, but we were afraid you'd been kidnapped or something."

"I wasn't able to leave when I wanted to. The men told us where to go and what to do. Then they tried to drug the girls so they wouldn't resist. When I said I didn't want to smoke the pipe, one of them hit me. I had to play along for a while. The only time I saw any money was when I was performing. I started hiding some of my earnings, which wasn't easy because they made me wear a two-piece swimming suit to perform in. They thought I would make more money that way."

Tom's eyes widened. "I didn't think it was that hot in San Francisco."

"It wasn't most days. I froze or I got sunburned. It took me weeks to stash away enough to buy a bus ticket. Then I went to a women's shelter and they gave me that dress to wear. I've been on a bus or waiting in a bus station for the past three days."

"This sounds horrific. But you're the one who took off and put yourself in danger. I don't know if you understand the effect this had on me or your family. I don't know how you expect me to trust you."

Linda stopped eating. "You don't trust me? You're not my parent."

"If I'm in love with you, the least I would expect is that you try to take care of yourself."

"I don't want to talk about this anymore, okay? I wanted to get back before college classes began. It's time for me to get back to normal. So, you can stop worrying about me, old man."

Tom stood up, put his plate in the sink, and ran water over it. Maybe Linda was too unconventional for him.

They didn't talk much after that. Her parents came and fussed over her and took her away. When he went back to his room, he found the T-shirt and the thermal pants on the floor. Why did he feel like he'd lost her all over again?

CHAPTER THIRTY-NINE

Tom didn't call Linda all week. It was a busy first week of classes and he still had lawn work scheduled around his classes. He figured she needed to spend time with her parents and recover.

No, that was an excuse. His neck muscles tensed every time he thought about her behavior. Had he said or done something to make her think this was acceptable? Was it all a reaction to her disillusionment with her father?

She'd been so reckless. She paid some consequences apparently and he wasn't very comfortable with any of those details either. But she still didn't seem to understand his feelings about it even now. And worse, she didn't seem to care.

Saturday night, and he had plans. There was a street dance on campus and he was meeting Trey and a few other guys. It was tough being twenty when you couldn't get served at a bar under twenty-one, but a street dance was a chance to meet a few girls who were probably in the same situation. So, he'd cleaned up after working all day and put on some new clothes. "Back to school clothes" his mother would have called them. He was hoping they were "time to get laid again" clothes.

Not that he'd been living like a monk this summer. First, there was Tina, a neighbor girl Trey had hired, who developed an instant crush on Tom. She'd cornered him in the back of the greenhouse the first week she worked there and kissed him silly. It seemed natural when things progressed at his apartment a few days afterward. What seemed odd was that she quit her job a week later. Then he looked at her employment application and discovered she was, yeah, seventeen. Not again.

And he found out that there was a reason for the cliché about middle-aged housewives. Muriel was not only looking for a greener lawn, but greener pastures, and thought Tom was it. He assumed Muriel was a young widow until her ex-husband showed up as he was finishing trimming her hedgerow.

Tom was about to leave when someone knocked on his door. Linda was back, only this time, she was dressed to the nines. Her hair had been trimmed and styled, and maybe even lightened. She had a face full of makeup, more than he'd seen on her. It made her eyes stand out and her lips practically glow. And then there were those impossibly tight blue jeans and towering sandals with cork soles which made her legs look even longer than usual. Her ruffly red blouse seemed to catch reflections from every source of light and bounced it back to her blushing cheeks. If he'd thought she looked anemic a week ago, she was the picture of health and energy now.

It was such a contrast that he could only admire her for a moment, as she waltzed into his apartment without an invitation.

Tom cleared his throat. "I was going out. What's up?"

"You have a date, Tom? You do look nice. I've never seen you wear a button-down shirt. Is it new?"

He narrowed his eyes. "Yeah, new shirt. What are you doing here?"

She sat down on his couch and curled one leg under her. "I haven't heard from you. I thought you might be mad. I know I was kind of a downer last time I saw you. But I feel much better now that I am eating healthy food and taking vitamins. And I like my classes so far. College is much more exciting than high school."

He sat next to her. He supposed they might as well have a frank discussion tonight as another time. If only her intoxicating scent didn't make his head start swimming. "Look, I've been thinking about what you told me and the way you ran off and—"

"Isn't that water under the bridge? We're finally in the same school. Do you want to go see what's happening downtown? Or maybe we should catch up with each other. Tell me about what's happened with your business."

He sighed. "I don't want to talk about work right now. Although, business has been booming. And we sold all of those extra T&T Lawnscapes T-shirts you ordered. I never would have guessed women would want shirts with a photo of Trey and me on them."

Linda turned her body toward him and put one hand on his chest. "That's because you were wearing tight white undershirts and you were all sweaty and dirty like you'd put in a hard day toiling away in the sun. That photo was very sexy. I told you it would sell."

Tom looked at her hand and then took hold of it. "Linda, we need to have some kind of understanding here. I'm still pretty upset about what you did this summer. You weren't thinking about me, your parents or even your friends. We all thought something terrible might have happened to you. I don't know if I can be in a relationship with someone that cavalier. Or someone who wants to take risks with her safety."

She cocked her head and lowered her lashes. "I thought you wanted to live a little dangerously. I thought I was dragging you down because I was too young."

"No," he said crinkling his brow. "Well, maybe too young for some things."

"I'm grown up now, well sort of. Maybe it freaked you out hearing about me using drugs and doing that love-in thing. But I got that out of my system. Not doing that again. I'm sorry if I scared you." She pulled her hand back and put both of them around his neck, climbing into his lap.

"You know you could have some residual effects from that. How do you know you're not pregnant? Those men in the commune could have had diseases, you know, that you could have gotten."

"You think I picked up an STD? Jeez, I hope not. But not

pregnant, I'm sure. The only thing I held onto was my birth control pills. Which was lucky considering I didn't know who was doing what to me most of the time."

"See that's the kind of statement that scares the shit outta me." Tom slid her back taking her face in his hands. "And makes me angry too. You acted like you were afraid of sex after you had the abortion, and now you tell me you had no problem having some sort of orgy with strangers. I don't get that at all."

She smiled. "How do you know I didn't make that up?"

He blinked. "You made it up? Why would you do that?"

"I just said, how do you know? You're pretty gullible."

"Gullible? What I am is trusting. If I can't trust you, I can't be with you. Tell me what happened in that commune."

Linda pursed her lips. "I did tell you, what I remember. A lot of it is a drug-induced haze. I had no choice. Not about the drugs or the sex. But I think I could have imagined part of it. And now you think I'm tarnished somehow, don't you?"

"No, not...tarnished. I feel like you're not always telling me the truth."

"I have told you the truth. You don't like the truth, isn't that the problem?"

He leaned his head back on the couch. "I guess that's accurate. That doesn't mean you shouldn't stick to the truth."

"You know," Linda said, dropping her hands to his shirt and unbuttoning the top few buttons. She smiled when she saw his bare chest. "I came over here to have a little fun. I thought we could both use that."

"Fun? What kind of fun?" He could feel his irritation fading as her fingers roamed down his midline.

She dropped her voice to barely above a whisper. "The kind of fun you've been angling for since we got back together last winter. I was planning it for your birthday in July, but I missed that. Tell me it's not too late."

He didn't resist this time when she offered her lips to him. He tugged his open shirt out of his jeans.

"You sure about this, Linda?" He slid her off his lap onto her back and leaned over her. In response, she unbuttoned her own blouse and revealed a new pushup bra in a colorful purple and red print.

"It's time, Baby," she said.

"Way past time!" he said, pulling her shirt apart. He planted a kiss on her stomach.

Sometimes you have to live in the moment. What's the worst that could happen?

CHAPTER FORTY

July 8, 1986

Linda opened the box of floating water-lily candles, and placed each one on a table next to the pool. She had many things to do before her guests arrived later that evening, but some of them couldn't be done too far in advance.

She heard the noise of the trimmer and glanced over to the elaborate garden that Tom had designed. He was doing some trimming and weeding, and their son, Matthew, now fifteen, was mowing the lawn. The gazebo where their wedding had taken place was centered in the garden.

She was setting up tables in the recreation room when Tom came in. He was shirtless, sweat glistening on his chest. He pulled the bandana he'd wrapped around his forehead off and mopped the sweat dripping into his eyes and fogging his glasses. They were wire-rims now, lighter weight, but more apt to get damaged with work like he did today. Linda thought he was even more handsome than the day they'd gotten married, with specks of gray invading his dark tousled hair and the more mature and powerful build of a man, not the boy she'd gotten involved with.

Someone should be tapping that. I guess I had my chance.

"You ready for tonight?" he asked.

"I think so. The caterers are bringing the food at six, it should be a pretty simple setup."

"No, I mean are you READY for tonight?" Tom scrutinized her face.

Linda sighed. "I don't know. I'm still rehearsing the speech in my head. I'm afraid it will come out all wrong."

"Nah, you'll be fine. These are your oldest friends. What are they going to say?"

"I know. I keep telling myself they'll understand. I guess you did."

He shrugged. "I'm leaving. Matt is about half-done with the yard. Have a nice party."

She sat down on the new sectional she'd bought last year. Matt and his friends had enjoyed many parties down in this rec room watching games around the big television. Linda had purchased the house from her father when he relocated to Chicago to be CEO of an even larger conglomerate. Her mother was now back in Atlanta, and Sarah and Gavin had moved to Kansas City. When they had a chance to get together, they all enjoyed coming back to her childhood home.

It was a familiar setting for her high school friends to return to as well. It was time to discuss how their lives evolved.

CHAPTER FORTY-ONE

May 18, 1973

"I wish Nancy was here," Linda said as Sarah released the hot rollers that were turning Linda's long fine air into a cascade of full blonde curls. The highlights Sarah had insisted Linda needed adding to the shimmer and texture. Sarah ran her fingers through Linda's curls to intensify the frothy fullness. Then she enveloped Linda's tresses in a cloud of hairspray.

"If you waited to get married until Nancy got back from Germany, that baby would have already arrived," Debbie said. "And I would have moved to South Carolina." She posed in front of Linda's full-length mirror sashaying in her long pink muslin dress featuring a square neckline and fagoting stitches connecting ever-widening tiers under the empire waist.

Yvonne sat in one of Linda's overstuffed chairs with her bare feet propped on the antique coffee table. She was wearing a dress matching Debbie's in yellow. "I am happy for you and Tom, and that you are having this baby," she said.

"It's a little crazy, even for me," Linda admitted. "I still have nearly a year left on my undergrad degree, then three more years before I can practice dentistry. But Tom was confident we could make it work since he's finished school. His sister, Theresa graduated last week, and she'll help with babysitting too. I suppose we'll have to juggle."

Sarah was patiently trying to apply eye makeup onto Linda. "Why did you never learn to be serene and relaxed like a lady?" Sarah held Linda's chin with her hand while she applied mascara.

"Not my nature, Sarah. You must have figured that out by now."

"Okay, done. You can blink." Sarah leaned back and put the makeup away. She was wearing a bridesmaid's dress like the

275

others only in baby blue.

Linda stood facing the mirror and smoothed her hands over her slightly-protruding belly. Her ecru cotton lace and muslin dress was in a style similar to the bridesmaids' dresses, with an empire waist, exaggerated bell sleeves, ruffles around the neck, and a lace-up bodice. Only her mother could find a designer wedding gown that looked so Bohemian. It fit Linda to perfection.

The florist came in and placed flower crowns on each of their heads. Linda's was mostly white miniature roses and baby's breath. The others had a mixture of pink, blue and yellow. The bridesmaids didn't have to carry bouquets, Linda figured they were wearing them. But she carried a single long-stemmed red rose. It had become almost a running joke between her and Tom and represented the first flower he'd ever given her.

The garden Tom had created in the side yard of her parents' home was a testament to his love and talent as a landscaper. In front of a stately white gazebo, Tom had planted a mixture of tulips, daffodils, and iris so something would be blooming throughout the spring. Beyond the gazebo were raised beds with a mixture of flowering and variegated perennials and ornamental grasses. A path of pavers led from the swimming deck to the gazebo itself, which would serve as the aisle. The gazebo had been adorned with climbing roses and ivy by the florist since it was too early for natural blooms.

There were folding chairs set up for the seventy-five guests they'd invited, including Tom's family from Gordon. Tom had even invited Buck Henderson and his new wife, and they came from Montana. There was guitar music provided by a couple of friends of Tom's, along with a drummer.

When it came time to walk down the aisle, they played "You Are the Sunshine of My Life," a recent hit by Stevie Wonder. Linda insisted the bridesmaids dance and twirl down the aisle and it made everyone laugh. Linda wanted to do that too, but she hadn't convinced Michael Bridges who would be escorting her. She compromised and let her dad sing to her all the way to the front. She couldn't keep a straight face.

Tom was wearing a black tux, black cowboy boots, and a new white Stetson, his formal hat, he called it. The groomsmen, Trey, Jerry, and Brent were all wearing white dinner jackets and black pants. The officiant was from Tom's home church in Gordon, and he was a good-humored, good ol' rancher friend of the Case family.

When Linda got to the gazebo, Tom took her hand and said, "You're barefoot!"

She laughed. "Barefoot and pregnant." The guests chuckled, but most of them already knew about her condition.

The ceremony was informal, with the minister making a few jokes along with his good wishes for the couple. The musicians sang the Carpenters' "We've Only Just Begun" as they left the gazebo. The contrast between Linda's wedding and her sister Sarah's was apparent. Sarah and Gavin were wed in a church and the reception was at a country club. There were 250 guests, many of whom were Michael Bridges' business associates. Linda wanted things kept as fun and casual as possible.

Tom's only demand was that he could dance to some country music. The reception was around the pool area, and a parquet floor covered some of the cement for better dancing. They did their first dance to Loretta Lynn's "Love is the Foundation." Jerry Case had been charged with playing individual tracks on the albums the bride and groom wanted to hear on the Bridges' stereo system, which had multiple speakers in the pool area.

After the newlyweds were toasted with champagne, they mingled with the guests. Tom hadn't had a chance to talk to Buck before he and Linda greeted him.

"Tommy, this is my wife, Geraldine. She was my sponsor in

AA. I got my three-year chip a few months ago," Buck said proudly.

"That's marvelous, Buck," Tom said. "I'm glad you're doing so well. Nice to meet you, Geraldine. And I guess you've figured out that this is my wife, Linda. Boy, does that sound funny!"

"Get used to it, Husband." Linda elbowed him. "And you're Buck. Tom told me about you. How do you feel about being a grandfather?"

Buck sucked in his breath. He glanced at Geraldine, then at Tom, and back to Linda. "I guess I never thought about it."

Tom tightened his grip on Linda's hand. "I guess genetically, she's right. This little bugger might look like you."

Geraldine smiled. She was maybe five years younger than Buck. She had a calm manner that was probably crafted by years of turmoil. "I know it would mean the world to Buck if you let the child know him, even if it is long-distance."

Tom stiffened. "I think we might be open to something like that. No reason we couldn't send you some photos."

Linda reached out and took Buck's hand and put it on her belly. "Just there. Hold it still," she said.

Buck's eyes widened. "It moved! I think I felt it move."

Linda's eyes crinkled. "I think there's something in there!"

Tom shook his head. "She makes me do that every night in bed. And it's not really where I want to put my hands."

"Tom, stop!" she said hustling him away. "You're a married man now. You can't go around talking like a sex-crazed teenager."

"Oh, I think married men get to be even more sex-crazed," he laughed and kissed her. The guests started cheering. "See what I mean?"

They danced, drank, and laughed until midnight. Robert and

278

Debbie polished off some of their old dance steps. Yvonne and Trey initiated a limbo contest, and Linda managed to win it, even though she was nearly six months pregnant. Sarah and Gavin demonstrated the waltz they did at their wedding. Tom and his family tried to teach the others to do the Swing.

And when they decided they'd better call it quits before the neighbors complained about noise, Jerry stepped up to his brother. "Tom, I think you'd better practice carrying your bride over the threshold."

"Practice? Why should I practice?" Tom laughed.

"Well, she is a little heavier now that she's got a passenger on board. And you're probably not nearly as strong as you were when you had to do heavy farm chores every day," Jerry smirked.

"Hell, I'm stronger than I was when I was doing ranch chores. I've got to load pavers and soil and all sorts of heavy stuff. And Linda still weighs about as much as a twelve-year-old."

"Okay, show us," Jerry said. "Pick her up!"

Suddenly this was a chant. Most of the guests still in attendance joined in saying, "pick her up!"

Tom shrugged. They were standing near the pool, but he swept Linda off her feet in a traditional bridegroom's carry. "See, not that difficult." Jerry and Brent lurched forward. Tom started to back up but he was too late. Tom and Linda went tumbling into the swimming pool.

They came up sputtering. "You okay, Baby?" he asked his bride.

Linda laughed. She turned to her attendants. "Don't stand there. Come and join us!"

Tom leaped up and grabbed Jerry's leg and pulled him in. Yvonne and Trey jumped in laughing. Soon, there were a dozen people in the pool, fully dressed.

"I think this means it's time to go home," Mary Jo announced surveying the chaos. There are extra pieces of cake wrapped up if anyone wants to take some home. I can't do much to help you with your wet clothes but we have some pool towels you can use on your way."

The official wedding photographer had left, but there were plenty of Instamatic shots of the wedding party in the pool.

"Mrs. Case, I don't think anyone will forget our wedding," Tom said as he shook the water out of his tuxedo jacket.

"Funny," Linda said, "That's exactly what I was hoping for."

CHAPTER FORTY-TWO

January 1974

Linda rocked baby Matthew in the maple rocking chair her parents had bought for them last summer. She could put him down on his mattress most nights without rocking him, he understood it was time to sleep. But she relished the closeness of a warm baby on her shoulder. He smelled like formula and baby shampoo and made little gurgling noises as he drifted into slumberland. It was a good way to relieve stress for both of them.

She never expected to enjoy being married or having a child. It went against what she thought she wanted from life: freedom, financial security, and meaningful work. It was love that changed her mind. She'd underestimated love.

And this little bundle certainly personified love. To carry a child inside you and then watch him change daily was much more enchanting than she imagined. When she looked at her baby, she saw Tom's features first and foremost. She supposed that was common with sons. But there was a certain orneriness to his expressions that made her identify with him. Tom complained the baby waited until you changed his diaper and then soiled it as soon as you picked him up, as a prank.

She had to grab these moments of joy. She knew she'd taken on a lot when she went back to school three weeks after giving birth. Tom tried to do paperwork at home in the mornings while she went to class, then his sister, Theresa, or another caretaker they'd hired came in for a few hours until she got home in mid-afternoon. She'd try to study and prepare dinner while caring for a newborn. It was difficult, but she'd had to balance priorities before.

Tom seemed to be very happy with this arrangement. She'd never wanted to cook but found herself reading through the Betty Crocker cookbook she'd received, and trying out recipes. It wasn't as difficult as she'd expected. She always thought her mother created magic in her kitchen; turns out she simply followed directions well.

Tom had purchased snowplows for their fleet of landscaping trucks, so after a snowfall, he rose in the pre-dawn hours to help plow parking lots. He'd also learned to be a tax accountant, and spent the winter months helping clients with tax returns. He often helped the same customers with their landscaping and their taxes. She had to admire how enterprising he was. He'd find work to do in any economy.

And she knew he loved her. She often wondered about her parents' marriage once she'd realized that her father had been unfaithful over and over again. Did her mother feel alienated by his betrayal, or had she come to accept it as the price she paid for a lovely home and two children? She knew her mom was able to go to any store in town and charge things on credit or write checks as she pleased, never worrying about having enough money to cover her expenses.

But did Mary Jo ever feel emotionally bankrupt? When she retired to her bedroom early in the evenings, was she enjoying a book? Or crying into her pillow?

Linda laid the sleeping infant on his tummy in the crib, as Dr. Spock recommended, and covered him with a comforter. She hoped her connection to her child would be more open and honest. They needed to be able to share their feelings, especially as he got older and dealt with the pressures of a complicated life.

Tom was in the living room when she closed the door partway on her son.

"Did he settle down okay?" Tom asked, patting the couch next to him.

"Out like a light." She snuggled in next to him. "Tom, how do you think our marriage is going so far?"

282

He laughed. "You want a critique? I think we are doing pretty well to keep our heads above water. I mean, in the last year, we got engaged, found out you were pregnant, got married, had a baby, and moved into a house. And you kept going to college and I kept my businesses afloat. That's a lot for two people. I'd give us at least a B plus."

She nodded. "I suppose we have accomplishments. But tell me how you feel about it."

His brows knit. "I dunno. I guess I'm proud that we pulled it off. What is it you want me to say?" He put his arm around her and pulled her closer.

"Are you glad we got married? Would you do all of that over again if you had a chance?"

He started. "Of course. I assumed we'd get married after we were together for a few years. It's kind of what people do after college. They get married, raise a family, buy a house. Didn't you expect to do that?"

She turned to face him. "No. I didn't. I realized that I needed to have a good job to have what I wanted in life, so going to school all these years seemed like a necessary concession. I thought I'd be traveling in my spare time. Or racing cars, jumping out of planes, something crazy. It seems very odd to me that I am married and have a baby. That is so conventional. So old-fashioned."

"Well, I like it. It feels normal. I like having a wife to wait on me when I get home from work." Tom was trying to hide a smile.

"Don't even start with that. Tomorrow, you can cook. Maybe I'll hit the bars after class."

"Just kidding. You know that." He pulled her into his lap. "Linda, you're happy with where we landed, aren't you?" She looked at his serious eyes as he took off his glasses and set them on the coffee table at their feet. Before she could answer, he pushed her down on the couch and crawled on top of her. "The best part is that we get to do this whenever we want." He kissed her softly, then more deeply. "You want to be unconventional? We could have sex in the living room. How about the kitchen table?"

She laughed. That wasn't what she had in mind. Sex between married people seemed conventional no matter where it was. She loved her husband. She loved her home and child. So, what was she missing?

CHAPTER FORTY-THREE

October 1977

"What do you mean, you want a divorce?" Tom asked. They were sitting in the living room after putting four-year-old Matthew to bed like they'd done countless nights before. Almost every night since they'd purchased a three-bedroom house on Eastridge Drive four years earlier.

Tom set his glass of wine down on the end table. "Is this one of those things you cooked up in a therapy session?"

Linda scooted into the corner of the large sofa, pulling her legs next to her and barricading herself with a throw pillow. "No. I have to change therapists. Dr. Heller is finding someone new for me."

Tom scowled, "So you're quitting your therapist and your husband? When are you going to figure out that the problem isn't your relationships? The problem is you."

Linda sighed. "I know the problem is me. I'm in love with Dr. Heller."

Tom started, staring at her. "Oh." He looked at the ceiling. "This is one of those things we saw on TV where the doctor helps the patient and they think it's love but it's really gratitude, appreciation. What did they call it? Transference."

Linda cupped her jaw in her hand with her elbow on her knee. "She said the same thing. And I know Dr. Heller is married to a man. But when I told her I had a romantic attraction to her, she said I needed a new therapist. Someone who is a specialist in this area."

"A romantic what? I guess Dr. Heller is rather nice-looking. I don't think of her that way. But how could you have any feelings of attraction to her? She's a woman."

"Yes, Tom. I'm trying to tell you I'm attracted to women."

"No, Baby. This must be some new phase of your neurosis rearing its ugly head. Surely Dr. Heller told you that."

Linda waited, hoping he'd start processing her words. She had been battling depression on and off since the baby was born, but the medication she'd been on had helped her cope with the usual routines in her life. But over the past several months, she'd realized she hadn't been as excited about their love-making as she had been previously. She'd been attributing that to the stress of graduating from dental college and joining a busy practice.

But when she realized she wanted more from Dr. Heller than treatment, she thought she was having a breakthrough. It wasn't Tom's fault. He had been patient and caring. Which was why she had to set him free. But how could she make him understand?

"Dr. Heller said there are women who prefer other women like there are men who would rather have another man as a partner. She said some doctors will try to 'cure' the patient if they don't want to accept this about themselves. But other therapists can help the patient explore their feelings and try to find relationships where they can be fulfilled."

Tom stood up and walked away from her, raking his hands through his hair. "No, no, Linda. This is just the latest kooky thing you want to try. Didn't the doctor tell you your medication might affect your sex drive? I think that might be what this is about. Maybe you need to stop taking that." He turned back to her and his face sagged. He blinked slowly. "I know you haven't been as eager in bed for a while, but you used to be happy. It's probably some hormonal problem."

"My sex drive is alive and well, thank you. It's now redirected."

Tom sat back down and faced her. "I still don't understand."

Linda pressed her lips together. She loved her husband. There was no way she could avoid causing him this pain.

"I want to be with women. I want to give you a chance to find a woman who wants to be with you."

He narrowed his eyes. "But you can't have sex with another woman. You know that, right? It's obvious."

"I can and I have."

His eyes widened. "What? But uh…that's kind of missing the point. Literally."

Linda put her legs back on the floor and leaned forward, putting her hands on his. "The point, as you put it, is somewhat different for men than it is for women. You can't conceive a child with another woman, but you can have enjoyment, you can reach—"

Tom put his hand up to stop her. "Wait. You're saying…I didn't think you wanted me to do that…thing. But if you want to try something different…"

"Tom, no. You're not hearing me. You're a man. I need to be with a woman."

He shook his head. His shoulders tensed and his eyes grew cold. "This is not happening," he hissed. "You absolutely need a new shrink." He got up and picked up his jacket that was lying on a kitchen chair. He started toward the carport.

"Where are you going?' Linda asked.

"Out. I dunno. I need some space." He went out the door to the carport and she heard the car start. They'd traded in his Jeep for a station wagon after Matthew was born but he mostly drove a pickup with his company logo on it.

Linda pressed her fingers to her eyes. This was going to take time. She couldn't expect him to change his mindset quickly. It had taken her months, after all. But at least she'd been honest. He'd always asked her to be honest.

CHAPTER FORTY-FOUR

Tom gritted his teeth. He didn't want to be here. Walking on hot coals sounded more comfortable.

"Linda tells me you're having trouble accepting that she wants to be with women. Is that how you feel, Tom?" Linda's new therapist, Sue Hastings, looked at him over her reading glasses.

He studied Ms. Hastings. She wasn't a medical doctor or a Ph.D. Linda said her specialty was validating and advocating for patients with sexual orientation issues. Whatever that meant. And this therapist was at least forty-five years old and he would describe her as frumpy. He didn't think Linda was going to be having any sordid thoughts about this one.

"You haven't known Linda very long," he began. "She has impulsive tendencies. Did she tell you about the time she hitchhiked to California and lived in a commune?"

"Do you think this is an impulse for her?" Ms. Hastings asked.

Linda was seated next to him on the couch in the therapist's office. She shook her head slightly.

Tom grimaced. "I don't think Linda knows what this is. She hasn't thought this through. I'm not going to break up our marriage and then find out six months later she's come to her senses." He tapped his boot rapidly on the braided area rug. "Especially when there is a little boy involved."

"Fair enough," the therapist said.

"Tom comes from a conservative family out in the Sandhills. Even the idea of getting a divorce seems revolutionary to him," Linda said.

"We've only been married four years," he said. "Couples go through rough patches."

"Is that what you think this is?" The therapist wrote something in her notebook.

Linda rolled her eyes.

"All I know is that what she has told me so far doesn't make sense. She wants to be with women. I don't know what that even looks like. Does she want to date women or live with other women? She even implied she'd sleep with women. How would she do any of that with a four-year-old boy living with her? I mean this could have some real consequences for a child."

"Matthew wouldn't know anything different is going on." Linda sat up straighter.

"He would notice if his father wasn't living with him." Tom felt his throat closing up on him as heat sprang to his eyes.

"Tom, I should tell you that my role is not to be a marriage counselor. You may want to go to marriage counseling," Ms. Hastings said. "I am trying to help Linda make you understand her position, her feelings, and how they may have changed where you're concerned."

"See that's another thing I don't get. She was attracted to me. The first time we had sex she was only seventeen and she was into it even then. She did go through a phase after she had an abortion where she wanted to be celibate. But then we started sleeping together again and it seemed pretty normal to me. I mean, I was with other women before we married. I know when someone is interested. I don't believe she's been faking it. Although, since Matt was born, it's been kind of off and on. I thought it was due to her depression and the meds she was taking."

"Did it occur to you that she was questioning her sexual orientation during those times you thought she was uninterested?"

"No, that never crossed my mind. I still think it could be a chemical imbalance or hormones." Tom furrowed his brows. "I'm not a goddamned doctor, how do I know what's wrong with her?"

Both Linda and Ms. Hastings drew in a breath simultaneously.

The therapist leaned forward. "Are you saying that if your wife prefers women over men, if she is, in fact, a homosexual, there is something wrong with her?"

Tom sniffed. "Is that a trick question?" He stood up and crossed his arms. "Hell yes, that means there's something wrong with her."

Linda threw up her hands in the therapist's direction as if to say, "I told you."

Tom's glare swept from Ms. Hastings to Linda. "I'm getting the feeling that you two don't care what I think or how much this is hurting me. You want to convince me I'm the one who's in the wrong."

Linda stood up and put a hand on his back. "I don't want this to hurt you, Tom. I want to stop hurting you. I want you to understand so you can move on."

He took hold of her arms. "I don't want to move on. I love you. I want what we had again. I don't want to get a divorce. Why do you think that what you want matters more than what I want?"

A tear rolled down her cheek. She let him pull her to his chest.

The therapist cleared her throat. "Maybe there are some ways you could ease into this situation. I know this will sound unorthodox, but maybe Linda could go out on a date with a woman while you're living under the same roof. Or have you started seeing someone, Linda?"

Tom pulled back and studied her face.

"No, I'm not dating anyone. I had what you might call a one-night stand, but I didn't expect anything permanent to come from that. I'm not even sure how to meet other women who might be receptive."

Tom turned around and walked to the window. The therapist's office was in her basement, so the window was mostly obscured by a window well. His voice was just above a whisper. "You're killing me here."

Linda tapped a finger over her lips. "See this is why your suggestion wouldn't work. He'd be upset or jealous and we'd end up fighting."

Tom scoffed. "Maybe I'm the one who should go out with another woman. I know where to find one who would enjoy the company of a man. Pretty much any bar in town."

"I couldn't blame you," Linda said.

Tom turned back to the women. He felt the flush igniting his face. "And then all of a sudden, I'm the bad guy. I'm the cheater. The way I see it, I'm screwed no matter what happens, and not in a fun way." Tom walked back to the couch and picked up his T&T ball cap he'd left there. "Ms. Hastings, I appreciate that you were trying to help, but I don't feel like we made any progress. I'll start looking for somewhere else to live. Don't expect me to be there when this whole fantasy life of yours blows up, Linda."

CHAPTER FORTY-FIVE

Linda sat on a folding chair in a circle of twelve women in a church basement. She studied them as they introduced themselves. All of them appeared to be older than she was, some in their fifties, others in their forties or thirties. They were all shapes and sizes, one Black lady, one of Asian descent, some thin, others plump, some attractive, and one person Linda couldn't determine whether they were male or female. Androgenous, she thought was the word to describe them.

"Welcome to our group," one of the older ladies began. "We operate a little like Alcoholics Anonymous. We don't have an addiction of course, but we share our stories about how to navigate the world where 'heteros' are the majority. Feel free to ask questions; we're here to help each other. We suggest you do not give out your full name. You can use a complete alias or use your first name and no last name. There may be other life details you want to keep to yourself too. It's okay. That being said, the girls here know me as Monica."

"My name is Linda," she said. "I am very new at this, so I hope to learn from your experiences. I don't even know how to meet someone whom I might want to date."

"It's not easy," a woman who called herself Ann said. "Most of us have partners now or have had one. I'm pretty sure there are a few bars and coffeehouses in Omaha that are hubs for lesbians. I think I have the names of those written down at home."

A younger woman called Sylvie told her, "Sometimes there are private parties. I can get you invited to some of those. They're usually in Omaha or Papillion, in the metro area. Gay men come to the parties too. We generally have a blast."

"Are you married or do you have children?" Bonnie asked.

"I'm married, recently-separated. I have a four-year-old son."

292

The women glanced at each other. "Did you tell your husband about your new lifestyle?"

"Oh yes." Linda crossed her legs. "He thinks I'll get over it."

"So, you're trying to get over him?" Monica asked.

"I feel guilty about what this is doing to him. He didn't deserve it. But eventually he'll be better off with someone else."

"What happened that made you decide you were a lesbian?" Gaylene asked.

"Wow. You kinda get down to it, don't you?" Linda chuckled rubbing a finger over the bridge of her nose. "I guess there were hints even when I was in high school. I kissed a girl once. She acted like she was grossed out, but I liked it. I had a crush on my art teacher, she had such amazing features. I always thought girls were so much more interesting to watch than boys. Then right before college, I was in a commune, and everyone sort of slept together. No one got to shower very often, but the girls smelled better than the men."

The conversation turned to other topics and most of the group shared what had happened the last week. Linda found it to be a safe place to talk and listen.

She was getting into her station wagon when she noticed a young woman leaning on a light pole, smoking.

"You part of that meeting downstairs?" the woman asked. She had long dark hair and big eyes. Linda guessed she was about her age.

Linda wasn't sure if the group was supposed to be confidential, but what other reason would she have for being there? "Yeah. First timer."

The woman came up to her and looked her in the face. "Funny, you don't look queer."

Linda's brows shot up. She supposed she needed to get used to insults. Then the other woman laughed.

"I'm in the club, too. Don't get mad. I like to tease, that's all."

"You weren't in the meeting though," Linda squinted at her.

"No, I have been before, but those ladies are a little old for me. Say, how would you like to go get some coffee? I'm here to pick up my mom, she works as the church secretary but she's not ready to leave yet. I'm Stephanie, by the way."

Linda lifted her chin and surveyed the surrounding area. "What about your mother?"

"Oh, I already gave her the car keys. She can leave without me."

"All right. But give me your purse first," Linda said, remembering one of the self-defense rules she'd learned in a class. She opened Stephanie's bag and found the usual assortment of makeup, keys, and cigarettes, plus some breath mints. No weapons unless you counted the cigarette lighter.

"You looking for my gun?" Stephanie snickered.

"Don't see one," Linda smiled, handing the bag back to her.

"Of course not," Stephanie said as she got into the passenger seat. "I keep that in the small of my back."

Linda quickly learned that Stephanie joked a lot. She supposed it was a way to deal with nerves. But once the ice was broken, she enjoyed talking to Stephanie. She had some great stories including some about women she'd dated. It sounded like Stephanie had been mostly unlucky in love.

Stephanie became Linda's new best friend. She was twenty-seven to Linda's twenty-five. She worked for a bank downtown and had time to play on the weekends. They did some hiking and bike riding. Stephanie seemed to enjoy working out and exercising.

After a few weeks, they went on a camping trip when Tom had Matthew for the weekend. It was their first chance to get intimate, and Linda thought it had gone well enough.

When Linda looked back on this time, she realized that there were some warning signs she'd ignored. Stephanie didn't volunteer to pay for anything. She didn't have a car. She lived with her mother. If Stephanie had been in a long-term relationship, she hadn't mentioned it. But they had begun to share personal information and Stephanie had been to Linda's house when Matthew was gone.

Six weeks later, she was back at her women's circle. One of the ladies told a funny story and they were all laughing.

"I'm surprised you don't have more younger women coming here. You ladies are so entertaining," Linda said.

The room got as quiet as a mortuary.

"We had another young woman but she caused a problem," Monica said.

"Oh yes," Gaylene said, "you mean Stephanie."

Linda's eyes bulged. "Stephanie?"

"Her mother works upstairs. She came to our group for about three weeks before latching onto the gal who seemed to have the most dough."

"What does that mean?" Linda leaned forward, trying not to be obvious.

Ann said, "The other woman, Mary Ethel, was a divorcee with a nice settlement. She made the mistake of bragging about buying an expensive new car. Stephanie became her constant companion, her girlfriend, I guess."

"Then something went wrong. We're not exactly sure what it was. Mary Ethel called me in tears one day," Monica said. "She told me never to let Stephanie come back. She was trying to decide whether to press charges against her. I got the impression Stephanie stole money from her, but she was vague."

"And Mary Ethel hasn't come back to our group, even though we've tried to contact her," Ann said.

"I thought about talking to Stephanie's mother about it, but it's probably out of her hands since Stephanie is an adult." Monica pulled a tissue from her purse.

"That's certainly unfortunate," Linda said. She had been much too trusting with Stephanie, she decided.

After that, she didn't contact Stephanie and didn't return her calls. After a few nights, Stephanie showed up on Linda's doorstep. Matthew was still awake and had come to the door with Linda.

"Oh, thank goodness you're home, Linda." Stephanie had a small suitcase at her feet. "My mother kicked me out and I need a place to crash."

"Um, Stephanie, I don't think you can stay with me," Linda said.

"Why not?"

"The ladies told me about you and Mary Ethel. I didn't like the sound of it."

"That old bat? I borrowed twenty bucks from her, and she went a little nuts when I couldn't pay her back for a week. I had to wait until payday."

"I'm going to have to be cautious, Stephanie. I have a young child to watch out for. So, we'd better say good-night." Linda shut the door and hoped Stephanie got the hint. Her gut told her there was more than twenty dollars involved. Maybe she should try to talk to Mary Ethel. But cutting things off with Stephanie seemed to be the easiest out.

The next afternoon, before the last patient left, the receptionist came to talk to Linda.

"Dr. Bridges, there is someone in the waiting room who asked to speak with you. She said to tell you it's Stephanie."

Linda's eyes widened. She'd never even told Stephanie where she worked. She supposed her last name was evident in many places in her house if she'd left mail sitting out.

Once the patients were gone, she let Stephanie come back to one of the treatment rooms.

"I'll make this quick, Doc." Stephanie let her fingers trail across the ceiling-mounted retractable light. "You've got a nice setup here. This equipment alone must cost a fortune. I'll bet your patients like you a lot."

"What do you want, Stephanie?" Linda pursed her lips.

"I wonder how your patients would feel if they knew their dentist was a deviant? That she's divorcing her husband because she prefers...well let's just say I would be quite graphic in my description. I may even have to get the dental licensing board involved. Don't they have a morals clause? I'm sure the mothers of young children wouldn't let you alone with them."

"This sounds like extortion."

"I'm going to need $10,000 to forget I ever knew you. That's pretty cheap to protect your reputation, don't you think?" Stephanie smirked walking around the room picking up dental instruments.

"Get out. I'll think about it and call you."

Or I'll have my husband come slam his fist through your face. It's his money too.

"Okay, but so you know, I already have a list of some of your patients. Your office staff isn't very careful with what they throw in the trash. I'll give you two days." Stephanie waved and walked out of the office.

Linda sank onto one of the rolling chairs she used in treating patients. This was her worst nightmare. After considering her options, she called Yvonne. She didn't go into details but explained someone was trying to blackmail her. When Daniel got on the phone, he assured her he could take care of it.

By the time she spoke to Daniel the next day, he already had a rap sheet on Stephanie Sanders and had sent her a certified letter. His threat of legal action was enough. Stephanie left Linda alone.

But after that experience, Linda was hesitant to trust anyone again.

It was nearly a year before she accepted an invitation to a party in Omaha. She went with Sylvie, one of the younger members of the support group. Sylvie introduced her to a few people she knew. It was an eclectic mix of both men and women. The music was lively, the food was trendy, the booze was plentiful, and people flowed back and forth between the large great room and the patios outdoors.

Linda was about to knock on a bathroom door when it opened. The occupant emerged and they nearly bumped faces.

"Brian! Brian Walker? What on earth are you doing here?" Linda clapped both hands on Brian's cheeks.

Brian looked different. Older, broader, with fierce brows and one earring. He was wearing eyeliner. His longish hair was swept off his face and held with some stiff hair product. But unmistakably, still her Brian.

"Lindy Marie! I can't believe it. I tried to look you up but you got married. Yay!" Brian wrapped her in an embrace and they bounced together in celebration.

"You left Chicago?" Linda asked.

"Oh, ages ago, Darling. When I graduated from Loyola, I moved back here to Omaha. I'm working at the Joslyn Art Museum. You should come to see what we're doing."

"I'd love that! I can't believe you're at this party! I thought it was mostly men who were, you know…"

"Light on their feet? That's me, Sweet-ems. I finally figured it out after high school. And look who you grew up to be? You're looking fabulous!"

"My God. Remember that time we tried making out on my bed?"

"Now we know why it never went anywhere."

The party was twice as fun after she started walking around with Brian. She met nearly all the men and at least most of the women through his contacts, and exchanged phone numbers with dozens of people.

It wasn't always easy keeping in touch with Brian. They both had busy lives and he lived fifty miles away. But three times a year, they made a habit of meeting for a long dinner, at a restaurant or one of their homes, and hashing out what had happened in the previous months. When he met and moved in with the love of his life, Will Hayes, he sometimes brought him along. Will was dashing and worked in commercial real estate where he could charm anyone into buying or selling property. Linda was thrilled to see how happy they were together.

CHAPTER FORTY-SIX

July 8, 1988

Linda watched Rose milling around the party space, checking to make sure everything was "just so." She reminded Linda of Mary Jo sometimes her attention to detail. It was because of Rose, with her generous spirit and calm manner, that Linda was able to face this party tonight. She could be more open than she'd ever been in her life. What would have become of her if Rose hadn't come into her life?

It had been six years since they'd met. Rose was a professor at the College of Dentistry, and she'd reached out to Linda to do a presentation for a seminar. Rose hadn't been there when Linda was in dental school, she'd been hired later from a school in Iowa. After Linda's presentation, Rose sent her a lengthy and heartfelt letter of thanks. Linda reached out to her and they had an instant connection over dinner.

After that, they seemed to fall into a relationship. Rose was a year younger than Linda and had been raised in Kentucky, but they had so much in common, it was often spooky. Once she'd become a fixture in Linda's life, Matthew accepted Rose and after a year, she moved into the house in Piedmont with them.

Tom even liked her. By this time, he'd remarried to a woman named Sheila, and they had a daughter, Cassandra, who was now seven.

Rose put her hand on Linda's shoulder. "Sit down, Sweetheart. Relax. Your friends will be here soon. Do you want some wine?"

Linda sank onto the sectional. "I'd love some. I probably should get a head start on getting giddy."

"Are you going to tell them about last year?"

"You mean when I had a nervous breakdown? I don't know. Telling them about you might be information overload."

"I tried to get you to call Nancy at least when you were down and out. Maybe she could have reached you."

Linda took the wine glass Rose offered. "You know I liked rosé before we met, but it tastes better now. I didn't want to bother Nancy last year. She had three kids to worry about. And I think her father was in the hospital around that time."

Rose sat next to Linda. "I know what will help you relax," she said, pulling Linda in for a kiss.

"Yuck, no mommy make-out sessions! Child in the room!" Matthew had cleaned up and was wearing a T-shirt, shorts, and sneakers. "I'm gonna ride my bike over to Jason's, so you old ladies will have the house to yourselves tonight. Okay if I come home by eleven?"

"Eleven is okay, but be careful riding after dark. At least it's not far away," Linda said, watching him scramble up the stairs.

"You know he's going to be dating before you know it," Rose said.

"Oh, I think his father has a big sex-ed lecture prepared for the occasion," Linda laughed. "Better that's on Tom."

Nancy, Yvonne, and Debbie arrived nearly at the same time. They all knew their way to the pool deck where the loveseats and chairs had been arranged for conversation.

"I can't believe you own this place now, Linda. Wasn't it hard for your parents to give it up?" Yvonne asked.

"The nice thing about me owning it is that they can come back to visit. But technically my dad still owns it. He financed it so I pay him the mortgage. We have an informal agreement that I can let him have it back after Matt moves out, which might be after high school or college. Dad assumes I'll want a place with less maintenance then."

"It does have a huge lawn," Debbie said.

"But I have an ex-husband who has a lawn service, so it works out fine." Linda got up to open some wine, and the other women helped themselves to the appetizers that were on the bar.

"Who is coming tomorrow, Linda?" Nancy asked.

"I was so lucky everyone could come. Barbra, Joann, Melissa, and Dawn all said they'd be here Saturday evening."

"You heard about poor Dawn, didn't you?" Nancy said. "I mean this has been years ago, but she joined the Dirty Dick club."

Linda laughed, "The what?"

Nancy shook her head. "I know it's hard to believe but she met Dick Dunn at Iowa State. She was a freshman featured twirler and he was a senior football player. I'm sure they discovered their families lived in Lincoln, but he probably didn't mention his history with not one, but two other twirlers at Capital High."

"Oh my God! How long did she date him?" Yvonne asked.

"I guess you didn't see their engagement announcement in the newspaper. My mother sent it to me in Germany so I guess it must have been about 1972 after he graduated. I didn't realize it was him at first, his name was Richard Carlyle Dunn III. My mom had recognized Dawn's name. Later, I heard from Rosemary Atkins Lee that Dawn caught him cheating with a friend of hers. Big surprise there! At least she didn't marry the jerk."

"That is too weird. Dawn is married now, though, isn't she?" Debbie asked.

Nancy paused until she finished her bite. "Yes, her husband is very nice. He's a science teacher,"

"And Barbra married John Anthony and they're running a travel agency," Yvonne said. "They booked our trip to Hawaii last year."

"Joann isn't married, is she?" Debbie asked.

"Joann is a cardiologist. She probably makes more money than anybody's husband," Linda said.

"And doesn't have to pick up her husband's dirty socks." Nancy sipped her wine and smiled.

"I was sorry to hear about you and Tom," Yvonne said. "It sounds like things are okay between you now?"

"Oh, absolutely. I still think of Tom as family. Divorce is never easy, but I adore his wife and little girl. We spend most holidays together." Linda knew this discussion was going to lead where she needed it to go.

"That's surprising. I don't think I'd be as understanding after my husband left me. And isn't it awkward now with you being alone, and him remarried?" Debbie asked.

"Oh. That's not what happened. Tom didn't leave me, I asked for the divorce. Sheila is a perfect wife for him, she's from a small town too. And I'm not alone." Linda took a big breath.

"You've been holding out on us! There's a new man in your life?" Nancy beamed.

Rose happened to come down the stairs then to check if any of the trays of appetizers needed to be refilled. "You gals have everything you need for now? Dinner should be ready upstairs in about fifteen minutes, Linda."

"Uh, Rose? Would you come over here for a minute?" Linda stood up and beckoned to her.

"Are you a caterer? I could use the name of a good caterer," Yvonne said.

303

Rose walked up next to Linda, who put her arm around Rose's back.

"Rosie, these are my high-school friends, Yvonne Adams, Debbie Washington, and Nancy Thompson."

"Nice to meet you all," Rose said.

The twirlers all murmured greetings, then waited for Linda to say more.

"Rose is my live-in girlfriend. My partner. You know like…Hell." Linda pulled Rose's face to hers and kissed her.

Rose laughed and put a hand on Linda's cheek. "You'd better take it easy on that wine, Babe. I'll check on the food." Rose smiled and went back upstairs.

All three of the other women had their mouths open.

"Surprise!" Linda said. She couldn't stop the blush creeping into her cheeks.

After what seemed like a long pause, Yvonne narrowed her gaze. "Are you trying to tell us you're a lesbian? Or was that another party trick like Spin the Bottle?"

"I'm a lesbian, yes. That's why I divorced Tom. I wanted to be with a woman, and after a few false starts, I found one who wants to be with me too."

"Knock me over with a feather!" Debbie said, wide-eyed. She glanced at the others to see if they were similarly amazed.

"How long have you been keeping this a secret, Linda?" Nancy's brows knit together. "You and Tom split up about ten years ago, didn't you?"

"Yeah, about that. It's not something you share with a lot of people. It can be risky."

"So, this is creepy but I have to ask." Yvonne wrinkled her nose. "You weren't like attracted to us when we were having sleepovers? You probably saw all of us undressed sometimes."

Linda grimaced. "Oh no, don't worry about that. I couldn't even identify my feelings until after I'd been married. But there are so many things people misunderstand. Lesbians aren't interested in straight women."

"How do you know the difference? Are you wearing some kind of sign?" Nancy asked.

"No, that would help. I went to a bar once where they had you put a piece of green tape on your shoulder if you were open to meeting men and yellow if you were open to meeting women. It was pretty helpful. People who weren't looking didn't wear any tape."

"I can see why it would be scary to reveal this to other people, including clients. I know Daniel and I talked about that crazy psychologist a few years ago who was making up rumors and statistics about gays and lesbians. It was in the newspaper, and even though he was exposed as a fraud, the proposed city ordinance prohibiting discrimination against homosexuals was defeated."

"I can't imagine being romantic with a woman," Debbie said. "It's like going against everything you've ever learned."

"Oh, you're right, Debs. Society tries to define us by our relationships with men. First, you're a daughter, then a wife. I felt like I was out there without any guideposts. I couldn't model my choices after my parents' relationship, although that wasn't perfect, as it turned out. They don't mention this same-sex preference in school at all. Although, do you remember Ms. Radcliffe, the art teacher? She was a lesbian. I saw her kissing her girlfriend in the parking lot."

"You did? And you didn't report her?" Nancy cried.

"No! I did think she was attractive. But I chalked it up to the fact that she made us study her face to sketch her. She was quite striking. I knew I had to keep her secret. That's one of the hard things. Lesbians and gay men have to be invisible most of the time. And you know, that doesn't work for me very well."

"Well, yes. People have been fired over it when it has nothing to do with their jobs. Remember those women who were discharged as military officers just because they came out?" Yvonne asked.

Linda nodded. "People have even been attacked, had their property vandalized. I would have gotten more politically involved except that I don't want to lose patients or have Rose subject to scrutiny at the university. It could even blow back on Tom and his business. Which is why I haven't mentioned this to any of you until now."

Over dinner, the other three women told their stories. Yvonne explained what happened with Michael Conyers.

"Is he still at Daniel's law firm?" Debbie asked.

"No, he was hired at a firm in Omaha. Daniel gave him a reference with the understanding that he would take the first job he was offered. I haven't heard anything about him since."

"That must have been rough if Daniel wanted to go to marriage counseling," Nancy said.

"I would recommend it. We learned to communicate with each other better. That can get lost with two young kids. And then we added Alicia to the mix about a year and a half later. It was chaos at our place for a few years."

"What about you, Nancy? Do you have a life lesson to share?" Linda asked, opening another bottle of white wine. This night may call for many glasses of wine. Rose had offered to drive anyone home who needed it.

"I think you all know the background of my story," Nancy said. "All three of my children were conceived outside of marriage.

It's kind of my thing. But my story is about the day my oldest decided I was a slut."

"No, she didn't!" Debbie said.

Nancy told them about the day Jennifer confronted her about Allison's birth certificate.

"What about Allie? Does she know?" Linda asked.

"Allie always considered Terry her father. What she didn't know was that I was still married to Pete. She seemed to accept my explanation a lot better than Jenny did. But then, she never knew Peter."

"Wasn't it hard naming your son after Pete?" Yvonne said.

"There wasn't much question about it. Terry and I knew we had to honor him that way. And the funny thing is that little Petey is very much his own person. He looks sort of like his namesake, he has that sandy-colored hair, but he doesn't have Pete's fighting spirit. He's more mellow."

"I'm not sure any of you can relate to my story. Oh, maybe Linda can, now that we know her secret. Growing up, I never expected to face discrimination like this," Debbie began as she told them about Jamal and his teacher.

"It's nice that Robert has a sense of humor about this, calling you 'Mama Bear,'" Yvonne said.

"Oh, he doesn't always. He was poking fun at me. But he's had to walk a line when it comes to how he's been treated professionally. Some people go overboard the other way to try to prove that they're not prejudiced. He finds that even more annoying. But Robert has learned to channel his frustrations into his city councilman role. Did I tell you he was elected to the city council last year? He has been trying to advocate for more minority bids for city projects, things like that. He says if you lift minorities economically, the power will follow."

"Robert is quite a gem. You know that, don't you, Honey?" Yvonne asked.

"I do. Yet I still have women ask me, 'how could you marry a Black man?'"

"They didn't see him on the dance floor," Linda smiled.

Debbie laughed. "Well, that is where he got to me. But even without that, once I got to know his personality, I knew I never wanted to be without him."

After dinner, they adjourned back to the pool area. Rose said she'd bring the cheesecake down to them after a while.

Linda's eyes surveyed her three friends. Was she going to scare them? "There's one more thing I wanted to talk to you all about. This part might be harder to accept."

"There's more?" Nancy asked. "I haven't recovered from your first revelation!"

Linda sighed. "It's something that happened last year. Did any of you know Brian Walker when we were in Eastridge Elementary? He was in my grade and lived across Lyncrest Drive."

The others shook their heads.

"He had several siblings, I thought you might have known one of them. Anyway, Brian and I were the best of friends all through grade school. He let me do 'boy things' with him, ride bikes, play baseball and football, horse around in the pool. My dad even took Brian and his dog hunting with us. We were still friends in junior high, but before high school, he moved to Chicago. I only saw him a few times after that when he visited his grandparents."

"Did he come back here?" Nancy asked.

"Total coincidence. I ran into him at a gay and lesbian party in Omaha. He worked at Joselyn Art Museum. It was shortly after I'd come out. That was in about '78 or '79. We kept in touch after that and got together a few times a year. He met a wonderful guy named Will Hayes, who we always called Hayes. They were together for three or four years and came up here and hung out with Rose and me. Matthew liked them too. They were his gay uncles."

"This story doesn't end well, does it?" Debbie said watching Linda's expression.

"One day Brian called me and told me Hayes was sick. He'd contracted AIDS. They had both tested HIV-positive a year before that, but they thought they were safe. They had a few friends who had already died.

"I meant to spend more time with them, but I was busy, and Rose was short-handed at work keeping her close to home. The next thing I knew, Hayes died and we were at his funeral. I had no idea how scared those men in his community were until I went to their apartment after the funeral. People were blaming them for getting sick. And it had already cost Hayes and Brian a lot of money. The landlord asked Brian to move out. I told Brian to call me if he needed help.

"It wasn't more than six months later that Brian called. He'd gotten AIDs too." Linda had to stop and drink some water as her throat was aching.

"Oh no!" Debbie said, patting Linda's hand.

"That's when things got crazy for me. I don't think I'll ever forget the day I brought Brian here to stay with me."

"What's going on, Linda?" Tom demanded. "Who are all these men in your basement, and what's with all this stuff?"

Tom had brought Matthew home after a weekend at his place and found multiple cars in the driveway. When he and Matt had gone downstairs, they found three men carrying boxes into her recreation room. Linda had been in the guest bedroom on that level, helping settle Brian in.

She quickly took Tom outside for privacy.

"Brian is sick. He lost his job because he couldn't work enough, and his illness is starting to show on his face. You know, those black spots. I told him he could stay with me."

Tom glanced back toward the house. "Brian is sick? His roommate died not that long ago. What's wrong with Brian?"

Linda took a deep breath. "He has AIDS too. I have no idea how long he has. I'll try to go to his next doctor's appointment."

"Brian has AIDS. And you let him into your house? Do you think he's going to live here? You know this thing has been killing people right and left?" Tom struggled to keep his voice down but the veins were popping in his neck.

Linda shook her head. "It's killing gay men, not other people unless they used infected needles. Brian is my oldest friend."

"You have done some pretty crazy things in your life, but I can't go along with this one," Tom said. "You are putting yourself, Rose, and Matthew at risk. This is a very scary virus you're dealing with. Haven't you seen on TV how the doctors have to put on HazMat suits to treat patients?"

"It's transmitted through bodily fluids. He got it through his partner, who probably got it from another man years ago. We're not going to be exchanging body fluids."

"You can't be sure. What if he sneezes? If he has to have an IV, there's blood exposure. Are you going to clean the bathroom? That's more exposure. You can't do this. Tell him to go to a hospital."

"He can't go to a hospital. He has no insurance and his money is gone. He had to pay for his partner's bills. I'm not turning him away."

310

Tom flung his arms out. "You're not even wearing any protective gear! But I can't force you. I guess it's your house. Don't think for one damn second, I'm letting Matthew stay here. He'll live at our house as long as you're taking in AIDS patients."

"No! Tom, he knows Brian. He's like family. And I don't want Matthew to be away. I miss him even when he spends weekends with you."

Tom put his hand up. "This's not up for discussion. Matthew goes with me. You don't like that; I can get a lawyer involved. You don't think a court would condone letting a child live in this environment, do you?"

"And Tom packed Matthew up and took him just like that. I hardly saw my son for months. It broke my heart. And then I had to watch Brian deteriorate." Linda said.

"I could see Tom's point. AIDS is like the plague, isn't it?" Debbie asked.

Linda nodded. "It was awful watching it suck the life out of someone. At the same time, my relationship with Tom went to hell in a handbasket. He wouldn't even talk to me for weeks. Men can be so stubborn. Especially one like Tom. I see the cowboy coming out when he starts to swagger and yell and throw his weight around. I think he enjoys getting sweaty and dirty to prove he's male."

"You see, Linda, most women find that appealing." Nancy raised her brows.

Linda smirked. "I was lucky to get Sheila to give me updates on Matt. She told me later that Tom had gone to an attorney but he hadn't done anything about the custody. Then on top of everything else, Rose's sister was in a serious car accident in Kentucky. So, she left me too for a couple of weeks. But at the time, I was trying to focus on Brian. His situation was desperate."

"This is getting hard on you, Linda," Brian wheezed. "I know exactly what you're going through. I was in your shoes when Hayes died. That's why I want you to do something for me."

"Anything, Brian. You know that."

"I want you to try to come up with some pills, a kamikaze combination. I've seen the list before, but I don't have it now. But one of my guys will know. Get the right mix of drugs and it will knock me out pretty quick. I don't want to suffer at the end or watch it in your eyes. When it's close, I want a quick exit."

Linda's eyes widened. "You're talking about assisted suicide? You do realize I'm a doctor of dentistry? That's illegal."

"We need to make sure I can take the pills on my own then. I have to be able to swallow. Gather up what I need. Surely you don't want to see me in pain."

Linda thought about it. She had a variety of drugs in her medicine chest that her therapists had prescribed. They changed prescriptions sometimes before she'd used them all. She did her research. What she didn't have on hand, she asked Brian's friends to supply.

A few weeks later, Brian asked again. "Babydoll, time is running out. You got the pills I asked for?"

"I think so. But I don't know if I should let you have them. You want to see your family first, don't you?"

"My family pretty much wrote me off when I told them I was gay. Mary reached out when Hayes died, but after I told her I was infected, I haven't heard from her either. Let's have my Omaha friends come by in a few days and then I'll take the pills afterward."

But two days later, she went downstairs to wake him in the morning. Brian had been sleeping a lot. This time, she knew he

312

wasn't asleep.

"I knew something was off as soon as I entered his room. His hand was hanging over the side of the bed. It was cold. I knew. It was over."

"God, that must have been horrible for you. What did you do?" Nancy said.

"I think I was numb. I went out and sat by the pool. It was June, so it was warm. I couldn't do anything for about thirty minutes. Then I called the police department to ask what to do if someone dies at home. They sent a coroner."

"That's so sad!" Yvonne watched Linda's face. She had a far-away look in her eyes. "Is there more?"

Linda nodded. "They took Brian away. I sat and thought about what he'd been through. How badly he'd been treated partly because he was gay, partly just bad luck. I was feeling so lost. Like I was losing Tom and Matthew. I thought Tom was using this incident against me. I missed Rose. For the first time in my life, I felt totally alone.

"My family wasn't close by either. My dad was more distant after I told him about Rose and me. My mother was cordial but I hardly ever spoke to her. I hadn't talked to Sarah for months either.

"On top of all that, it was June 17. The anniversary of my abortion back in high school. I had no idea whether I would have a child after that. I don't know how to explain my state of mind that day that Brian died; I snapped."

Nancy moved over and sat next to Linda on the loveseat. "What do you mean?"

"I lined up all those pills that Brian asked for. It was a pretty little colorful collection and I put them all on the bar over there. I was afraid they might get dirty, but then I realized I wouldn't know the difference."

Yvonne scowled. "You're not saying you attempted—"

Linda shook her head. "I must have heard my mother's voice in my head. She was always a stickler for thank-you notes. So, I decided to write thank-yous to some people. I hauled out the word processor. I wrote each of you a note to explain why I was doing this. I intended to write to Tom, to Rose, and of course, to Matthew." Linda went to the bar, pulled three envelopes out, and scattered them on the table in front of the group. "I got all of yours written. But as soon as I tried to explain myself to Tom, I couldn't do it. I pictured how pissed off he was going to be. I started crying and couldn't stop. You know me, I hardly ever cry. I took that as a sign. I needed more time. Darkest before the dawn crap." She wiped her eyes.

"I put the pills away and called to tell Tom and Sheila that Brian died. Tom sent a hazardous cleaning crew over here and they disinfected the whole house, especially the basement. The next morning, he let Matthew return. Rose came back before Brian's funeral."

"Did you tell them that you were thinking about ending your life?" Yvonne asked.

Linda pressed her lips together. "I told Rose. And my therapist. That might have been a mistake. The therapist made me come see her three times a week after that. But she forced me to talk about it. I have come to rely on therapy. Therefore, I'm turning into my mother."

The others snickered.

"How can you make me laugh when I want to cry, Linda?" Nancy asked. "I wished you had called me. I would have tried to help."

"I know. I'm sure you all would have tried. I said that in the letters. It's been a year since I wrote those, but I think I told you all

314

that I loved you, and how much I admired each one. Yvonne, not for your beauty and grace, but how you waited to marry the right man and to have his children when the odds were stacked against you. Debbie, you fought for your decision to have a baby at eighteen, taking on your family, defending your husband's family. You've become a real inspiration. And Nancy, you held tightly to your religious foundation, but you didn't let society's rules dictate when and with whom you wanted to make babies. I only hope I am half as good of a mother as all of you are."

Nancy rose and took Linda in her arms, and Debbie and Yvonne joined the hug.

"You know we've always loved you too, Sweetie," Debbie said, grabbing a tissue for her eyes. "Even though you sometimes marched to different music."

"That's true enough," Linda said. "We each had batons to twirl, and it doesn't get easier when you are out in the world."

"To continue your metaphor, if I had to step in formation with anyone, I'm glad it was the three of you," Yvonne said. She raised her wine glass to toast.

"To the fabulous twirlers of Capital High," Debbie said.

"May our sparkle keep shining," Nancy said.

And they clinked their glasses each to the others.

ABOUT THE SERIES

This is the fourth of the Twirler Quartet series. Previous books include *Catch It Spinning, Twirling Fire,* and *Learning To Twirl.* Although the main characters are high school majorettes, twirling is largely a metaphor.

I previously wrote a historical fiction novel using different time periods. One of the challenges of that type of writing is that you constantly need to check to see what expressions were in vogue, what clothing was worn, and whether such-and-such had been invented. After that, I thought it would be easier to write about a timeframe in which I had lived, and use a setting that I remembered well. I decided to pick the late sixties, and start as my main characters were finishing high school and learning about love.

Many social mores have changed in the past fifty years. The prevailing notion among school administrators and parents seemed to be that sex education in schools should be limited to the mechanics of reproduction. No one talked to teenagers about their hormones or feelings for fear of giving them "ideas." While some methods of birth control were available, they were never promoted, and this was before Roe vs. Wade. Consequently, teen pregnancies were at an all-time high. I had three friends who "had to get married," and they inspired me to write this series.

But teen pregnancy was only the starting point. I wanted to illustrate how widespread attitudes toward interracial relationships, military service, and homosexuality have changed. My characters at times display attitudes that are not politically correct today. This is less a reflection on the character than it is on the prevailing mindsets of the era.

When I was in high school and college, many young men I knew planned to join the armed forces. They were undoubtedly attracted by the benefits offered such as free tuition for college and travel. Their fathers had served their country. Joining the military had been considered noble and patriotic. I recall one boyfriend asking if he joined the navy, wouldn't I be proud of him?

One of my high school friends was killed in Vietnam. As the war became a political hot potato, the veterans of that conflict began returning and having to face the dual burden of the trauma they'd faced in war and the lack of appreciation from the general populace. Peter faces post-traumatic-stress syndrome in *Learning To Twirl* in a timeframe long before that became a catch phrase.

Homosexuality was rarely spoken about, especially involving women. It was the twenty-first century before I met a lesbian woman who was candid enough and had enough job security to be "out" at work. The lesbians I knew had mostly had hetero partnerships prior to declaring their preferences for women. Linda and Tom's story is fictional, but it illustrates a problem women might have leaving a loving husband.

It feels like we've made significant progress as a country in becoming more educated and addressing problems faced by Vietnam veterans and lesbians. The attitudes and treatment of AIDS patients has dramatically improved. I don't see the same progress in race relations. The widespread availability of cell phone videography has shone a light on instances where more work is needed. After writing *Twirling Fire,* I joined the local chapter of NAACP to try to learn what I could do to help bridge the gap.

I hope you have enjoyed the Twirler Quartet, and its intermingled storylines. I used a lot of real restaurants and other locations in Lincoln, Nebraska at the time. Feel free to contact me at https://claudiaseverin.net. I'd appreciate a review for any of my books on Amazon, Goodreads or other book sites.

—Claudia Johnson Severin

ABOUT THE TIMES

Spinning Sideways isn't an LGBTQ romance. The love story is between the man and woman until the woman decides to pursue a lesbian relationship. But as part of the series, I kept the emphasis on the more male/female couple, while giving both parties a Happy Ever After ending with new loves and successful co-parenting.

As Linda was coming of age, what were society's views locally regarding homosexuals and lesbians? I went back to the newspapers distributed at the time.

The Lincoln Gazette, Lincoln Nebraska, reported on August 27, 1975, "As of June 1975, six years after the Stonewall Riot in New York City that is recognized as the movement's beginning, gay activism has forced the legislative repeal of restrictions on consensual adult sex in 12 states.

"While the push for protective legislation continues, lesbians and gay men have been struggling and winning small, often qualified, victories on other fronts as well. Policy resolutions pressing for legal reform have been passed by a growing list of organizations including the American Bar Association, American Federation of Teachers, National Education Association, National Organization for Women, American Civil Liberties Union, and the Young Women's Christian Association.

"Last year, making a statement in support of gay civil rights at the same time, the American Psychiatric Association removed homosexuality from its list of 'mental disorders.'"

In the 1975 Nebraska Unicameral session, the lawmakers worked to update the state's sodomy laws. As a result of Legislative Bill 23, it became a criminal offense for a husband to rape his wife, and it was no longer illegal for unmarried consenting adults to engage in sexual relations. But as explained in *The Lincoln Journal Star* on April 8, 1975, "the lawmakers also decided that homosexuality should remain illegal in Nebraska."

It was difficult to find places to meet women with common interests. According to *The Lincoln Journal Star*, Lincoln, Nebraska, on January 29, 1975, "Gathering places for gay women in Lincoln are limited. The Women's Resource Center at the University on the Nebraska-Lincoln campus is one such place and the Commonplace coffee house on Saturday and Sunday evenings is another. There are no gay bars."

By 1980, *The Lincoln Journal Star* listed a Lesbian Support Group meeting at the YWCA and a Lesbian Teenager's Support Group meeting at UMHE. By 1984 there was a Gay/Lesbian Crisis and Referral line.

During the timeframe I was searching, there were numerous attacks on women who were supporting the National Organization for Women, and delegates to various related conventions were often called lesbians as an insult. One example is that the Ku Klux Klan objected to a women's movement conference claiming it was a haven for "all the misfits of society, including self-admitted lesbians." *Lincoln Journal Star,* September 2, 1977.

When I skipped forward a few years, I noted that one of the bellwethers of cultural change, Ann Landers, took a stand on homosexuality in her syndicated advice column of December 17, 1979. She printed a letter she received that said, "I chose to be what I am, and I am not ashamed of it. I don't flaunt the fact that I am a woman whose sexual preference is another woman, but neither do I try to hide it." Ann Landers' reply was "I am printing your letter because you represent a point of view that deserves to be heard. A great many people, however, do not believe homosexuality is 'normal and healthy,' and I am among them." Ann goes on to say, "I have received thousands of letters from male homosexuals (fewer from lesbians) who are desperately unhappy and would give anything to be straight."

But just three months later, on March 9, 1980, Ann Landers wrote, "As for a gay couple being permitted to adopt a child, it would not surprise me in the least. The literature I have read, the authorities with whom I consult, and the letters in recent years from gays, lesbians, and bisexuals have convinced me that eventually all legislation which discriminates against homosexuals will be abolished."

Yet even by August 4, 1984, when the same local newspaper did a series of articles interviewing homosexuals, this editor's note prefaced the first article: "There are hundreds, perhaps thousands, of homosexuals in Lincoln. It is a lifestyle that the majority of Lincolnites know little about, even though they may unknowingly work with or be friends with gays or lesbians...

"It is a subculture of hundreds. Gay men and lesbian women in Lincoln, Nebraska."

"People in the straight world would be shocked," said one Lincoln lesbian. Shocked at the numbers, shocked, perhaps, at who among their co-workers and acquaintances is gay."

If attitudes were becoming more tolerant in the mid-eighties, the AIDS health crisis, with seventy-three percent of its victims identified as homosexual men, created new fears and misconceptions.

MAJORETTES: Back Row—Mari Jo Cook, Sandie Holtgrewe, Rickie Hahn, Pat Kromberg. **Front Row**—Connie Becker, Claudia Johnson, Lynette Jackman, Jan Worley.

www.ingramcontent.com/pod-product-compliance
Lightning Source LLC
Chambersburg PA
CBHW051119190726
48290CB00006B/1608